HELEN ROW TOEWS

WHEN LOVE BLOOMS IN *Paris*

vinci
BOOKS

By Helen Row Toews

Chateau de Belliveau

One Golden Summer
A Garden of Promises
Moonlight Over the Cinque Terre
When Love Blooms in Paris
With Love From Paris

Vinci Books

vinci-books.com

Published by Vinci Books Ltd in 2025

1

Copyright © Helen Row Toews 2023

The author has asserted their moral right to be identified as the author of this work in accordance with the Copyright, Designs and Patents Act 1988. This work is a work of fiction. Names, characters, places and incidents are the product of the author's imagination or are used fictitiously. Any resemblance to actual persons, living or dead, places and incidents is entirely coincidental.

All rights reserved. No part of this publication may be copied, reproduced, distributed, stored in any retrieval system, or transmitted in any form or by any means, including photocopying, recording, or other electronic or mechanical methods, nor used as a source for any form of machine learning including AI datasets, without the prior written permission of the publisher.

The publisher and the author have made every effort to obtain permissions for any third party material used in this book and to comply with copyright law. Any queries in this respect should be brought to the attention of the publisher and any omissions will be corrected in future editions.

A CIP catalogue record for this book is available from the British Library.

Paperback ISBN: 9781036702885

Printed and bound in Great Britain by Clays Ltd, Elcograf S.p.A.

Chapter One

Lyam was gone. Gabrielle sat cross-legged on the cold cement of her tiny Parisian balcony with her eyes tightly closed, rocking back and forth. She took a deep shuddering breath, scrubbing at tears long since dried on cheeks that ached from the force of her pain and anger.

There was frost in the air. She shivered, but the chill that seeped into her bones went unheeded. On the streets beyond the black iron railings that surrounded her, twilight fell like a damp blanket. The fading light of a cold February evening marked the desolation of her heart.

Lyam was gone, yes, but she had ended it, not him. After listening to what Gabrielle had to say, the police took him away. She reached for her wine.

Two months later

Gabrielle stared at grey sheets of rain that splashed into puddles outside the café window. She watched as people hunched under bobbing umbrellas of all colours and sizes, hurrying to escape the deluge. Leaden clouds hung over Paris. Sidewalks glistened, and cars drove slowly, their headlights creating beacons of light in the rainy gloom.

Yet, a scent of spring was in the air. The smell of damp earth and the regeneration of leaves, grass, and flowers soon to bloom again in dormant gardens, wafted through the door each time it opened, welcoming in a soggy customer.

Gabrielle warmed her hands around a hot glass of mulled wine, glancing hopefully at a fire burning in the hearth not far from where she sat. But it was mostly for show. Very little heat reached her small round table. With a sigh, she closed the heavy book she'd been reading.

Steam rose from the beverage as she lifted it to her mouth, breathing deeply to fill her senses with the sweet, spicy scent of orange peel, cloves, and cinnamon. Tipping the glass, she allowed it to trickle down her throat, thawing her from the inside out. She closed her eyes.

It wouldn't be a good idea to sit here too long, she mused. Moving to check the time on her phone, Gabrielle looked down at her favourite moss-green cardigan. She knew it went well with her mane of ebony hair often twined into a thick braid running the length of her back. Though today she wore it down as an extra layer of warmth. The weather wasn't supposed to be this cold. The forecast had been clear. It was meant to be spring-like outside, as warm as summer. But then the rain had started, preceded by a rumble in the sky. Now, even the trees outside were cowering and the sidewalk tables were dripping and desolate.

It was dark for two o'clock on a quiet Saturday. She

wrapped her sweater around her, shrugged deeper into her jacket, and zipped it to the top. How she wished she'd grabbed her winter coat before dashing down the street for this much needed respite. The idea was to get some fresh air before heading home to study for final exams, not freeze to death.

"Gabrielle!"

A voice called her name, but it couldn't have been meant for her. There was no one she knew in Paris this weekend. Her friends had taken advantage of the time off to go home or spend vacation with their boyfriends abroad. She'd chosen to stay in the city to study. Besides, there had been no man in her life—since Lyam. She looked around. The place was almost deserted. How many other Gabrielle's could there possibly be?

Her back was to the door, but she heard footsteps approaching and familiar laughter ring out. Turning, despite herself, Gabrielle couldn't believe her eyes. She blinked uncomprehendingly, her mouth falling open. Three of her family members stood before her, grinning and folding away their umbrellas. She leaped up and regardless of their wetness, hugged each one tightly, kissing cheeks. The love in their embraces instantly lifted her mood.

"What are you doing here?"

"We came to rescue you from yourself," her cousin-in-law Angelina said with a grin. "We have a day planned you're going to love." She reached into a bag she had slung over one shoulder and withdrew two bottles of wine which she clunked onto the table before Gabrielle's startled eyes. "Compliments of Chateau de Belliveau," she announced with a grin.

"But..."

"Before you argue," Angelina interjected, "we're aware

you have to study. That's why we're only going to take you out for the day. We have a hotel booked for the night and our overnight bags are already there. It isn't far from here. No, don't say it..." She raised a hand to silence the protest on Gabrielle's lips. "You have all of tomorrow to yourself for studying." She moved closer to the fire and extended her hands toward the flame.

"Come on Gabby." Annette spoke up, using the childhood name she'd always used for her older sister. Her voice rose with excitement. "We 'ave a plan...the afternoon for shopping, and to end the day, dinner at an amazing restaurant."

Sarah, another cousin by marriage, beamed at Gabrielle too, the glow of the fire turning her freckles into golden constellations. Gabrielle couldn't help but admire how Sarah always appeared to light up a room. "We want to take you out on the town!" the young woman chimed in, her eyes sparkling with mischief. She pulled a bag from behind her back and set it on the table with a flourish. "And, we've got a surprise for you," she said, gesturing towards a cherry red dress, just visible through the plastic.

"Ooh la la," Gabrielle exclaimed breathily, picking up the dress. "Thank you. *C'est incroyable.*" She dabbed at her eyes, overwhelmed and unable to prevent tears from flowing at the sight of these women she loved. "I can't believe you came all this way for me."

Annette winked and said, "What's family for if not to pounce on you when you least suspect it? We 'ave shoes for you also, but they were too heavy to bring from the hotel. It is decided that we will all prepare for our evening at the 'otel. *D'accord?*"

Gabrielle nodded. Happily, she gulped the rest of her wine, and paid her bill, while the group prepared their umbrellas to brave the dreary Parisian weather. She was so pleased to see them. She would have agreed to almost any idea they came up with at this point.

"I want to take my books back 'ome, first," she said, sliding the heavy volume from the table into a worn leather bag at her feet. "It will only take a moment."

Huddled close together, conversation flowed freely amongst the women as they trekked along the blustery street. Drawing near to her apartment, Gabrielle glanced up at the building she'd lived in for almost four years. Made of creamy white brick, it was typical Parisian and boasted intricately wrought steel railings at her balcony and kitchen windows. Although the rain had dampened its appeal for the moment, she loved her little sanctuary on the top floor.

Stopping at the tall, navy-blue doors leading to the foyer, she keyed in her passcode. They clicked open and her family piled through behind her.

Five flights of stairs later, they entered Gabrielle's tiny apartment and filled *la salle de séjour* with lively chatter.

Gabrielle felt a sense of comfort wash over her. She'd missed her family—the acceptance and love of home, especially lately. She looked at each one of these precious women, thinking how much they'd changed in small ways since she'd last seen them. They grouped before her as she dropped her bag on the floor beneath the coatrack, popped the *vin rosé* wine into her small refrigerator to chill, and grabbed something warmer to wear.

Annette, her sister and the youngest of this generation, was always vivacious with glossy, chocolate brown, shoulder-length curls. Her hazel eyes sparkled with warmth as she glanced at Sarah through oversized glasses and grinned, revealing a set of pearly white teeth. She was petite and wore an outfit that belied her love of fashion—baggy jeans that boasted more holes than material, a cropped, sky blue t-shirt, and well-worn trainers. She had an air of confidence that could only come with being eighteen and freshly graduated, ready to begin art school at university in the fall.

Sarah's long, golden hair tumbled to her waist in soft waves, a perfect complement to her bright blue eyes. She'd gained a few pounds since Gabrielle had seen her at Christmas, but it only served to enhance her lovely hourglass figure. Married only a few months earlier to Gabrielle's cousin, Raphaël, she looked perfectly happy. She wore chic, yet comfortable high-waisted skinny jeans, a grey cable-knit sweater with a matching scarf knotted around her throat, and chunky heeled boots.

Gabrielle let her eyes drift toward her cousin Julien's wife, Angelina. In her late thirties now, she still radiated youth. Her shoulder-length, dark brown hair was tied back with a mauve ribbon at the nape of her neck and her petite frame was clad in lightly faded jeans, cinched at the waist with a brown leather belt and topped with a simple but elegant white blouse. Contentment saturated the air around the group as Gabrielle slowly buttoned her jacket, absorbing the conversations of the women.

She relaxed for what felt like the first time in months as she hung the dress her family had brought for her to wear. Tears stung her eyes for the second time that day. She hadn't dressed up and gone out for a long while. Her degree in psychology had always come first. And of course, there'd been Lyam. He hadn't liked going anywhere in the evening —unless it was by himself.

"So, it is nice to chat and catch up, but we should go. We are in Paris after all." Annette waved at the door, turning to look at each woman in turn. "I'd like to wander along Rue de Rivoli and do some shopping. I think it's even stopped raining." She leaned back to glance out the balcony window. "What do you say ladies?"

No one needed any more urging and they piled back down the corkscrew staircase to the darkened foyer below. Gabrielle snapped on the light and caught sight of the post boxes. She hadn't checked her mail in days.

"*Une minute, s'il te plaît*," she called out.

The others paused by the huge doors leading to the street as she dug into her purse for the key. Yanking the small metal door open with a protesting squeal, she reached inside and grabbed the envelopes, giving them a cursory glance before slamming it shut. Amongst the pile there were the usual bills and a flyer advertising real estate in the area. However, one envelope stood out from the rest. It looked personal and addressed by hand. Who would be writing to her? Even her parents sent texts or called. No one had ever written her a letter—except Lyam, but those were in the early days of their relationship. They'd been left for her to find around the apartment, filled with lines of poetry and sentiments of young love. She didn't want to think about any of that. Yet, the handwriting looked eerily similar.

A trickle of fear shivered down her spine. *No. It couldn't be him, could it?* Gabrielle refused to allow anxiety or memories of the past, mar this perfect day. None of her family were aware of the circumstances surrounding the breakup and she wanted to keep it that way. The less they knew, the safer they were. She stuffed the wad of papers to the bottom of her voluminous bag, along with her concerns, and forced a grin on her face.

"Ready?" she asked. The four women stepped onto the street. Linking arms, and giggling, they headed for the nearest métro, the transit system that served all of Paris with a complex web of underground trains.

They spent the next few hours wandering in and out of stores and tiny boutiques on Rue de Rivoli. Everyone but Gabrielle bought something. Another pair of boots for Annette, a top and two sweaters for Sarah, and Angelina purchased clothes for her daughter, Celeste and Philippe, her young son. Tired, but happy, they returned to Gabrielle's apartment.

The four women filled the small entry. Somehow, the space managed to house Gabrielle's coats, her neatly organized shoes, a miniscule washer/dryer that was tucked into a corner, and high shelves filled with boxes. They left their wet things to dry a little before they moved into the living space which consisted of a mere two rooms. They weren't grand, but prettily decorated and cozy.

The tiny kitchen held everything she needed, with a small round table at the center where a bowl of fresh pink peonies reposed. Long narrow windows were pushed open to allow a breeze to waft through filmy white curtains when the weather was sunny. The cupboards on the left and a squat buffet on the right were painted a deep forest green. They would have darkened the room if not for the gold swirls of metallic paint Gabrielle had used to lighten and accentuate them. The floor was a checkerboard pattern of green and white tiles. White ruffled drapes ran around the base of the cupboards, masking the presence of larger utensils and pots.

Gabrielle opened the wine and poured each of them a glass. Handing them around, she took an appreciative sip. It was like a taste of home.

They moved into the salon and occupied every available seat. Annette spoke excitedly about her latest art project and gossip from home. While Sarah teased Annette about the cute young desk clerk at their hotel, and Angelina relayed news from Chateau de Belliveau, the estate where she and Sarah lived with their husbands, Gabrielle's cousins.

Two high-backed wing chairs, covered in a pale gold fabric, stood on either side of balcony windows that were almost replicas of the ones in the kitchen only bigger. A small, paisley-patterned sofa in soft blues, golds, and creams was tucked between a tall bookcase filled to overflowing with books and several antique figurines her parents had given her as a child, and what must have been a working fireplace in its day. A few art nouveau paintings she'd picked up from a gallery she'd visited with Lyam graced the walls, and a small flat screen television hung overtop the mantle, but Gabrielle seldom used it. She preferred to read whenever she wasn't studying, which wasn't very often.

"I can 'ardly wait for you to take the dress out of the wrapper and try it on," Annette gushed, from where she perched on one of the two chairs in the salon. "I want to see if Sarah guessed your size correctly." The young girl leaned back and assessed Gabrielle's figure. "Can a woman be slender and voluptuous at the same time?" Annette swivelled around to ask the other two, holding her glass between thumb and forefinger.

Sarah balanced on the other chair, closest to the long windows leading to the balcony. She answered with a chuckle.

"That *is* a bit of a contradiction." She tapped a finger on her chin, also giving Gabrielle a once-over. "But in this specific instance I'd have to say it fits." She grinned and spoke pointedly to Gabrielle. "I don't think you understand how absolutely gorgeous you are. Back when we first met, and I thought you were dating Raphaël, I wanted to hate you for how beautiful you were. But I couldn't since you were just too sweet." Sarah hurried across the room to hug her cousin-in-law and released her just as quickly.

"It's true," Angelina added with a smile from where she reclined on the tiny sofa. "You have a way of turning heads everywhere you go, but it's your inner beauty that truly shines." She became serious, reached across, and laid a hand over Gabrielle's own. "Just so this is absolutely clear, we're here for you whenever you need us, okay?" She nodded encouragingly. "I don't know what happened between you and Lyam, but if you ever need to talk…"

Gabrielle felt the love roll off these women in waves. She looked between them, not trusting herself to speak, and blinked rapidly. With a swift intake of breath, she gave each one a wobbly smile.

"*Merci beaucoup*. You 'ave no idea what it means to me that you came 'ere today." She jumped to her feet, almost spilling her drink. "Now, let's get ready and go to dinner! I'm ravenous."

They lost no time in leaving, and soon stood in the spacious but plain, adjoining rooms of the hotel in the tenth arrondissement where the women were staying.

Considering four women were getting dressed at the same time, with only one bathroom, it didn't take them long. There was laughter, good-natured teasing, and a lot of perfume before the dust settled, but soon they were ready.

The fitted red sheath they'd gifted her, hugged Gabrielle's curves to perfection. She gazed at her full reflection in the mirror she'd been allotted, knowing she looked her best despite feeling stressed with finals and the whole relationship turmoil she'd gone through with Lyam. She flipped her long black hair over her head and brushed it vigorously. It needed trimming, she noted, tipping it back and smoothing the flyaway ends. It had grown well past her waist. As a final touch, she put on some gold hoop earrings she dropped into her purse as she'd left the apartment, and then added a matching shade of red lipstick before sliding into the glossy black stilettos they'd thoughtfully included. *Done.*

"Ready," she called, lifting a long black, double breasted trench coat from the back of a chair and entering the miniscule salon where the others were waiting. Throwing it over her arm, she smiled. Sarah wore a fitted, knee-length, dusty rose dress with a long slit reaching mid-thigh, a square neckline, and bows tied on each shoulder. It set off her long blonde hair perfectly. Angelina looked almost regal in an emerald, green midi. Large, embossed black flowers covered the A-line skirt and long sleeves.

"*Oui! Je suis prêt.*" Annette poked her head around the corner of the bathroom with curls bouncing. She did a little twirl to show off the frills of her short, frothy concoction of white chiffon. "*Allons-y.* Let's go, I'm starving." She snatched up her coat and grabbed her purse. "By the way," she called over her shoulder as she hurried out the door, "Sarah was correct in picking out your size. You look so 'ot."

"*Merci*," Gabrielle said with a smile.

Closing the door, she waited while Angelina checked to make sure it was locked before following the clattering group along the corridor. She fell behind, pushing away thoughts of her recent ordeal, and of the letter that lurked at the bottom of her bag. Nothing would spoil this night. As the door banged shut behind them, Gabrielle stepped forward to hail a cab splashing its way toward them on the glistening street.

As they had hoped, it was a wonderful evening. The four of them spilled onto Boulevard Saint-Germain-des-Prés after a leisurely meal and several glasses of champagne. What they were celebrating, Gabrielle wasn't sure, but it was fun. She forgot her troubles, and that was all that mattered.

Sarah waved to a taxi who pulled up to the curb. They sobered, realizing that this was goodbye. Gabrielle kissed each face several times and hugged her family tight.

"I don't want to let you go," she said, stepping back and crossing her arms. "It 'as been a perfect day. Thank you so much for coming."

"How will you get home?" Annette asked with a worried frown, hanging back when the other two had climbed into the car.

"Same as always, the métro." Gabrielle hugged her little sister one last time and ushered her into the waiting cab.

Just before the car pulled away, Annette rolled down the window and called to her. "I'll be back soon for a visit. Just you and me." She blew her sister a kiss as the car sped into the night.

Gabrielle's spirits deflated now they were gone. She draped the long strap of her purse around her shoulders, tucked her umbrella under one arm, and set off for the

Saint-Germain-des-Prés métro station. She wished she'd thrown a pair of thin flats into her bag.

A blister was starting to form by the time she spotted the unassuming red sign and began to descend the stairs into the bowels of the earth. Echoing up from the tunnels, Gabrielle heard the horn blast, signalling that the train was closing its doors and leaving. Her shoulders sank. *Zut!* She'd have to wait for the next one.

Slowing her pace, she entered the open area where the trains squealing along their dark, twisty rails, emerged to be loaded, and found a hard plastic chair to sit. It was ten o'clock, and not too busy. She glanced at the other waiting passengers. A mother with two young girls laughed over something on their phone, an older couple sat on a bench facing her across the wide gap of rails, and a nearby group of teenage boys pushed one another back and forth as they loudly recounted their evening's fun.

Her gaze shifted to a man consulting a blown-up version of the Paris métro map on the wall nearby. He traced streets and train lines with a finger, his speech low and uncertain, and then, shaking his head, he started all over again. He was an unusual figure since he was probably the only person she'd ever seen in real life wearing a cowboy hat. It seemed to belong on him, too.

He looked so out of place and disoriented that she briefly wondered if she should offer to help him. Except another train was already coming, and she was tired, wanting to get home. Besides, when the train skidded to a halt and the doors slammed open, he climbed on behind her. His brown leather bomber jacket creaked as he lifted a huge duffle bag into the railcar. A guitar case poked over his shoulder. She wondered if he was a country western entertainer visiting the City of Lights as a busker.

She shifted her regard. The man must know where he was going. He sank into the first chair he saw, still muttering. Only now she could make out it was an address he repeated over and over, a sound of desperation in his voice.

She took a seat on the other side of the wide entrance and watched him curiously from beneath her lashes. He was attractive, she decided. He wore snug-fitting jeans with boots like she'd only seen in old Westerns, and had sandy-coloured hair, short at the back and longer over his forehead. His face was kind, if somewhat confused. He looked rumpled as though he'd been up all night and badly needed a shave. Large, strong hands clutched the long canvas handle of the bag resting at his feet. He looked like a man who worked outdoors for a living, maybe cutting down trees and hauling them from the bush on his shoulders or chucking boulders out of the way to build roads through uncharted territory.

Inwardly, she smiled at her fanciful ideas. His eyes were a vibrant blue beneath the black felt of his hat, set in a ruggedly handsome face. He scanned the other passengers as though looking for someone. A moment later, they alighted on her watching him. Quickly she lowered her gaze, but it was too late.

Reaching out to secure a grip on the pole at the center of the car, he staggered across the open area, dragging his heavy-looking bag behind him as the train lurched around a bend. He dropped into the seat next to her.

"Par-lay voo...English?" he asked with a hopeful expression.

Inwardly she chuckled. Really, his French was so terrible it was cute. "Yes," she answered calmly. "I speak quite good English."

"That's fantastic." He breathed a sigh of relief and flopped back on the seat, closing his eyes briefly. "Do you suppose you could help me figure out if I'm on the right train?" He straightened one long leg as he dug a hand into his jeans' pocket. "I've had visions of wandering the backstreets of Paris until morning." Straightening, he swivelled on the seat to explain, holding a folded piece of paper. "I flew into Charles de Gaulle Airport late this afternoon and had worked out how to take the train into the city."

He waved the paper. "I managed that part okay, but then fell asleep on the next train. When I woke up it was the end of the line, somewhere out in the suburbs. Anyway, I couldn't make sense of where I was…and no one spoke English, so I got on a train going the opposite direction and changed trains a few times till I ended up here…" He sighed heavily. "For the last three hours I've been endlessly riding the rails to my doom."

The man grinned at her from close range. "Sounds like the lyrics to a sad country song, or the opening line of a third-rate sci-fi novel. Doesn't it?" His brows raised and she nodded bemusedly at him.

"But that's what happened." She admired the colour of his eyes, an icy shade of blue, lightly creasing at the corners with good humour, and found herself smiling back. The man was charismatic. He thrust the tattered paper at her. "Could you tell me how to find this address?"

She accepted it and smoothed the creased scrap of paper over her leg to examine it more closely. It was a map he must have printed from the internet, but it had been folded and handled so often that the street names were fading. He appeared to have nothing else to guide him on this journey.

He reached over, caught the end of the paper, and flipped it. "I wrote the address on the back."

She looked up at his hopeful face and wide, trusting eyes. "*Oui*," she said. "I know exactly where it is, and you are on the right train." The train skidded to a stop and the doors flew open as several people rushed on and hurried to find a seat.

"You're kidding! I had it right?"

"You did. Five more stops and we will arrive at the Étienne Marcel métro station. Both of us will get out there since it 'appens to be close to where I live as well." She folded the paper and handed it back. "I will point you in the right direction once we are on the street."

"Unbelievable." After all his chatter he suddenly appeared to be at a loss for words. He shoved the printout back in his jeans' pocket.

"You are staying in the Marais," she added, in case he wasn't aware. "It is a popular area for tourists."

"Yeah, I was told that when I booked the place, but I'm not a tourist as it happens. I mean, I am…in the sense that I've never been to Paris, or really anywhere before. But I'm not just coming to look around."

"Oh…" Gabrielle wondered why he was here, but felt it would be rude to enquire. Instead, she asked another, safer question. "Where are you from?"

"Canada," he said shortly, his eyes following their progress on the map above the doors. "Grew up on a ranch in southern Alberta. Ever heard of Calgary?"

She shook her head. "No. But I 'ave family members who lived in Manitoba and Sastisk…Satisk-a…" She stumbled over the word.

"Saskatchewan?" He looked surprised when she smiled her agreement. "That's wild. It's the first province east of Calgary, Alberta." His big grin revealed even white teeth as he leaned toward her conspiratorially. "This is where you're supposed to ask me if I know so-and-so, who also lives in Canada. And since it's just such a small place we must all be friends." He broke into derisive laughter. "I've been asked that question today a couple of times. As though I'd know a guy called Brad Larson, who lives in Toronto, three provinces away."

His laughter was infectious, and she chuckled along, not fully understanding the joke. "By the way, we haven't introduced ourselves," he said, sticking out his hand to awkwardly grasp hers. "My name's Andrew Filmore. I'm happy to meet you and thankful for your help."

"I am Gabrielle Dupont," she replied, shrinking a little from the strength of his grip and his unorthodox greeting. "You do not 'ave a phone with GPS to give you directions?"

He shook his head apologetically. "I have a phone, but no data. It's pretty useless right now, at least till I can buy a SIM card."

Even as her mouth opened to make the offer, her head was telling her to let him find someone else to help. Still, she knew how disorienting it could be to wander through the maze of tiny streets, late at night, searching for an address. "Then, I will walk you to your apartment if you wish."

Andrew's eyes widened. "You'd do that?"

She shrugged. "Welcome to Paris, Andrew Filmore."

"That's really nice of you. But for all you know, I could be a mass murderer. Or turn into a crazed maniac once I'm above ground."

"Will you become a…" she paused over the words, "crazed maniac?" She arched her eyebrows.

"No," he said, tapping a finger thoughtfully on his chin, his eyes alight with mischief. "I'm a pretty safe guy."

"Then would you like my 'elp?"

"Very much," he said, becoming serious. "I can't tell you how much I'd appreciate it."

As the train rolled to a halt with a sudden lurch, Gabrielle looked through the window for the name of the stop painted on the wall. There it was *Étienne Marcel*.

"This is where we get off," she said, jumping up and lifting the latch to open the door. Hoping she wouldn't regret it, she said, "Follow me."

As they exited the métro and headed down Rue de Turbigo, Gabrielle took a deep breath of fresh air. The city was a tapestry of dark and light, with long shadows cast by the occasional streetlight. There weren't many pedestrians about, but cars flashed past them, their headlights still glistening off the wet pavement. Gabrielle marched determinedly along, wincing with each step.

"Why don't you just take them off?" Andrew's deep voice cut into her thoughts. He hadn't spoken since they'd arrived at street level.

She faltered, the pain of the shoe biting into her heel was worsening by the minute. He was right. Why didn't she? Spying a bench just ahead, she aimed for it and gratefully sat down to pull the offending heels from her feet, rubbing each aching foot in turn.

"*Quelle bonne idée*," she said, forgetting for a moment that he couldn't understand. "Sorry. I said that was a good idea. Thanks." She lingered for a moment, enjoying the cold, wet pavement beneath her burning feet. A sigh escaped her lips.

"So, is it far?" he asked, standing like a dark sentinel beside her. He gazed out at the traffic whizzing by, despite the late hour. "I guess a city never sleeps, heh?" he mused, half to himself.

"It's only a few minutes' walk," Gabrielle replied, standing to continue with a shoe in each hand. Andrew fell into step beside her. "And no, it's never really quiet here. People are always on the move. You said you live in the country?"

"Yep. That's where I grew up, although my roots are here in France. On my mother's side."

Gabrielle looked at him in surprise. France? This man looked as though his heritage was about as far away from French as it was possible to get. His large boots thumped loudly with each step, the cowboy hat jutted from his face, and he strode along as though the enormous bag and guitar case hanging across his back were stuffed with feathers. He was about as country as it got, at least in her limited knowledge. She really only had movies to go by. She shook her head, focusing on the sidewalk as the incongruity of the situation suddenly striking her as funny. Here she was, dressed to kill in her red dress with stilettoes, now exchanged for barefoot in puddles, leading a lost cowboy along the streets of Paris. Unsuccessfully, she tried to stifle a giggle.

He glanced at her. "Something funny?" he asked. "Oh, I get it..." his face took on an expression of mock horror as he paused under a streetlamp. "*You're* the mass murder, luring an innocent traveller off to his death." He took off his hat and dragged a forearm across his brow. "I should have known. It's always the raven-haired beauties you have to watch out for."

Gabrielle broke into a fit of uncontrollable giggles. She hadn't laughed like this since—since who knew when? "*Désolé*, uh...I mean, sorry!" she sputtered and then hiccupped, still chortling. "You're perfectly safe. In fact, we're almost there." She pointed ahead. "We should cross here." Looking both ways, she darted across the road in her bare feet with Andrew loping along behind her, his guitar bobbing up and down. Somewhere in the distance a siren wailed. They continued to walk in silence.

"This is Rue Saint-Denis. That is your street, correct?" He nodded in the dim light, his face registering admiration. "Now, we find your building, but I don't think it's much farther."

"You're awesome," he said. "You made it look so easy. Without you, I bet I'd have ridden that train to the end of the line again."

"You will learn 'ow it works soon enough," she stated

modestly, as they trudged along. "There are small métro maps you can pick up at the ticket offices. Pick your destination and figure out which colour-coded lines you need to piece together to get you there. It's 'ard to explain, but the main thing to keep in mind is that you follow the direction you need to go based on the end destination." She stopped. "I could show you if you had a map, but we 'ave arrived, and you don't."

"We're here?" Andrew peered into the gloom with wonder as Gabrielle picked out the number plate on the side of the building with the flashlight on her phone.

"Do you have the passcode?" she asked.

"Yes." Throwing his duffle bag to the ground, he fished in his other jeans' pocket. He finally came up with a similarly rumpled bit of paper and handed it over.

She held up a hand, waving him forward. "It's best if you do it yourself," she said. "After all, I won't be here to open the door each time you go out."

"You could," he countered with a grin. "I wouldn't mind." She shook her head, his light-hearted innuendo making her smile again.

Andrew committed the code to memory before he pressed the corresponding buttons. When an answering buzzer sounded and the door unlatched, he pushed it open. Leaning back, he grabbed his bag and reached for her hand, grasping it within his large strong one. This time he didn't squeeze though. He brought it up to his lips and kissed it with gallantry.

"Thank you, fair lady," he said, as if quoting Shakespeare in a school play. "You've saved a poor, lost cowboy from a fate worse than death." He dropped her hand with evident reluctance, but made no move to leave, holding the door wide. "All dramatics aside, you really did come to my rescue. I can't thank you enough. Could I perhaps take you for breakfast in the morning? Just to thank you," he added quickly. "Besides, I don't know where to eat so you'd be helping a guy out yet again. What do you say?"

The smile had faded from Gabrielle's face at the mention of breakfast. She wasn't in the market for another relationship. She'd had high hopes for the last one and look how that ended. But Andrew did seem sweet, and he was funny. What could it hurt?

"Alright," she agreed. "What time will you be up? You must be suffering from jetlag."

"Is nine, okay?"

"It's good." She pointed back where they had just come. "Did you see the red awning on the corner we just passed?" He nodded, craning his neck. "That café is where I will be at nine o'clock tomorrow morning, Paris time. *Bonne nuit.*" Waving, she stepped back and moved off into the night.

"Bun nuey," he called after her. "I'll be there."

Pulling the ties of her coat tighter, Gabrielle set off for her own cozy apartment on the fifth floor of a tiny *rue* only about fifteen minutes away. *Should she have done that? Probably not.* But lifting the hand he had kissed up to her cheek, she had to admit that some part of her, deep inside, was thrilled.

Chapter Two

Cobblestone streets glistened with the remnants of yesterday's rain, as the rising sun cast its golden light across the city. Gabrielle hiked along the sidewalk, avoiding men in long trench coats looking worriedly at their watches, and old women pulling two-wheeled shopping trolleys after a successful shopping expedition at the early morning market. She was making her way to the café where she had agreed to meet Andrew.

Birds sang from trees and balconies, as the sound of distant car horns echoed through the streets. The laughter of café-goers from their early morning conversations filtered into her ears in the clean, crisp morning as she arrived. Inside the café was bright and warm, a cozy haven on the corner of a busy street, but outside was soft and hazy with wisps of a light mist that melted away as the morning heat grew.

Gabrielle chose a small round table outside, in a patch of sunshine on this perfect spring day. The wicker chairs were well-worn from years of use and the servers cheerful as they began their day serving coffee to the regulars. Gabrielle often stopped here on her way to university, and they knew her well. She didn't need to place an order. The minute she sat down, a smiling young man placed a steaming cup on the table before her.

"*Bonjour et merci*," she said, returning his cheery greeting.

She'd dressed in a slim-fitting black blazer, white lace top, dark jeans, with a long, thin black scarf wound about her neck, and grey, well-worn ankle boots. Her long black hair was pulled into a ponytail with a thin red ribbon today. It could be a distraction when she was studying.

She sipped her *café au lait* and watched as people bustled in and out of a *boulangerie* across the street wielding long baguettes and bags of fresh pastries. Inhaling the scent was almost as good as indulging in a crisp croissant herself, but not quite. However, she would wait for the cowboy to join her before ordering. If he showed at all.

It was against her better judgement that she had come this morning, but good manners dictated that she should keep her promise after having agreed to it the night before. She leaned back in her chair and crossed her legs, squinting in the bright sunlight, but enjoying the feeling of warmth on her face. It promised to be a beautiful day. And, despite knowing she ought to be holed up in her apartment studying until all hours of the night, she planned to go on a pilgrimage to find cherry blossoms.

Those favoured trees, heavy with white and pink blossoms, could be found almost everywhere in April, but Gabrielle planned to visit Jardin des Plantes. It was one of her favourite Parisian gardens.

Reaching for her purse, hanging on the back of her chair, she dug through the contents for her phone, her hand finding the mail from the day before. She groaned with annoyance, having forgotten about the letters after seeing Andrew safely to his door. Her fingers curled around the thick wad, thinking she might as well open them while she waited. Her heart sank at the thought of opening the strange one, but her hand stilled as she heard her name.

"Gabrielle! You're really here," said a voice. Then, quickly correcting himself, Andrew added, "I mean, bun jure."

She dropped her bag and smiled. "*Bonjour*...good morning. Please, sit down."

Andrew pulled out a chair and lowered himself onto it, the round bistro table immediately looking small beside him. He wore the large black hat again today, but removed it as he sat, balancing it on his knee. She stared at it, mesmerized. Since the sheltered spot received the full force of the sun, he also removed his leather jacket, revealing a white t-shirt that strained over taut, muscled arms. "Did I say that right?" he asked. "I have to start learning French or I'm going to be in trouble."

"Trouble?" she asked. But when he made no move to answer, she continued. "It is pronounced, *bonjour*," she repeated slowly. "It's one word, not two, and it slides over the tongue without hard sounds to the letters. *Bonjour*," she repeated gently.

"Oh," he said, stretching his mouth into a number of positions to limber it up. "*Bonjour*," he said, sounding much improved.

"That's right," she snapped her fingers. "You will master the language in no time at all."

"Yeah, no problem. Should only take me the next twenty, maybe thirty years," he said with a nonchalant shrug. "How do we order something to eat?" He looked around then eyed her tiny coffee cup with amazement, picking it up between his index finger and thumb where it dangled like a toy from a little girl's tea set. "Why is it so small?"

"That is 'ow coffee is served in France." Gabrielle didn't know how else to answer this unusual man. "Do you want one?"

"If they're all that small I'd like about five of 'em to start," he said seriously, dropping the little cup onto her saucer with a clatter. "And something to eat, but I have no idea what. Could you choose for me, please?"

Gabrielle lifted a hand to her mouth to hide a grin as she waved for their server. "I know just what you would like," she stated. "At least, I 'ope I do."

When the young man reached their table, he placed her empty cup on top of the tray he balanced in one hand. She quickly ordered a *pain au chocolat* for herself and a *croque monsieur* for Andrew, along with *trois café au lait*. The server raised an eyebrow, no doubt wondering why she'd ordered three coffees when there were only two of them. However, he didn't question it, but soon reappeared with the beverages on his tray.

"That's really good coffee," Andrew declared, drinking the first in one gulp and reaching for the second.

"Did you even taste it?"

"Well, sure I did." He grimaced, delicately poking his pinky finger into the air, and taking a minuscule sip. "That better?"

She laughed out loud. "Are you always like this or am I just privileged?"

"Like what?" he asked, tipping the entire contents into his mouth and swallowing.

"Quirky—unpredictable—eccentric," she cocked her head to one side and frowned, staring at this man who clearly walked to the beat of his own drum. "Or per'aps all Canadian men are like you?"

"Pretty much," he agreed. "But we're not uncouth, if that's what you're hinting at. I'm just used to coffee served in a mug that holds more than a mouthful." He squinted into the cup as if hoping it would magically fill again.

Gabrielle watched him for a moment and then couldn't prevent herself from asking the question that had been burning on her tongue. "Why are you in Paris, Andrew from Canada?"

Leaning back, he stretched his long legs out in front of him, nearly crushing a passing poodle. "Well, I inherited a business," he said simply.

"A business?" Gabrielle felt as though she repeated half of what this man said with a question mark at the end. "What sort of business?" Her thoughts raced to when Lyam had told her almost the very same thing. His was antiques and curios coupled with working as a tour guide. Of course, she had never seen the shop he purportedly owned, and now knew him to be the most adept liar she had ever met.

"Yeah, selling wine. My uncle Olivier, my mom's brother, lived here all his life. It was his store. His pride and joy, really. But his wife passed away a few months back, and they had no other family. When he died, only a month ago, he left everything to me. I rented a private room for a few days until I can find out whether I could live in my uncle's home next door to the shop and what should be done with it all."

"Oh." Gabrielle was at a loss for words. "I'm sorry to 'ear this. Were you close?"

"He came to visit us a couple of times when I was a kid. But no, I didn't know him very well. Mom flew here every summer and spent a month with him. He was her only living relative. She's taking it pretty hard."

They both took a moment to digest this information during which time Gabrielle flagged down the server and ordered two more coffees. Andrew was an interesting and unique person.

"So, what will you do with this shop? Do you know much about wine?"

"Do I look like the kind of guy who knows about wine?" he countered with a lopsided grin.

"No," she said immediately. He most definitely did not.

"He pulled in his legs as a group of elderly ladies shuffled past on the sidewalk. "Give that girl a prize. You're right. Beer, I understand. Pilsner, Molson Canadian, Budweiser, Labatt's to name a few," he listed. "Or give me a shot of whiskey and I'm a happy man. I know nothing about wine."

"I see." She took another sip of her coffee while waiting for him to continue. Eventually, his face sobered and he did.

"I don't know what to do about the shop," he said. "It meant a lot to Uncle Olivier, and I'd hate to sell it, but this…" he spread his arms wide to encompass the whole of Paris, and continued, "is not me."

"Per'aps, you 'ave to find this shop and try to understand the life that gave your uncle such feelings of pride before you make your decision," she suggested.

Andrew turned to look at her, for once his eyes were grave. "Yes," he said. "It's important to me and to my mom. So, guess I'll be around for a while." He crossed his arms behind his head and leaned back with his eyes closed.

"Hey!" he reared up, startling Gabrielle so much she almost dropped her cup. "Do you need a job?"

"A job?" she said, then mentally kicked herself for parroting the man yet again. "What are you talking about?"

At that moment, their food arrived. A steaming plate was set before Andrew. On it was Gabrielle's favourite breakfast; two slices of rustic bread covered with ham and Gruyere cheese, then browned in butter on either side. Afterward the sandwich was smothered in béchamel sauce, sprinkled with more Gruyere, and broiled until the top was golden brown. The smell was mouth-watering and she wished she would have gotten one for herself.

But her crispy pain au chocolat was delicious too and she took a bite. Andrew stared at his plate for a moment as though to say, 'this is it?' but once he cut a portion off and lifted it to his mouth he closed his eyes rapturously as he chewed.

"That's great stuff. What do you call it?" Busily he sawed off another portion.

"*Croque monsieur*," Gabrielle said, pleased that he liked it so well. She allowed her attention to drift back to the bakery across the way. She had a nasty suspicion what he was getting at with his question concerning a job and no, she didn't want any part of it.

Andrew lifted a napkin to his mouth with a satisfied sigh. "That was wonderful, but I'm not even going to try repeating what it's called. At least, not in front of you." He winked at her. "Thanks for ordering it. And back to what I was going to ask you…I've decided I can't impose upon you any further."

He looked around at the slow progression of life on a Sunday morning in the Marais. "It's not at all like I'd imagined," he murmured. "I really like it here. But that's largely thanks to you." His icy blue eyes caught hers again and a slow smile spread across his face. "Your kindness has made all the difference in a difficult situation."

She flushed. "I only 'elped someone in need," she said. "Most people would 'ave done the same."

"Most beautiful young women would *not* have gone out of their way, late at night, to help some strange, and obviously desperate man find his way." He leaned his chin on folded hands and gazed at her admiringly, which only served to deepen her colour. "I think you're quite remarkable." Then with a laugh he sat back. "If the tables are ever turned, and you find yourself lost and alone on the Canadian Prairies, facing down a herd of restless cattle, I'm your man."

"I'll remember that." She laughed with him, the intensity of the moment dissipating. "Are you going to find your uncle's shop today?"

"Yes," he reached for his coffee cup and examined it to make sure there wasn't a drop left. Then, setting it down carefully, he wrung his large hands together, a worried frown creasing his forehead. "I expect it'll be an emotional day. No one has set foot in the place since he got sick and was taken to the hospital. The lawyer mailed me the keys along with a copy of the will and other paperwork. Guess there'll be a lot to do."

"I'm sorry." As before, Gabrielle felt a surge of pity for this man and his lost relative. She couldn't imagine what she would do in a similar situation. Especially in a foreign country where everyone spoke a language he couldn't understand. "Andrew, I'd like to…"

"No," he said emphatically, holding up a hand and dipping his head. "I won't keep you any longer or ask you to help me further," he said. "I'm sure you have things to do. I haven't even had the courtesy to ask you about yourself."

"You don't even know what I was going to say," she said, feeling indignant that he'd shut her down so sternly. If she wanted to help him she would!

"I could tell." He placed his napkin alongside his plate and pushed away from the table. "Now, how do I get the bill for this meal?" He pulled a credit card from an inside pocket of his jacket and flourished it in the air.

"You can ask your server for the bill like this, *l'addition s'il vous plaît*," she said, enunciating slowly. "But honestly…" she giggled, "in your case I think, I should just accompany you today and give you a few lessons." She held up a hand of her own as he began to protest. "No. Please do not argue. It is what I want to do. No one should be in Paris, doing what you 'ave to do without a friend. I will be that friend, for you. *D'accord?*"

His face lit up with a broad grin and his shoulders visibly relaxed. "If *de-a-cord* means, 'do you agree,' then yes, I agree and accept your offer. Thank you."

"First lesson," she said, wagging her finger at him with a shake of her head, "thank you is *merci*. Say it with me. M-e-r-c-i." She dragged it out purposely, encouraging him to repeat it with her. Laughing again when he made it sound like, *mercy*, she then continued, "We 'ave our work cut out for us, that is for certain. But now, we will pay and find your uncle's *petit caviste*. That is French for, small wine shop."

Nodding, but making no attempt to try the phrase, Andrew pushed away from their table. Gabrielle waved their server over and explained to him that Andrew wished to pay with, "…*une carte de credit*." Again, she enunciated slowly as she looked at Andrew meaningfully and pointing to the plastic in his hand.

"I was going to take a cab," Andrew said, handing her a

scribbled address on a piece of paper as they strolled away. "I wasn't going to fool around with that underground train again, but since you're here, perhaps you can find it. I chose an apartment in the Marais, because it was fairly close." He looked around in bewilderment. "I just have no idea which way to go from here."

Gabrielle examined the scrap of paper. "*Oui*, it is not far from 'ere." She looked at him and waved a hand down the street to her left. "We will walk, *d'accord*?

"Dah cord," he agreed, as they quickened their pace.

It didn't take long for them to reach the cobblestone lane where the shop was located and soon they stood in front of large windows in need of a good wash. A set of antique-looking keys jangled in Andrew's hand as they paused outside to take it all in.

To Gabrielle, it felt a bit like stepping back in time. They faced two ancient, wooden doors, side by side. One led into a darkened shop where she could see row upon row of bottles gleaming dully in the bit of sunlight filtering past the tall old buildings all around them. The other appeared to be a private entrance.

"That must be where Uncle Olivier lived…" Andrew said, staring at the door with a sigh. "Poor man. He was devastated after his wife died. Wish I'd have gotten to know him better."

Paint peeled from the wood surrounding the bricks that made up a majority of the walls, and a rickety sign squeaked to and fro over the door in the slight April breeze.

"*Caviste de Tremblay*," she murmured, reading the faded words that hung above them. She sensed the sadness Andrew was experiencing as he looked upon this place that led to him learning a part of his family's history.

Andrew took a deep breath and moved forward to unlock the door. It swung back on old hinges that would be improved with a dousing of oil. Gingerly, Andrew walked inside.

She noticed there was no light switch as Andrew groped around on the wall in the semi-darkness. Looking around, she spotted a thin chain hanging from the ceiling. Moving past him, she pulled it, and the room flooded with light. Andrew shut the door and leaned against it.

Gabrielle wasn't sure if Andrew felt the palpable sense of sadness in the stagnant air of the shop. She gazed around at the dusty bottles and derelict bins filled haphazardly with additional flasks down the center of the space. She rubbed the grime off a few and peered closely at them. Each one had a different label, from all over France.

The shop wasn't wide. She could have spanned the entire width of the store in five strides, but it was long and housed a lot of inventory. Both walls were covered, top to bottom, with bottles, and they ran right to the back of the store where there was an old counter and an equally old cash register.

"Do you suppose he was selling any?" Andrew asked quietly. He'd wandered in a few paces, but then stopped and lifted a hand to scrub the back of his neck. "It reeks of neglect and illness in here." His voice sounded anguished. "Why didn't he tell us? I would have come to help. I should have come…" His voice trailed off. Clearly he was blaming himself.

"Andrew, you can't take responsibility for something you didn't know about. Your uncle must 'ave 'ad his own reasons for not saying anything to your mother." She walked behind the counter where there was a tottery old stool, a wastepaper bin, and a roll of brown paper, presumably for wrapping each bottle of wine before it left the store.

"What am I supposed to do with this place?" he asked. She whirled around to see that Andrew had come to stand behind her, staring blankly at the cash register with his shoulders slumped. He poked a feeble finger at a few of the keys and a drawer slid out with the loud ring of an internal bell.

He jumped back in surprise and then pulled it out further to look inside. "Coins—a few euro, two buttons, and some string," he said, pushing it closed. Taking a deep breath, he straightened his shoulders. "Uncle Olivier gave this place and his home next door to me, his nephew. It was his love, his life." The deepening tone of Andrew's voice became more confident with each word. "According to mom, Uncle Olivier didn't make any decision lightly, which means there was a purpose to him entrusting all of this…" he flung his arms wide, and continued, "to me. And I won't let him down."

"*C'est vrai*," Gabrielle murmured. "It's true. I am certain 'e believed you would do what was best." She moved around the counter, unprepared for what would happen next.

Leaping forward, Andrew scooped her up and lifted her off her feet as he twirled her in the air. "Ooh la la," she screeched, catching her breath as his strong hands closed around her waist. Grinning, he set her down, ran a hand through hair that had fallen over one eye and fixed her with his piercing gaze.

"I'll do it!" he announced with fervor. "I have a long-stay visa in place. I'll take some time and put Uncle Olivier's shop back on its feet. I owe it to his memory. The future will take care of itself, as my mother always says. Yes, I may have to sell it down the road. Not really sure that a guy whose closest companions were cows, could even run a wine shop in Paris. I don't understand the language and don't know the first thing about wine, but…" he squared his shoulders. "I'm going to give it a damn good try."

Chapter Three

After showing Andrew how quickly he could reach his rented apartment from his uncle's store, Gabrielle returned to her own home. *Chambres parmi les étoiles*, or her rooms among the stars, as she liked to call her apartment on the fifth floor of the building on Rue Saint-Martin. She spent the afternoon cross-legged on the floor of the salon, finishing homework and studying for final exams. If she passed, it would secure her a degree in psychology. From there she could take on the problems of the world while waving her diploma in victory, or so she had imagined when she'd first started this journey.

She paused to search for a bottle of sparkling water that lurked at the back of her tiny refrigerator. Carrying it to the table, she laid the book she had been reading in front of her. Before opening it to her marked page, she considered the man she had agreed to help. Why had she suddenly changed her mind? Was she thinking of him as a psychology project? An interesting case study like so many she'd encountered over the last three years. Or simply a diversion from the recent chaos of her life, post Lyam. She didn't want to label the friendship she had begun. Instead, she fell back to poring over her books until the alarm on her phone rang, alerting her to the lateness of the day. It was almost four-thirty and she'd wanted to go for a walk before the sun slipped from the sky.

Grabbing her purse and jacket, she hurried downstairs. The idea crossed her mind that by now Andrew would likely need a break too. She strode along the sidewalk, humming a little tune, taking no notice of the appreciative stares she received from men she passed.

Arriving at his Uncle Olivier's neglected little shop, she noticed the store's two ancient windows had been lifted from the bottom and propped open by using elderly, black leather boots, set on end.

"*Bonjour*," she called, poking her head through the window that was open the widest. "'Allo? Andrew are you 'ere?" There was a distant scuffling sound from inside.

"Hi!" he yelled. "Come on in."

Pushing the door open, she noticed things were already taking on a brighter aspect. Fresh air had driven out the dank smell of sadness and dilapidation. The crumbling crates that ran down the center of the space, were gone too. Bottles, clean and sparkling stood in their place, and the sound of hammering could be heard from a back room.

Gabrielle paused to look at a few labels as she passed through and realized there was some really good wine here. She wondered if any were from Chateau de Belliveau, her family winery in Provence.

"Hey," Andrew greeted her from the floor where he was kneeling over a pile of old boards. A saw, bucket of nails, and other equipment lay around him. He sat back on his haunches and swiped an arm across his brow. "It's surprising what Uncle Olivier had back here. I think I can make something really nice from this." He waved a hand over the assortment of wood. "I may not know wine, but I can build almost anything; cow sheds, barns, fences, you name it. Surely I can put together a few display shelves or wine racks."

"I am sure you can too. I see you 'ave been cleaning."

"Yep," he picked up the hammer, waving it in her direction. "I just want to put this idea of mine together. Then we can see what it'll look like, okay?" She nodded. He stuck a few nails in his mouth and as he began hammering, she left the room to wander among the bottles. She picked up the cloth he'd been using and started dusting a few more. Fifteen minutes later, he called her back and she entered to find him standing over a rectangular, wooden container.

"It's a display box. Otherwise known as a manger, or a feeder for cattle." He grinned at her puzzled face. "Still, I think my uncle would have been happy with it." His pleasure was endearing, and his face flushed with pride. He hoped she would like what he'd created, and Gabrielle found her heart skipping a beat. He seemed like such a sweet guy. Of course, she'd believed similar things about someone else before too. And look how that had turned out. She cast her eyes away from him and toward the box.

He nudged his invention with a toe. "All I have to do is find some of that fake straw stuff to create a cushion, and bottles can be laid inside. Makes a beautiful presentation, don't you think?"

"I do. And I believe you are referring to raffia. I can find some for you at an 'ome improvement store." Despite her brain telling her to remain aloof, Gabrielle found it hard to admire the box instead of the man. "Would you like to take a break from your work and go for a walk? I promised myself I would find some cherry trees today. They are blooming all over the city."

For his answer, Andrew brushed off his knees and reached for the leather jacket flung on an ancient workbench. "I'd follow you anywhere," he said with a grin.

Gabrielle blushed, turning away quickly to lead the way back through the shop. She waited outside while he closed the windows and locked up. They then walked purposefully up the street toward the same métro station they'd arrived at late last night.

"Where are you taking me?"

"*Jardin des Plantes* on the left bank of the Seine River. Officially, it is the National Museum of Natural History, but I go there for the botanical gardens."

"Sounds great," he said enthusiastically. "I've never had too much time for gardens. As a kid I'd help my mother, but that was for vegetables, not flowers."

"You spent much of your time working with *les vaches*?" She grinned up at him as they strolled along Rue Saint Denis.

"If you're going to use French words I don't know, and then laugh at me," he said with a mock frown, "I may have to revert back to my earlier threat where I become a crazed maniac."

She made a sound of derision. "I wouldn't believe it any more than I did last night." But she made a show of distancing herself from him and he chuckled.

"Not even one day has passed, and already this girl's me figured out." Andrew directed his remarks to a plane tree growing through a square patch of earth on the sidewalk.

Laughing, Gabrielle said, "*Les vaches* means, the cows."

"Ahh, thought so. Yeah, I've spent a lot of time with them. Too much probably. Twenty-eight years old and still single." He kicked a stone from the sidewalk with the toe of his cowboy boot. "What about you? Did you grow up here?"

"No. Toulouse. It is in the south of France. I came 'ere to attend the University of Paris-Descartes. I will graduate with a degree in psychology soon. If I pass my finals," she admitted.

"I see," Andrew said, stroking a non-existent beard and frowning. "So, that's why you're being so nice. You're using me as a case study." Moving his hands as though he were picking up an invisible book, he shot her a sideways look, licked his finger, and turned unseen pages before reading aloud, "Chapter ten, paragraph three, and I quote, '*The inner workings of the primitive male, fresh off the farm are unfathomable to the gentile Frenchwoman. It is highly improbable that an uncultured, unrefined, almost boorish man could enter polite Parisian society without the intervention of modern psychological methods of treatment. See attached dossier for recommendations.*'"

"You are terrible," she quipped and laughed aloud, smacking him in the arm. "I'm doing no such thing." She looked coquettishly over her shoulder as she sped up. "I am taking pity on you, because I believe you are beyond conventional 'elp." Giggling, as he roared with mock outrage, she sprinted ahead, feeling happier than she had in —well, maybe in forever.

Gabrielle was pleased to learn Andrew had purchased the Passe Navigo card, used for all public methods of travel in Paris. Grabbing a small, free map of Paris from the ticket kiosk, they descended into the métro station and flashed their cards at the scanner. The gates clanged open, and they hurried along the cave-like hallways to where their train was screeching to a stop. The doors slid open, people poured out, and they hopped on.

The train was full of passengers who studiously avoided eye contact. Gabrielle led him through the crowd of people, who kept their feet planted wide to maintain balance, as the train lurched away with a squeal of metal. As they rode toward *Odéon*, where they needed to change lines, they fell into a friendly silence.

In a matter of minutes, they reached their destination, alighted from the train, and made their way along the winding corridor. As they climbed to street level, Gabrielle sighed rapturously, feeling the fresh breeze swirl down the steps to meet them.

The sky above was the colour of a robin's egg, and the sun shone with a gentle warmth that promised a serene spring day. As they wandered into the garden, shimmering butterflies floated through the air, moving like scraps of spun silk.

Flowers of every hue splashed across the landscape in riotous colour, each row painted as though with the stroke of an artist's paintbrush. Eagerly, she led her new friend to saunter along paths created for admirers of natural beauty, toward a cherry tree hanging heavy with pink blossoms. Its branches dipped low beneath the weight. The tree was so heavily laden with blooms, they nearly touched the ground, resembling a wedding cake covered in perfectly formed flowers.

"I can't even see any leaves," Andrew said with surprise. He left the path and ducked under the branches to stand beneath the blushing canopy, examining a branch at close range. "Flowers cover the entire tree."

Gabrielle laughed as he came back to join her, and they continued their promenade. "The garden was created in 1635 by the royal physicians of King Louis the thirteenth to grow medicinal plants," she said. "They brought herbs and plants from all over the world to be tested for their curative properties." She gestured ahead to where a long, creamy-white building, with domes at either end, spanned the open area. "That building is the Natural History Museum. I spend time there too, but we do not have time to go there today."

Other shrubs and plants rustled in the cool, blissful breeze, their new leaves glowing in the light like emeralds. The air was filled with the fragrant bouquet of sweet-smelling flowers and the earthy aroma of freshly turned soil.

"I can see why you wanted to come." Andrew drew a deep breath. "It's peaceful. Sort of clears your head." He turned his head to look at her face, seeking her agreement as they walked.

"*Oui*. When we were young, my parents would bring my sister and me to see this garden and occasionally the *Ménagerie*..." She paused to translate. "In English, it means the zoo. *Ma mère*, my mother, was from Paris and she would miss 'er life in the city sometimes. So, my father would bring 'er to visit. Walking through 'ere brings back special memories." She trailed her fingers along a tree branch filled with white cherry blossoms. They brushed across her skin like velvet whispers. She stopped, pulled a branch to her nose, and breathed deeply. The sweet smell of petals and pollen was heady. The breeze carried a chorus of buzzing insects and chirping birds. This was the balm she had wanted. It was perfect.

Tears welled up as she thought of her mother. The last few months had been hard. Sharing the burden with her parents would have been a relief, but she couldn't involve them in the mess that surrounded her relationship with Lyam.

Surreptitiously, she dabbed at the moisture on her lashes

and pasted a smile on her face. "My mother grew up not far from here, in that direction." She swung her arm. "In the fifth *arrondissement*."

"You have special ties to the city. Guess I do too, in a way, but we're worlds apart."

"Tell me about it," she prompted, clasping her hands behind her back as they wandered between beds of multi-coloured tulips.

"About where I'm from?"

"*Oui*, it interests me." She smiled at him.

"Nothing too exciting to tell," he said, hooking his thumbs into the belt loops of his jeans, his boots clumping on the broad sidewalk. "Dad met Mom in Normandy while touring France on an educational trip when he was in high school. It was his last year, so he must have been seventeen or eighteen. The two of them kept in contact through letters for a couple of years and then she came for a visit. They fell in love and were married within a few months' time. She came to live in Canada, on the cattle ranch where my dad grew up. The countryside is beautiful there," Andrew's eyes took on a faraway look. "Our farm is set in the foothills of the Rocky Mountains. Ever been there?"

"No, I 'ave traveled around Europe, but never to the Americas."

"You should go sometime. Of course, you need to have realistic expectations. When Uncle Olivier came to stay with us, he was disappointed there weren't cowboys on horseback, rounding up cattle on the streets of Calgary." He laughed.

"Anyway, like I said, they got married." He looked sideways at her and winked. "And that's where I came in."

"I would never 'ave guessed," Gabrielle said dryly. "Do you 'ave any brothers or sisters?"

"Yep, a younger brother. He loves the farm."

"Don't you love your farm?"

"Yeah, I do," Andrew shrugged. "But there isn't room for us both to work with Dad and earn a decent living. I was thinking of applying to take a course in carpentry when we got word Uncle Olivier had died. Then we were contacted by his lawyer, learned about the will…and, *whala*, here I am." He stopped and spread his arms wide with an infectious grin she couldn't help but returning.

"I believe the word you want is *voila*, but I must admit there is a certain earthy charm to *whala*." Gabrielle giggled behind her hand, hoping she wasn't offending the man. He really was too cute.

"Vella? Is that what you said? Or volla?" He cupped an elbow with his hand and tapped a finger to his temple as she repeated it again. "*Voila*," he ground out finally, bending at the waist to expel the word as though it had been stuck in his throat.

"*C'est parfait!*" she shouted with a laugh. "You did it."

"And what about you?" he asked with a teasing grin. "Tell me about yourself. Specifically, are you dating anyone? Married? Attracted to men wearing big hats?"

Gabrielle laughed. Scuffing the toe of her shoe through a drift of pink cherry petals, and scattering them across the paved walkway, she thought a moment before answering. She didn't want to say anything about Lyam. The less anyone knew of him the better. And she didn't want to open a door that gave Andrew opportunity to ask her on a date. She wasn't ready for that.

"I am single, yes." She chose not to remark on men in hats, but her lips curved with humour at his question. He was flirting with her, and the knowledge warmed her heart despite her misgivings. "And you?"

"Aww, I've dated quite a bit, but nothing serious. The girls were nice enough. We just didn't click."

Although not exactly sure what he meant by 'click,' Gabrielle dropped the line of questioning for a safer topic. He did too.

"You seem to know a few things about wine," Andrew said. "Is that true of all people who live in France?"

"My father's side of the family owns an estate in Provence with vineyards and olive groves. They produce both wine and olive oil. Growing up, I spent most of my summers there, so I suppose you could say I have some familiarity with it." She shrugged expressively. "I would be interested to know if your uncle carried any of their wine. It is a delicate *vin rosé* created by *Chateau de Belliveau*."

"Hey," Andrew said with a deep chuckle. "I don't even need an interpreter for that. *Rosé* wine." Sobering he said, "I'll certainly keep an eye out for it. Not sure how I'm going to sell wine to Parisians when I know nothing..." He sighed. "It might be best to put the shop up for sale right away, but somehow, I feel as though I'm supposed to stay for a while...at least try to make it work."

She led him out the other side of the park and onto the street, ending up on Boulevard de l'Hôpital.

"That wasn't much about you," he said. "I still know nothing. You're the only friend I've got in this whole country, and I'd like to get to know you better." He looked at her with genuine interest, something she'd never experienced before from the male species. Sure, they looked at her beauty, but the men she'd known only wanted to talk about themselves. *Did he really want to know the real Gabrielle?* She felt at a loss to know what to say.

After a long pause, he said jokingly, "I'll start you off. What's your favourite colour, food, and music?"

Gabrielle giggled despite herself. He was so comical, so animated...so different from the brooding, enigmatic man she had dated for the last year.

"*D'accord.*" She stepped closer to him, allowing a lady walking three dogs to pass, and then began. "I love red... crimson to be exact, and I like American pop as well as some traditional French music. I like to travel, and ski, although I am not very good at it. My favourite season is springtime, as you can tell." She lifted an arm to trail her fingers through the bright green leaves of a young sapling. "I 'ave one sister, named Annette, who is younger and still lives at 'ome with the best parents a girl could ever 'ave. I swim twice a week and ride *une velo*, otherwise known as a bicycle, for exercise. My birthday is in December and my age will remain a mystery...although I can say I am a little younger than you. I am passionate about 'elping people and understanding the 'uman condition." She drew in a deep breath. "Oh, and I adore cassoulet, but it is not so good for the figure." She patted a slim thigh.

"I don't think you need to worry about your hips." To her embarrassment, Andrew backed away to examine her more closely, then fell back in stride. "Thank you for sharing that information." He tapped the side of his head. "It's gone into the memory banks, although I'm left with a few questions. Like, what the heck is cassoulet?"

"Sometime I will make it for you," she promised rashly, then wondered why she was offering such a thing. She certainly wasn't following her own advice.

"Actually, we should eat," Andrew said suddenly, looking at the many bistros and restaurants on the street. "All this talk of food has me thinking it's been a long time since breakfast. Are you hungry?"

Gabrielle hadn't noticed, but now that he mentioned it,

her stomach growled loudly. Dusk was falling upon the city and the breeze had a bite to it.

"*Bien sûr*, I know just the place." She glanced both ways up the street. Tossing the ends of her scarf over one shoulder, she sprinted between traffic, leaving Andrew to follow as best he could. She pulled up short on the other side to look back. Andrew was loping along in her wake, a car skimmed past him with an irritated honk of its horn.

"Oh sure, *now* you check to see if I'm still alive," he said in a playful tone, lurching to a stop beside her. "Lot of good that would do if I'd been mashed to a pulp out there."

She found herself stifling a giggle, yet again. She turned and led the way to a little hole-in-the-wall restaurant she remembered from time spent in the area with her family. She strolled onto a narrow street lined with cars, hoping the place was still there.

Unfortunately, Gabrielle focused so eagerly ahead, she failed to notice a raised cobblestone at her feet and rammed her boot right into it. She yelped. Sprawling forward, she flailed at the air, struggling to make her feet catch up to her body. But just before her hands took the force of her fall, a strong arm curled around her waist from behind, preventing catastrophe.

Andrew pulled her upright and spanned her waist with both hands. The heady scent of his cologne combined with his leather jacket assailed her senses. He bent down to search her face. She shook her head, as though to clear it, and pulled away.

"You okay?"

"Yes—Yes I'm fine." She glared at the problematic stone, which had dislodged even further. "Thank you for catching me."

Brushing errant hair from her face with a gentle finger,

he looked at her, his blue eyes filled with concern. "Maybe so," he said firmly, "but let's not take any more chances." With an exaggerated motion he extended his hand, palm up, and waited.

Against her better judgement, Gabrielle placed her small hand into his large one. She watched, mesmerized, as his fingers closed around hers, warming her whole being with his caring touch. Her heart leapt.

Calm down, she told herself. *The last thing you want is to start something.*

But as they continued to walk, she felt a spring in her step that hadn't been there before. She peeked at him from beneath her lashes. He was sweet, she decided, quite genuine in his wish to hold her hand and it made her feel safe.

Of course, she guessed there was more to his request to hold her hand than just to keep her safe. Despite that, she sensed no ulterior motive, as she often did with other men she'd dated. Gabrielle had no false illusions as to why most men wanted to go out with her. She knew she was an attractive woman. Sometimes it felt more like a curse than anything.

She glanced at the door beside her, shaking off her musings, and realised they were passing the restaurant she sought. *La Petite Licorne* was written in a flowing, gold script over the door of a tiny building, tucked in between two gigantic apartment blocks. There was one window, cut into the ruddy-coloured brickwork that made up the facade, looking in on an interior that glowed with light and life.

"This is it." Gabrielle said with surprise. Her memory had served her well. She stopped abruptly and pulled him to the entrance. Andrew reached around her and yanked the heavy oak door open, gesturing, with a low bow and a sweeping gesture, that she should proceed him.

The door creaked and then banged shut behind them, causing Gabrielle to jump in the tiny, dark foyer. But as they stepped through another door into the restaurant itself and gazed around, Andrew removed his hat and gave a low whistle of appreciation. The space was charmingly quaint and inviting. Soft music eddied around them, mingling with a murmur of voices, but their eyes were immediately drawn up.

High above them and at the ceiling's center was a large, circular piece of art that stretched from one side of the room to the other. The sculpture resembled a stained glass rose window, such as might be seen in Gothic architecture. Vibrant with hues of orange, red, and yellow, the swirled patterns were set apart by ornately curling slivers of thin, darkly polished wood. Lit from within, it glowed with almost an ethereal beauty.

The wall opposite them was a bright crimson, but the others, including a high arch leading to the kitchen, were sedate in their creamy whiteness. Bell-shaped lampshades, looking as though lacy red scarves with long trailing fringes had been draped around the exteriors, were suspended from the ceiling, adding a soft warmth to the room.

Glass cabinets lined the wall closest to them, each boasting something either pretty or appealing. One flashed in the light with crystal stemware, another chilled carafes of water and multi-coloured drinks, while still another housed a delectable selection of desserts.

Long, wooden tables, rustic in their smooth, simple finish, filled every available space. While richly carved chairs, covered in red velvet were pushed beneath, awaiting customers. Already a few tables were filled, but several tables were empty. Gabrielle breathed a sigh of relief. She remembered the food had always been good in this establishment and seating would be at a premium.

An older woman, dressed in a swishing floral skirt and red blouse, scurried from behind a swinging door at the back, only pausing to snatch a small chalkboard from where it rested on a drinks' counter. Her jet black hair, in contrast to her lined features, was knotted tightly in a bun atop her head. But as she hurried toward them, a broad grin nearly split her face in two, lending beauty to an otherwise tired face. She held the board, etched in chalk with the day's menu, in two hands and looked enquiringly from Andrew to Gabrielle before speaking in a gravelly voice.

"*Bonsoir, bonsoir,*" she said, waving at the few available tables. "*Une table pour deux?*"

"*Bonsoir madame. Oui, pour deux s'il vous plaît.*"

The petite lady nodded briskly and wound her way through the complicated configuration of tables to a secluded spot in the corner where she propped the chalkboard menu on a chair and left them with a smile to attend to other guests who were arriving.

"We were lucky to get 'ere when we did," Gabrielle leaned across the small square of wood between them, her hands folded under her chin. "Only Parisians know of this place. I think it was always very popular." She looked around with interest, but her gaze quickly shifted back to rest on Andrew's animated face.

He was tanned, rugged, and good-looking. He had the sort of face that later in life would earn its wrinkles from hard labor under a hot sun. Or contrarily, from braving the blast of winter weather that was said to dip below -40 Celsius in Canada. His jawline was strong with a faint shadow of whiskers dusting his cheeks. His blue eyes danced with excitement as he bent to place his hat under the table. Then, he gazed around the charming French restaurant, finally coming back to catch Gabrielle staring. He grinned.

"I'm counting on you to translate that." He jerked a thumb at the hand-written menu beside them.

Gabrielle smiled. Reaching out, she turned the chalkboard to face her since Andrew couldn't read any of the French words scrawled neatly on the *prix fixe*. Scanning quickly, she translated with ease.

"There are two options of three courses each that I think you might like. First, a lentil salad topped by fresh goat cheese with a lamb and prune *Parmentier*, which is a French version of what you might call a shepherd's pie, and to finish, Crêpes Suzette flambéed in Grand Marnier..." As he opened his mouth she held up a restraining hand, took a deep breath and continued.

"Second, a curly endive salad with a poached egg and lardons. That's chunks of bacon, to you," she cocked her head sideways to look at him before continuing. "Then, savoy cabbage stuffed with *boulettes de saumon*, which is fancy French talk for salmon dumplings, served in a pink crayfish sauce. The dessert course is a runny chocolate-chestnut cake, which actually sounds better when you say it in French." Assuming a lofty expression, she repeated a description of the sweet treat in her own language. "*Gâteau coulant chocolat-marrons.*"

She peered at him, a chuckle bursting from her throat as he pretended to consider, tapping a finger on his chin, and looking at the beautiful artwork above.

"That sounds like a heck of a lot more than two choices of three courses each. I barely remember where one ended and the other began." He slapped his head in mock horror. "You decide. I'll be happy to eat whatever you choose."

Was he joking? He was too easy to get along with. Shaking her head as he looked away again, clearly pleased to accept whatever she ordered, she read the neat handwriting once more and made a decision.

"*Voila*," she said, as the server, a slim young man in black pants with a crisp white shirt, plunked a basket of sliced, brown baguette on the table. He also placed a bottle of water and two glasses in front of them. Then he wrote down their order and hurried away to the kitchen.

"Salmon it is. I 'ope you will like it." She waved a hand at the bread. "Please, 'ave some. It is fresh and we can ask for more if you wish."

Andrew's eyes grew round. "More?" he said in a disbelieving tone. "I didn't exactly put in a hard day's labour. This will be just fine." He picked up the basket and offered it first to Gabrielle before taking a slice for himself and biting into it with thoughtful consideration. "What a great idea. It's crusty, yet soft on the inside. How do I say, delicious, in French?"

"*Cette baguette est délicieuse.*" Gabrielle closed her eyes, kissed her fingers, and then opened them with a dreamy smile.

Andrew chuckled. "Okay, but I think I'll start with the words rather than the gesture. Don't want to offend someone by accident." He took a breath. "Set bag-et hey, delisers."

Gabrielle covered her mouth as she collapsed against her chair in a fit of merriment. "*C'est t-terrible!*" she spluttered, at length. "But I love it."

"I have a long way to go until I can be trusted to say anything beyond, thank you, hello, goodbye, and please," Andrew said with twinkling eyes, his attention resting on her. Suddenly, he grew serious and reached across the table, taking her hand in his. His bright blue eyes looked like a stormy sea in this light. Her gaze flickered between them and his mouth that always appeared to be curved into a smile of good humor. "I want to thank you, Gabrielle. You've done so much to help me already and made me feel so welcome. I really think I can pull this off if I have you as my friend." He squeezed her hand gently and let it go. "At least, I want to try, for Uncle Olivier."

His eyes drifted across her face. "You really are a remarkably beautiful woman," he said, half to himself. "And unbelievably, kind." He appeared to flush and cleared his throat as he looked away.

Her hand felt cold after the warmth of his touch, and she lowered it to her lap where she twisted both of her hands together. Swallowing, she said, "You are quite welcome. I am so glad I was there at the right time to 'elp you." A hush fell over them; her eyes cast down, and his remained fixed on the decorative ceiling. The mood turned sombre.

"So..." she paused dramatically. "I require some vital information from you."

His head whipped around with his eyes opened wide. "You do?"

"*Oui*," she said, lifting one shoulder. "What is your favourite colour, food, and music?

"Oh." He grinned, his features lightening. "Pretty standard selections for a guy, I guess. I like all shades of blue. And thick, juicy cheeseburgers covered in fried onions and mushrooms. Steak too, of course. But my choice of music isn't what you might expect from a cowboy." He leaned forward slightly as though divulging a great secret. "I'm not a fan of country." He raised his eyebrows, clearly expecting her face to register shock. When she merely nodded encouragingly, he continued.

"I like 60s folk music with a dash of Celtic thrown in. Sometimes a little jazz is nice, too." He settled back in his chair, arms folded over his chest as he added this last, startling piece of information. "I also play the fiddle, guitar, and I sing a little. Mainly play the same sort of tunes as I like listening to."

She *was* a little surprised at this last fact. It felt out of character with the rugged man's appearance who sat opposite her. Involuntarily, she noted his work-roughened hands. "You're right," she said. "That does surprise me although I saw you arrive with a guitar."

"Yeah. I never leave home without it." He quipped. "I'm not a professional or anything, but I've performed for events like weddings and dances…and appeared at a few gigs in Calgary during the winter, when the farm wasn't busy."

"I would like to 'ear you play." Gabrielle shook out her napkin and laid it on her lap.

"I'd love to play a song for you," he said thoughtfully. "I know just the song. Anyway, it'll help to pass the time when I'm not working on the shop. It's pretty daunting to take over a business you know nothing about. Especially a failing business in a foreign country." He sighed.

"But I'm determined to bring it back to life, and then I'll see how it goes from there. At least the shop will be easier to sell once it's fixed up…if that's what I decide. My mother told my uncle when I set my mind to something I stick with it. Maybe that's why he left it to me."

Andrew glanced toward the kitchen where the door was swinging open. "Did you order wine? I'm asking because our waiter is carrying a bottle and two glasses this way with a purposeful look in his eye."

"*Oui*," she turned her head to watch the young man's progress. "It is customary to enjoy wine with the evening meal. In this case I chose a crisp white to accompany the fish. It is *Pinot Gris*, from the Alsace region of France."

"Interesting."

The server dispensed a little for Gabrielle to taste. Then, after her nod of approval, the young man poured a measure into both glasses.

Mimicking her, Andrew lifted the glass to his nose and sniffed. Then, holding the goblet by the thick stem, he swirled the liquid and took a sip.

"Not bad," he said, holding his glass to the light and squinting at it. "I like it. Not sure why I like it. I mean…I can't describe it like I've heard people do in movies, but it's nice."

Gabrielle chuckled. "You are *tres honnête*, very honest. I like that," she said, turning back to the wine and launching into some information she hoped would help Andrew learn more. "There are different styles of pinot gris. For example, if the grapes are allowed to properly ripen, the wine will be naturally low in acidity and high in sugar."

Andrew feigned patting his pockets for pen and paper. "I should be taking notes from the master," he fussed, a smile lurking about his mouth.

"If you tease me, I stop," she announced with mock severity.

"Okay, okay," he laughed. "Please continue. And I'm serious when I say I should be writing this down."

"*D'accord*," Gabrielle pursed her lips and went on. "Pinot gris is usually less aromatic than, for instance, a sauvignon blanc. Also, it is drier than chardonnay wines.

This particular bottle is..." she paused to take another sip before adding, "rich and spicy, but not so aromatic, making it a perfect accompaniment for food."

She glanced at his face. He looked lost, so she relented. "I can write a few things down for you," she admitted, "and per'aps we could buy you a book or two on the subject. In English, of course." She peered at him over the rim of her glass.

"Yeah. Thanks, that would be great...Hey," he said with obvious relief, "I think our dinner is arriving." Quickly, they made space for the hot food to be set in front of them. Andrew leaned over his plate, drawing a deep breath appreciatively. He looked up, puzzled. "This is odd, though. Doesn't salad usually come first?"

"Not always in France," she said, lifting her fork. "It is believed that the salad course can assist with digesting the heavier dish." She paused, flicking the end of her utensil toward his plate. "Please, try some. I am anxious to know if you like it."

Obligingly, Andrew cut into the tiny, perfectly formed cabbage to reveal several creamy and colourful layers within. "The salmon?" He poked at a thick peach-coloured portion near the center. It crumbled at his prodding.

"I think so."

He cut a small portion, swirled it in the sauce at the bottom of the dish, and lifted it, dripping, to his mouth. "Hey, this is really good," he said, chewing vigorously. He sounded shocked.

Gabrielle released her breath, startled to realise she'd been holding it in anticipation of his verdict. "*Tres bien*," she said. Grasping her knife and fork, she sliced into her own meal and savoured the delicate flavours of the salmon in its perfectly paired sauce.

They ate in a companionable silence. The buzz of conversation from the other diners, the soft lighting, and the gorgeous canopy of glowing artwork, all added to a romantic ambiance.

The main course was cleared away, and they waited for the salad. Andrew gushed again about how tasty it had been, but his expression became pensive.

"Is something wrong?" Gabrielle asked, smoothing the napkin on her lap.

He ran a hand through his sandy hair leaving it rumpled and untidy. "You're trying to prepare for exams and live a life that I have no idea about. So, I won't ask you to help me with my uncle's store. It wouldn't be fair." He arched one eyebrow, hopefully. "But I would like to see you again."

The arrival of their salads allowed her to think about her response for a minute. She knew her feelings for Lyam were long since dead, but the betrayal was still raw. She didn't think she could ever trust someone again.

"I don't mind 'elping you learn some French and per'aps a little about wine," she said finally. "It would be a distraction from the constant pressure of my studies." Purposely, she avoided his request to see her in the sense of dating.

"Then, I'll leave it up to you." Andrew's cheerful smile returned. He placed both hands on the table, as though making a decision. "Come by the shop whenever you have time or need a break. The most important thing is that we're friends. Okay?"

She nodded, feeling relief wash over her. He was indeed a remarkable man. Sensing her reticence, he had backed away without applying pressure or expectation.

They enjoyed the salad without speaking.

"I think I might have to loosen my belt buckle if this

keeps up," Andrew joked, pushing back from the table with a contented sigh.

But only a few minutes later a plate of chocolatey goodness was deposited in front of them. Gabrielle glanced up, not having noticed the server return.

"Mercy!" Andrew mispronounced the word for thank you with such energy that the young server did a double take before recomposing himself.

"M*erci*," she said to the retreating server. She picked up her spoon and prepared to attack the dish, giggling to herself.

Letting a morsel of gooey chocolate melt upon her tongue, she closed her eyes rapturously and then opened them to remonstrate with Andrew. "You must learn to say the word correctly. At the moment, it sounds as though you are begging forgiveness for some serious crime." She wagged a finger at him and smiled to soften her words.

"Nope." Andrew shook his head in denial. "I *meant* to say mercy just as it sounded. As a cry for help. This is all too delicious and filling." She watched him spoon a bite of dessert into his mouth and then take his time to swallow. "Mercy," he said again, with more emphasis.

She rolled her eyes.

"Mare-cee," he said again. "Meercee. There, that was better wasn't it?"

"Maybe a little, but still not good. Watch my mouth."

"Oh, believe me, I'm watching it," he accompanied his words with a great bark of laughter that caused people to turn and stare. "I've been watching it for a while now."

"Stop being silly and concentrate!" She frowned, took a calming breath, and repeated it again. "*Merci.*" The word rolled off her tongue like melted butter.

Andrew's forehead furrowed with effort. "*Mercy!*" he hollered, as though he were leading an army into battle.

She sighed. "I think that is enough for today. Shouting, *thank you*, back and forth, louder and louder each time is beginning to attract negative attention." She ignored a couple who scowled at them over their aperitif, took one more spoon of her chocolate dessert and placed her napkin on top of the dish. "I am too full to eat more."

Andrew dropped his spoon onto the plate and sat back contentedly. "You're right. Rome wasn't built in a day, and I doubt I'll learn to speak French in a millennia. I'll try again tomorrow." He winked at her, then looked around for their server. "Now how do I ask for the bill again?"

"*L'addition s'il vous plait*. But I think I will just do it for you if that is okay? I believe, along with the book on wine, we should sign you up for a few French classes." She reached across and patted his arm. "There is no way you could know 'ow to pronounce these words. But you 'ave the desire to learn and that is the most important part." She sent him an encouraging look. "With time and practise you will learn."

Andrew insisted on paying and soon they made their way back onto the main street. The setting sun, like a blood-orange gem, had painted the sky in hues of red, gold, and icy pink, and turned the world below into a kaleidoscope of glowing colour. Spring flowers bloomed in apartment balconies high above and fresh young leaves shivered in the trees beside them.

Without looking at her or making further comment, Andrew held out his hand. She slipped her own inside, feeling an instant warmth fill her body. His strong fingers curled around hers.

She breathed deeply. The sweet scent of spring rain

lingered on the evening air. And, as they came to the steps leading into the métro, and started to descend, the symphony of horns, laughter, and merry chatter were left behind on the street.

Once through the barrier, the hallway broadened and appeared to go on indefinitely. A family, obviously American, shuffled along the corridor in front of them. Each parent was dragging a large suitcase and struggling to keep track of their tired, irritable offspring. The father was thin and moved sluggishly, wisps of blond hair peeking out from beneath a ball cap pulled low over his ears. Knee-length shorts slopped around his bandy legs, the hemline meeting up with long, white athletic socks that ended in a pair of thick, brown leather sandals. He held tightly to the hand of one tow-headed youngster who was bent almost perpendicular to the ground in a futile attempt to have his father move faster.

The mother, plump and arrayed in a long flowery dress with a matching pink cardigan, scuffled slowly along. A sobbing child of about two years old clung tight to her legs, impeding her progress.

The lady looked harried and distracted. She stopped abruptly as the smallest child collapsed to the floor, weeping, and repeating one word, over and over, "Puppy, puppy, puppy." The father was oblivious to their plight, his attention trained solely on corralling the older child who had broken free and ran ahead, laughing gleefully. The mother was forced to stay where she was, entreating the distraught child to stand up and keep walking a little further. When that failed, she stood the suitcase upright and set her handbag on the concrete to gather the toddler into her arms.

Even as Gabrielle called out a warning, two men

approached from the other direction. Quickening their pace, they came alongside. One of the men bent, snatched up the lady's handbag, and both took off at a run.

The father, realising what had happened when his wife screamed, whirled around to look on helplessly as the thieves sped away. The woman waved frantically at passersby. She tried to catch their attention, pleading for assistance, pointing at the fleeing men who had stolen her purse. Her cries for help mingled with the howling of her baby. But it appeared hopeless. There were only a few people to hear her, and evidently no one at all who cared. They gave her and the child a wide berth as they hurried past with heads down, minding their own business.

All people, except for Andrew.

Pulling the cowboy hat from his head, he tossed it aside, whirled around, and took after the culprits. The hard leather soles of his boots echoed loudly along the corridor. At the sound of this unexpected pursuit, one of the thieves cast a look over his shoulder. His face contorted into fear. Yelling something to his partner, the pair redoubled their efforts to escape with the stolen property. But it was to no avail.

Gabrielle only had time to take a strangled breath before Andrew leapt forward, tackled both thieves, and all three crashed to the floor. They rolled together, slamming against the wall of the corridor with cries of anger and pain. Andrew took the worst of it. Yet he came up on his feet first, with one steely arm around the neck of the thief holding the bag, pinning him tight. The man writhed, kicked, elbowed, and hollered for help from his partner. But his pal had disappeared. Andrew yanked the thief's arm behind him with one hand and grasped the man by the scruff of his neck with the other. Then, he marched the culprit with the bag, back to where the lady stood holding her howling baby. She sobbed with shock and relief.

A small crowd of interested onlookers had gathered by this time. Unwilling to help the woman themselves, they were nonetheless intrigued by the single-handed capture of this scourge of society.

"Hand it over," Andrew growled into the man's ear as they reached the family. The robber snarled threats in a language Gabrielle didn't recognise, ending in a strangled gurgle as Andrew tightened his grip on his collar. The greasy scoundrel thrust the stolen bag at the woman. The crowd of bystanders began to clap and whistle as the thief was forced to return what he had taken.

Fingers trembling, the lady reached out to take her voluminous purse. With wide, frightened eyes, she looped it over her neck before hastily stepping away and hugging her baby close to her chest. Her husband slid an arm around her, shaking his head in disbelief.

"Thank you!" he exclaimed, looking close to tears himself. "I can't believe you did that for us. You're a regular Superman."

The lady gave Andrew a wobbly smile, patting the bag at her side. "This bag has all our passports and my wallet with our bank cards. I don't know what we'd have done if it had been stolen. We can't thank you enough." She subsided into fresh weeping, leaning into her husband's embrace.

"You're welcome," Andrew said, still firmly restraining the thrashing thief. "Glad I could help. But I think you should keep your valuables in a safer place. I've read that pickpockets in big cities make a good living off unsuspecting tourists like yourselves."

"We read about that too, in our travel guide, but when the baby started crying..." The woman's voice trailed off.

She blinked rapidly, took a deep calming breath, and caressed the child's head.

"Thank you again," the husband said. "The name's Mel Jackson, from Wisconsin. We just flew in today. If everything had been stolen…" he paused to take a ragged breath. "Well, we'd have been in real trouble. Can I offer you a reward? Some money perhaps?"

Mel stepped back hurriedly as the thief doubled over, attempting to throw Andrew off guard and break his hold. There was a slight skirmish and then Andrew straightened, the thief still held erect in his steely grasp.

"No," he said breathlessly. "Just glad I could help. I better get this guy to the authorities." Andrew nodded to the couple. Then he added, "You should give your contact information to my friend here. The police will likely want to talk to you."

As if in a dream, Gabrielle stepped forward as Mel hastily wrote their names and the address and telephone number of their hotel on a paper napkin from his pocket. He pressed it into her hand.

Andrew spoke once more. "You take care and have a good trip. Paris is a beautiful city, and the people are great." Andrew shook the man in his clutches. "Just, not this one." As the family gathered their luggage and moved slowly away, the toddler waved goodbye over its mother's shoulder.

The crowd clapped again, a few of them cheering and shouting in French.

"Well, guess I should get this guy to the authorities. Where would that be exactly?" Andrew looked placidly over the shoulder of the captured man as though he'd picked up some loose change and wanted to turn it in at the front desk.

Gabrielle still stood in shocked silence, her mouth

hanging open. She'd never seen anything like it. The vision of Andrew tearing down the corridor and tackling two men at once, was something she'd never forget.

"I—I have…I mean, I have no idea if there are authorities nearby." She shook her head as though the dreamlike image would disappear in a puff of smoke. "Maybe at the ticket office there will be a guard?" She stared at the assembled crowd, a few teenagers turning to follow them as she mindlessly led the way back up the tunnel to the ticket desk.

Unbelievably, two policemen were on the other side of the exit doors, talking to a group of ticket inspectors. Gabrielle pushed through the gates, holding them open for Andrew. Still gripping the thief, he shoved him through, still spluttering obscenities and fighting to escape. She approached the uniformed men, and addressed them in French, explaining what had happened. After some measure of disbelief, and a few rapid-fire questions, the pickpocket was handcuffed and led away by one of the policemen.

The remaining officer asked to speak to the couple who had been robbed. Again, Gabrielle explained. Although displeased that Mel and his wife were not available for questioning, he took the paper bearing their names and stuffed it into his jacket with a frown.

Three young men from the group of cheering onlookers, had tagged along. Now, they pushed forward and spoke to the policeman in excited voices accompanied with much hand waving.

"They are telling 'im you are an 'ero. A powerful man who brought down a gang of thieves single-handedly." Gabrielle whispered a loose translation to Andrew from the side of her mouth. "They are recounting what they saw and asking to go to the station to also make a statement. Apparently, they feel ashamed for not 'elping the woman themselves."

The tall policeman detached himself from the group and beckoned to Andrew with an imperious hand. "We will need your statement, *monsieur. À la commissariat*," he said in French, his eyebrows knitting together in a frown. "You 'ave done the city of Paris a great service, so it seems. Follow me, *s'il vous plaît*." He strode toward the entrance, followed by the three teens.

"Guess I have to go to the police station," Andrew said ruefully. "Who knew doing a good deed would end our evening so abruptly."

"It might take some time," she said, handing him his hat. "These things seldom move quickly in France. Will you be able to find the way back to your apartment?"

"Sure." He slapped the hat across his thigh to clear the dust, before ramming it low over his ears, one hand unconsciously smoothing the brim. "You get back to your studies. I can figure out the métro now." The policeman coughed meaningfully from the stairwell leading to the street.

But Gabrielle couldn't move. She still felt in a state of shock. Could all of this really have happened?

Andrew took a step to leave, then turned abruptly, grasped her gently by the shoulders, leaned close and whispered. "There's something missing here. In all the movies I've seen since a boy, when the hero saves the day he gets to kiss the prettiest girl in the world." With a lopsided smile, his face came closer, and she looked deep into his deep blue eyes as his lips softly brushed her own.

"Thanks for everything." His hands slid away. Wheeling around, he hurried after the law.

Chapter Four

Gabrielle slumped on a seat in the lecture hall of the University of Paris-Descartes, listening, but only half hearing what the professor was teaching on the subject of social behavior. She smoothed the scarlet material of her skirt over her knees and looked down, admiring the white kitten-heels she'd found at a tiny boutique in the Marais. She pulled the two sides of her denim jacket together, wondering why she'd taken such care with her appearance today. She felt a bit overdressed. Usually, she threw on a pair of jeans, a t-shirt, and trainers to scurry off to class. But this morning, she'd applied makeup, donned a pale pink, fine-knit sweater, and scrabbled through all the hangers in her closet for this particular A-line skirt. It flattered her figure, if the looks she was getting were anything to go by.

Her thoughts slid from the bizarre scene in the métro last night, to the dimly lit shop filled with dusty bottles of wine where she knew Andrew would be working today.

Shaking herself from this stupor, she straightened. This kind of distraction and behavior were not allowed. She wanted nothing to do with a relationship this soon after Lyam. Tucking her hair behind her ears, she focused on the professor, poising her pencil to scribble notes. The class would conclude in thirty-five minutes. Then, she would take the information home to study.

As students poured from the classroom, chattering amongst themselves, Gabrielle hugged her books close to her chest with her head down, and walked purposefully to the exit. She had several good friends here, but she wanted to make the most of today's studying, while the information was fresh, and not stop to visit. Friends had texted, asking if she wanted to meet up later, and questioning what she'd done over the weekend. She smiled to herself. They wouldn't believe it if she told them. The smile faded as she considered what had happened with Lyam. Nothing would shock her friends if they had known anything about that fiasco.

It was late afternoon when Gabrielle rubbed her eyes and blearily consulted her phone for the time. Four o'clock! Tossing her pencil aside, she slammed her textbook shut, gathered the notes she'd taken, and stacked them neatly on top before standing to stretch. She deserved a break.

At that moment she heard a strange noise at her door. Almost sounded like someone writing on the wood with a rough implement, perhaps chalk. She stopped, heart pounding as she listened intently, but the noise stopped. Tiptoeing to the door she peered through the tiny peephole her landlady had installed a year ago after someone had forced their way into an apartment downstairs, demanding money from an elderly man.

Nothing. There was no sign that anyone had been there at all. Could it have been a child outside the door?

Telling herself it had been her imagination, she decided she needed fresh air. She had no destination in mind. Just a quick walk around the neighbourhood to clear her head and then she would return.

Running a brush through her long black hair, she refreshed her lipstick, and grabbed her handbag before stepping into the hallway. Turning around, her stomach clenched as she read the words scrawled on her door.

Vous avez un jour pour le trouver.

Her hand instinctively went to her throat. 'You have three days to find it.' Find what? Could this scribbled missive have been meant for her? Surely not. The words meant nothing. Whoever it was for had been given a limited amount of time to find something, but it couldn't possibly be directed at her. Hurrying back inside, she ran a cloth under the tap and squeezed a liberal amount of dish soap over it. Then, she rushed back to her door, scrubbing at the words until they were obliterated. Tossing the rag back into her sink, she took several cleansing breaths and strove to push the fear away.

Since the fiasco with Lyam, her senses had been on high alert. But knowing he had been incarcerated for his crimes helped. Still, even though she felt alarmed, she decided to keep the incident to herself. It likely had nothing to do with her.

She locked her door and checked it three times, just to be certain, then exited the building. Wandering without purpose, or so she thought, she surprised herself when she stopped in front of the dilapidated little shop, Caviste de Tremblay.

"Hi!" Andrew grinned as he poked his head through the

open window that once again was propped open with one of his uncle's old boots. "Saw you coming. I was hoping you'd show up. I want to show you something." He disappeared and she moved to the doorway feeling some sense of normalcy return. After unbolting the door, he stepped outside, grasped her shoulders, and swung her around.

"Oh!" she exclaimed, half laughing and half embarrassed that the people living in the neighbourhood should see such abandonment. "Put me down, Andrew."

He did, with a laugh, but held her by the arms, leaning back to take a good look at her. "You are a beautiful woman Gabrielle. But I'm not just referring to your looks. I mean, you're stunning, no doubt about it, but it's who you are on the inside that's most attractive."

Gabrielle felt her face flush for the second time in five minutes. No one had ever said such things to her before, apart from her parents and family, of course. But her relatives were obligated.

"*Merci*," she said, ducking her head in a mock curtsy. "Now, what is it you 'ave to show me?" He gestured that she proceed him inside the shop. She did, noting that one long wall was bare and all the bottles from it were sitting in the center of the room under several threadbare looking sheets.

"I'm cleaning and then I'll repaint," he said flinging an arm wide to encompass the long narrow space. "It needs brightening up. Think I'll build a few shelves and add new lighting too. I visited several other wine shops today and took notes." His handsome face took on a mischievous look. "Don't worry. I didn't offend anyone with my language skills, I hope. All I tried was a polite *bun jure*."

Gabrielle lifted her eyebrows and pretended to wipe perspiration from her brow. "That is a relief. I would not want you to tarnish your reputation as, what did the man call you? Ah…Superman?"

Andrew laughed, then turned to make his way along the narrow path between covered bottles. Actually, Gabrielle couldn't help but agree with the label. This man towered above her, his shoulders broad and his muscles bulging beneath the rolled-up sleeves of his plaid, button-up shirt. The cowboy boots had been replaced with a pair of grey, rather run-down looking trainers, but his usual snug-fitting jeans were still in place, belted securely at his waist.

She lifted her eyes to the back of his head, realising too late he'd been speaking. What was wrong with her? That was the second time today she'd been daydreaming.

"*Désolé!*" She cut into his discourse apologetically. "Could you repeat that? My thoughts were wandering."

"I said, I explored a little more of my inheritance today. It was pretty enlightening," he flicked a glance over his shoulder. "The more time I spend here, the closer I feel to my uncle and the sadder I am. Sure wish I would have known him better."

Andrew passed through the back room where he'd built more display crates and stacked them in a teetering pile. There were two closed doors on either side of the room.

"That one leads to the cellar where he kept the inventory that wasn't on the shelves." He pointed, then stopped in front of the other door, tucked away into the far right corner. Grasping the handle, he turned it with a protesting squeal and shoved, motioning that Gabrielle should enter.

She wandered into the gloomy space; hearing Andrew flick the light switch behind her. The room was thrown into stark relief. Facing her was a rickety single bed with a few blankets tossed over it in disarray. The pillow looked flat and lumpy. At one end of the room was a counter on which sat a kettle, microwave, a small one element cooker, a toaster, and a stack of clean dishes. A tiny refrigerator balanced on a table nearby.

One tired looking armchair sat in the corner, and next to it a small table on which a lamp, a stack of books, and an empty wine glass resided. In the other corner was a free-standing rack of old suits and shirts, two pairs of shoes, and behind that another door, presumably leading to a bathroom.

"He lived here," Andrew said, stating the obvious. The room fairly reeked of melancholy. Uncle Olivier had not been a happy man when he died.

"But didn't he own an apartment next door?" Gabrielle was puzzled. "Why would he live here? It's not nice at all."

"We'll never know for sure," Andrew said with a regretful twist of his lips. "But I have a theory. That's the other part of what I want to show you."

He waited for her to exit the dreary little room before switching off the light and shutting the door. They retraced their steps through the shop and out to the street. Andrew drew the set of ancient keys from his pocket, locked the shop behind him and strode to the door leading to his uncle's other home, fitting a key into it he explained his theory.

"I talked to my mother last night. She told me that six months before my uncle's passing, his wife, Clarisse, had died. I remember Mom flying here to be with Olivier for the funeral. She said he was distraught. Mom said Uncle Olivier and Aunt Clarisse had been the happiest couple she'd ever known. They adored one another. The one great sorrow of their lives had been that they never were able to have children. Consequently, her death left him alone in the world."

Gabrielle and Andrew passed through the door, closed it behind them, and began to climb a steep set of creaky wooden stairs to the next floor. With each step, her skirt swished around her bare legs. Feeling the coolness of this dark, entrance she shivered and crossed her arms over her chest.

Andrew, several steps ahead of her, spoke softly, yet in this silent tomb-like entry, his voice carried loud and clear. "Mom said their love for one another was apparent in everything they did. They held hands, even after sixty years of marriage, treated one another with great respect, and shared their lives together with joy. When Clarisse died suddenly of a heart attack, Uncle Olivier was devastated. Mom stayed here with him for more than a month. At his request, she cleaned the upstairs apartment and cleared the kitchen of all food, bringing it downstairs to the shop. I think it was at that point that he closed his business, Caviste de Tremblay, and retreated from the world. Six months later, he died..."

Andrew paused as he reached the landing and the keys jangled again. "I believe he died of a broken heart."

"Oh, that is so tragic." Gabrielle felt tears prick her eyes. The poor man. She could only imagine a love such as that.

With his hand on the knob, Andrew drew a deep breath before continuing his tale of true love. The dim light from an old-fashioned, shaded bulb on the landing cast shadows over the grim set to his jaw. He blinked rapidly. The retelling of these events had caused an emotional response in the man, and Gabrielle liked him all the better for it.

"It's also my belief that Olivier never again darkened the door of the home he had shared with Clarisse. I don't think he could bear it. He must have taken up residence in the dark little room behind their beloved shop until he died." With a sigh, Andrew twisted the doorknob and gave it a push. "Please...enter."

As she stepped inside, Gabrielle sucked in a breath at the sight that greeted her. It was nothing like the dull, dingy place she had expected. She stood in a grand entryway, surrounded by mirrored doors where coats and shoes must reside, hidden away so as not to detract from the aesthetic beauty of the space. She walked a few steps to peer around a corner to the right.

A huge salon opened up, flooded with light from ceiling to floor windows that had been thrown wide open. Late day sunshine and the rustling whisper of outside trees danced on a breeze throughout the room, while sheer, white curtains fluttered across the polished parquet floor. It was a magnificent period property, classically decorated. Cream-coloured walls led to vaulted ceilings, ornate with embellished mouldings. A long, tan-coloured sofa sat against the far wall with a softly curving back, arms that curled inward to hold its occupants close, and a multitude of colourfully matching pillows for comfort.

Opposite the sofa, three deep armchairs in shades of fuchsia, picked up rose-pink colours from the cushions. A cozy rug spread across the center of the floor and on it was a low coffee table of light-coloured wood that matched two other end tables holding antique lamps. Reading glasses adorned a stack of books at one end of the sofa, waiting patiently for their owner to return. Artwork graced the walls, picking up hints of the rose colour. Two palm trees sat on either side of the windows, long since dead; stark reminders of the life that had once thrived and loved within these walls.

It was clear the room had been lovingly decorated by the hands of Uncle Olivier's late wife. Gabrielle felt tears rise in her throat once more. The room ached to be loved again.

"It's beautiful," she said, her voice hushed and reverent as though they stood in the presence of Clarisse herself.

Andrew shuffled over to stand beside her; hands shoved in his pockets.

"I would never have suspected this was here when I looked at the shop and those back rooms." He shook his head. "The rest of the house is just as beautiful. I'll show you another day."

"The poor man gave up 'is 'ome when she could not share it with 'im," Gabrielle said musingly. "It is so sad."

"I know." Andrew ran a hand along the archway beside him and gestured into the adjoining room. "The kitchen's all up to date, and spotlessly clean. But the air was stale when I first came in. That's why I opened the windows. I'm sure no one has been in here since my mother cleaned out the fridge." He sighed.

Following her instinct, Gabrielle walked toward him, holding out her arms. Andrew moved into them, and she hugged him tight, feeling his body shudder.

"Guess I could move in here right away, and save myself the money for a hotel," he said, resting his cheek against her hair. "After all, it belongs to me." He pulled away and gave her a tremulous smile. "But somehow, it feels sacrilegious. I think I'll just clean up the back room of the shop and camp in there for a bit."

Gabrielle nodded. She would feel the same way now that she'd seen the upstairs.

"Anyway," Andrew said, as he walked across the room to pull the windows shut. "I'm hungry and there's no food down there. None that's edible," he qualified. "If I asked really nice, do you suppose you'd show me a good place to buy some groceries and cleaning supplies? Then, I think I'd like to see the Eiffel Tower and take you for dinner. Is that a lot to ask, friend?"

"I don't think it is possible," she said, shaking her head and noticing his attempt at a smile fade. Quickly she added. "The order of operations is incorrect. If you are going to live in France you must get your priorities straight. First we shop, then eat, and after, we sightsee. *Comprenez vous?*"

Andrew relaxed and the smile she was becoming so fond of, returned. "If you're asking if I agree, then yes. I get it. So, you'll come?" His boyish hopefulness was nearly her undoing. She fought back an unreasonable urge to take his face in her hands and kiss him. But that would not be a good idea.

Instead, she said, "*Oui*, I will take the evening off from my studying, but let us go now. *D'accord?* It grows late."

They were ravenous by the time they left the Monoprix, the closest store to where Andrew was staying. Hurrying, they unloaded cleaning supplies and the small amount of food he'd bought into the tiny room at the back of Caviste de Tremblay. Fortunately, there were plenty of good restaurants nearby. Gabrielle freshened up a little while Andrew changed his clothes and added his ever-present boots, hat and leather jacket. Then, they were off.

Andrew held out his arm encouragingly. After a moment's hesitation, Gabrielle decided they were friends and deemed it natural to link her arm through his as they strolled along the street in search of somewhere to eat. As a rule, Gabrielle didn't go out much, so she had no idea where to take them. In the end they let their noses guide them. The delectable scent of fire-roasted pizza won them over and they found themselves stopping beside the outdoor patio of an Italian restaurant boasting an authentic Neapolitan pizza experience.

The April evening was fragrant with the sweet scent of blossoming trees and the mouth-watering smell of fresh bread and spicy Italian food. The street bustled with the sound of laughter and conversation from this and several other eateries. People were enjoying the opportunity to get outdoors and enjoy the warm evening air. They seated themselves outside at a tiny table for two and picked up the menus that lay in wait for them.

Surreptitiously, Gabrielle watched Andrew from beneath her lashes. He looked with interest at the lively happenings around him, people going about their business, dog walking, visiting—all hazy with the fading light of the sun. He had barely glanced at the cardboard menu.

"Do you need some 'elp deciphering the words?" she asked. Their server, a grizzled, gray-haired man wearing baggy black pants and a white shirt with a red bandana around his neck, came to take their order. He waited patiently with pencil poised over a small notepad.

"Naw. For once I don't need help" Andrew said with a twinkle in his eye. "I took a course in Italian back in high school."

She arched her eyebrows and smiled up at the server. "*Bonsoir Monsieur. Une pizza Margherita, s'il vous plaît.*"

The man scratched busily on his pad. "*Oui, mademoiselle. Et pour vous monsieur?*"

"*Bonsoir,*" Andrew said in an almost perfect imitation of Gabrielle. He winked at her before continuing "An all-meat calzone, please." Andrew pointed at the item on the menu card, just to be sure the fellow understood. He then jabbed at a drink on there too, holding it up for the man to see. "And a bottle of Zinfandel."

The man leaned close, squinted at the paper, and then nodded, his face breaking into a wreath of smiles. *"Oui, monsieur."* He whirled around and hurried back inside the building.

Andrew sat back with a self-satisfied smirk on his face.

"Indeed, it is a proud moment." Gabrielle chuckled. "I almost hate to puff your 'ead any larger, but I 'ave to admit you are learning." Changing the subject, she asked, "Tell me, what are your plans for tomorrow?"

"More cleaning. I think I should focus on the back rooms, so I can move in as soon as possible. It'll make working there a lot easier. And you? Do you have classes every day?"

"No. Not every day. The semester is drawing to a close. But I must devote myself to studies every day if I want to pass my exams."

"I see. And what will you do once you pass them?"

The question took her off guard. She'd been so focused on her finals that her plans to take on the troubles of the world had been quite vague. It had remained an obscure time somewhere in the future that would never arrive, yet that very moment was almost here. She watched an older, gray-haired woman and two small children approach along the sidewalk. The lady walked slowly while the children bounced excitedly around her.

"I suppose I will look for a job, per'aps in an education setting, working with teens."

"Here in the city? Or would you return to where you grew up?"

"I love Paris," she said simply. "It is where I want to stay. What about you? Are you missing *les vaches*?"

"The cows?" He laughed. "No. I miss the wide open spaces, but when I left Calgary there was still snow on the ground. You've got flowers and green grass. I don't miss winter one bit."

"What is it like to 'ave so much cold weather and snow?" She leaned her chin on one closed fist to await his answer.

"You get used to it, I guess. As long as you dress properly, a person can withstand the cold. The worst part is how long winter lasts. Sometimes it stretches into seven months of the year."

She shivered. It sounded intolerable. At that moment their meals arrived, sizzling hot. After the wine was poured, they applied themselves to the food.

To reach Gabrielle's favourite spot to view the Eiffel Tower for the first time, she led the way back to their usual métro stop of Étienne Marcel. Though they had to change lines twice in order to reach her chosen destination of École Militaire.

Once up to street level, Andrew dragged his feet. He was clearly interested in the majestic buildings that greeted them, but she urged him onward.

"The buildings are all part of the military training school of Paris. We are in the seventh arrondissement, southeast of the Eiffel Tower," she said. "But we need to keep moving if we are to see the tower before darkness engulfs it."

They were running out of time. She hoped, if they hurried, to have a few minutes of light before darkness fell and the tower was illuminated. Hemmed in on both sides with tall buildings, she led him down the sidewalk at a fast pace. Soon they reached a spot to cut across the street. They entered Champ de Mars, a huge landscaped green space filled with burgeoning flowers, shrubs, and lofty trees that glowed red in the deepening shades of sunset.

She sighed. The light was magical. The setting sun had painted the sky in a wash of pink and gold.

Andrew was so focused on his immediate surroundings; he didn't notice the great structure looming before him. Granted, it was partially hidden behind trees, but it amused her that he didn't see the spear-like tower stretching into the heavens.

He reached for her hand, and she allowed it to be engulfed in his own, filling her with a sense of security she had never known before. She should pull away, distance herself from this man who was becoming too dear to her, and far too quickly. But she didn't. A stab of fear rose inside her as memories of her recent past flooded her mind, including the eerie message scratched on her door, but she quickly quelled them. This man was nothing like Lyam.

They hurried on. She mused as to the point at which he would see the reason for the journey, wanting him to discover the Eiffel Tower without her aid. Only hoping he would catch on before it began to glow with the golden lights for which it was so famous.

They crunched along a gravelly path on the east side of the park. Still, the whispering leaves of the many trees that lined the trails appeared to hide *la tour Eiffel*. The rosy glow of evening was upon them. Soon, it would be dark and Gabrielle could wait no longer.

Slowing, she nudged him with an elbow. "Attention, Superman, I think your x-ray vision is slipping. Look up there."

Dutifully, Andrew squinted through the gathering dusk. "Hey!" he exclaimed. "We're almost on top of it!" Without her urging, he quickened his steps and led them now. Out to the center of the park he strode, to a place where his view was unobstructed and magnificent. He pulled up short and gazed at the huge tower. "That's fabulous," he murmured.

As they watched, the tower came to vibrant, golden life. Andrew flinched with surprise. She stared at him, enjoying his reaction. He dropped his head and gazed down at her. Their eyes met and locked as he slowly turned, his thumb beginning a mesmerizing circle on the palm of her hand as he caught her other arm and drew her inexorably toward him.

As his face moved closer, Gabrielle's eyes fluttered shut. Her heart thrilled with anticipation, and she was not disappointed. His lips captured hers in gentle exploration, taking his time, drawing out the moment as he tasted her sweetness. With a shudder, he gathered her to him and the kiss deepened. She lifted her hands to his chiselled jaw and pulled him closer, arching her back as she fused herself to this wonderful man who was stealing her heart.

When at last he broke away, she clung to him, grateful for the darkness that surrounded them so he would not see her desire. He took a ragged breath and squeezed the hand that he still held. "I should get back to my hotel, and you need a good night's rest, so you can do justice to your studies tomorrow."

"*Oui*," she said in a small, shaken voice, knowing she sounded as though she wanted nothing of the sort.

He brought her hand up to his mouth and kissed the palm that still tingled from his touch. Then, he drew it through his arm and tucked her close to his side. "Will you come visit me tomorrow?" She nodded, not trusting herself to speak. "What about the next day, and on into infinity?"

She giggled then and the spell was broken, as he had obviously meant for it to be. He was smart enough to know not to push her for more than she could give. She took a cleansing breath. "I will come each day to check on you," she said. "If only to give you a few French lessons and make sure you do not get yourself into trouble."

"Good," he patted her arm where it rested against his side. "Now, can you get us back to where we began? I'm starting to feel that Étienne Marcel métro stop is home."

They retraced their steps, sauntering along and chatting like old friends. In no time at all they were back at his street, Rue Saint-Denis, and saying good night.

"Would you mind giving me your cell number?" Andrew asked, releasing her hand to reach for his phone. "You'll be pleased to know I went out, alone, and bought a new SIM card. I'm now the proud owner of a European phone number."

She hesitated and he continued. "Or maybe you'd rather take mine and then write me if you feel like it," he added casually.

It was uncanny how he perceived and accepted her reticence. It didn't even make sense after the way she'd kissed him in the park, that she would back away now. Despite that, his request brought up a memory of Lyam asking the very same thing. If only she had refused back then.

"Of course," she said, with forced brightness. "I'll send you a text right now and then you'll have it." Digging into her purse, her fingers grazed the forgotten letter she'd received two days earlier. How could she have overlooked it? Unaccountably, she shivered. Grasping her phone, she drew it out, tapping it to life, and entering the number he recited.

"*C'est complet*," she said, clicking the phone off and dropping it back into her bag. His phone *pinged* almost immediately, and he smiled at her in the light of the streetlamp.

"Are you sure you don't want me to walk you to your door?" he asked for the second time since they'd left the métro. "I don't like thinking of you on these dark streets alone."

"Paris is a safe city," she assured him with a shrug. "I 'ave done it a thousand times. Until tomorrow then, *oui?*"

"*Oui*," he said, but he made no attempt to kiss her again, or to touch her in any way before they parted. "Sweet dreams," he said before melting into the shadows.

She turned and continued walking. It wasn't far to her own apartment. A brisk fifteen-minute walk was all. But maybe it was the threatening message on her door, her own imagination at work, or that Andrew had expressed concern for her. Yet she had the uneasy feeling that she wasn't alone as she strode along the empty, darkened street. She squinted at shadows that had never caused her anxiety before, and glanced furtively over her shoulder, all the while telling herself there was no one there. Why would there be? What would anyone want with her? But she couldn't shake the feeling she was being watched.

Hurrying to her apartment, she tapped in the passcode and pushed open the heavy door to the foyer. With relief, she heard it snap shut, then climbed the corkscrew stairs at almost a run. The light would click off before she reached the top unless she was quick, she told herself. That's why she was taking them at a pace faster than she ever had before. Pressing the automatic light switch as she reached the top level, Gabrielle rummaged for her keys, turned them in the lock, and shoved impatiently at the door. Breathlessly, she slammed it shut behind her not caring what level of noise she made in the quiet hallway.

Snapping both deadbolts, she flicked on the tiny overhead light, and collapsed against the door, breathing heavily. She was safe. Lifting a hand to her heart she patted her chest, willing it to slow its racing clamour. Then with a sigh, she pulled off her jacket, hung it on one of the hooks by the door and kicked off her shoes. Her feet were killing her. The day had been long, but good.

She smiled to herself as she pushed upright. How foolish she'd been to think someone was following her. Then she froze. Something moved in the salon followed by a slight noise. Were her ears playing tricks on her? She stiffened, immobilized by a sudden, gripping fear. There it was again! A shuffling sound, along with a low groan.

Frantically she looked around for some sort of defense. The hammer! She kept one in a closet by the door in order to hang pictures and make small repairs. Soundlessly, she reached into the cavity and felt for it, nearly knocking over her umbrella, but she caught it just in time. Her fingers curled around the long wooden handle. She drew the hammer from its place and felt the weight in her hand as she lifted it and crept toward the dark salon, her arm raised. Her breath caught and held as a figure stirred on the sofa, sitting up, and rising to their feet.

"What in the world do you think you're doing?" a voice screeched.

A woman?

"Gabby? Is that you? What's happening?" the voice spoke again, each consecutive sentence delivered at a higher decibel.

"Annette?"

"Of course, it's Annette," the young woman said irritably, flopping back on the couch and shading her eyes as Gabrielle flipped on the light. "Who did you think it would be? A mass murderer?"

Gabrielle wobbled into the room and dropped into an armchair, the hammer slipping from her grasp and clattering onto the floor.

"*Mon Dieu!*" Annette flung a hand over her mouth and her eyes grew huge. "You did think I was a murderer. But why? I told you I was coming for a visit, and you gave me a key yourself, a long time ago."

Gabrielle's heart was still racing like an outboard motor. It took everything she had to muster up a sickly smile. She hoisted herself onto feeble legs and teetered to the sofa where Annette was still curled up under a blanket.

Gabrielle bent, holding out her arms to the younger woman. "I'm so sorry sweetheart. Hope I didn't scare you."

"It's alright. I guess I might feel nervous too if someone suddenly appeared in my apartment." Grabbing Gabrielle's hands, she pulled her onto the sofa. "Are you surprised?" she probed and then giggled, drawing her pajama covered knees up and wrapping her arms around them. She didn't appear to notice how drawn and pale her sister looked. "Don't worry, I promise not to interfere with your studying. You won't even know I'm here. Do you have classes tomorrow?

"I don't. We can spend the rest of the day together if you allow me the morning to study." She motioned toward the table where several piles of books were stacked before placing an unsteady hand on her forehead. A nasty headache was forming at her temple.

Annette leaned in to examine her up close. "You don't look so great," she observed, finally taking note of her sister's appearance.

"I wasn't expecting you, that's all. For some reason I felt nervous tonight." Gabrielle pushed a dark cloud of hair from her eyes and mustered another smile. "Probably just because I'm tired. I think we should both get some sleep." She stood, offering a hand to Annette, and pulling her sister upright. "The sofa makes into a bed, remember? You could have made yourself more comfortable."

"And have you think the mass murderer was sleeping in your bed?" Annette laughed; her good humor restored. "I don't think so."

Together they moved other furniture out of the way, tossed aside the cushions and pulled the innards out of the sofa to create a bed. Once Annette was settled, Gabrielle kissed her on both cheeks and wished her good night before retiring to her miniscule bedroom.

She undressed in the darkness and felt under her pillow for her nightgown. Tonight, she didn't care about washing her face or applying moisturizer. A lingering feeling of dread still hung about her as she hopped into bed and pulled the covers around her ears despite the warmth of the room.

It wasn't until she was almost asleep that she remembered the letter. But her purse was by the door where she'd hung it under her coat. She wasn't sneaking through the salon, and disturbing Annette for that. It could wait till tomorrow.

She had a feeling she wasn't going to like what it said anyhow.

Chapter Five

Gabrielle groaned. An alarm clock buzzed relentlessly on the bedside table. She flopped close to the edge of the bed and extended an arm to yank the plug from the wall. When the noise stopped, she rolled onto her back and stared at the ceiling. Fear immediately clutched at her heart although she struggled to recall why, until the events of the night before flooded back. Oh yeah. That horrible, prickly feeling as though someone had been spying on her.

Yet, daylight was peeking through her window and such fears felt distant now. It must have been her imagination playing tricks on her last night. Good thing she hadn't clobbered her sister with a hammer because of it.

A clattering sound from the kitchen had her out of bed and reaching for her dressing gown. Annette must be up. Now that she thought of it, she could smell the comforting aroma of fresh *café*.

The sofa had been returned to its previous state and the cushions were all arranged prettily. She passed through, tying a knot at her waist. Padding into the kitchen with bare feet, Gabrielle grinned at the sight of her little sister, busy filling two white porcelain cups with the steaming beverage from a coffee press and adding hot milk.

"*Voila*," Annette said, placing them on the table along with two warm croissants. She dusted off her hands, clearly pleased with herself. "I ran down to the bakery on the corner. They bagged them still hot from the oven for me."

"Mmm, it smells delicious. Just what I needed." Gabrielle pulled out a chair and slid onto it, thankful her headache from the night before was gone and overall, she felt pretty good. She picked up the frothy drink and allowed the vapours to tantalize her senses. Sipping it, she rested back on the chair, dipping her head from side to side and rubbing her neck to ease the muscles.

"I've decided to go out for the morning to a few of my favourite spots. That way you can be completely alone." Annette peered at her over the rim of her cup, tucking a stray corkscrew curl behind her ear.

"A few of your favorite *shopping* spots?"

"Maybe," Annette looked purposely evasive, staring out the narrow kitchen window, a slow grin widening on her face. "Alright, yes..." She rolled her eyes with resignation. "Of course, it's for shopping. You know me and my love of clothes."

Gabrielle reached for a croissant and tore a flakey piece off one end. Popping the buttery morsel into her mouth, she considered her sister's outfit as the young woman hopped up to get them each a napkin. She was dressed all in black. Her long-sleeved, cropped jacket featured large gold buttons down the front, matching a pair of shorts that fastened in the same way. She wore a pair of black patent loafers that were *tres chic* this year, and her legs were sheathed in gossamer black stockings sprinkled with velvety black dots. A small black shoulder bag, slung with gold chains, and a pair of sunglasses lay ready and waiting on the table beside her.

Annette's hair bounced with a healthy sheen, the chocolate curls a perfect foil for long gold earrings that swung to and fro as she seated herself again. Her face glowed with youth and vitality. Also, from a lot of bronzer, if Gabrielle wasn't mistaken. She squinted and looked closer at Annette's tanned face yet pale white hands.

"Do you approve?" Annette asked with a toss of her head. She dropped onto the other chair, her hazel eyes regarding Gabrielle solemnly.

"I love it. It's a really cute outfit." She decided to say nothing about her sister's unusually brown face.

They caught up on family news, had a second cup of coffee, and enjoyed one another's company for the next half hour. Finally, Gabrielle pushed away from the table and stood, tightening her robe.

"I'd best get to work." She glanced at a clock that hung next to the pretty green cupboards. "It's nine. That will give me three solid hours. Is that okay? You can be back here at noon, and we'll go out to Chez Hélène for lunch."

"Ooh, I'd love that." Annette reached for the cups and the empty plate, swiping crumbs onto a crumpled napkin. She waved away her sister's help. "No, you get dressed and start to work. I'll see you soon."

Gabrielle gave her sister a hug and hurried from the room. She planned to study first and shower after. Quickly throwing the rosy pink spread across her bed and plumping the pillows, she dressed in a yellow track suit and opened the window for some fresh air. It would be hot today. The sun already beamed into her room from a tiny round window near the ceiling, wrapping her in its warmth. She stepped around the bed and grabbed her cell phone from the dressing table.

Opening it, she saw that her friend, Sandi, a girl from the USA, who was in Paris studying French, had written to ask if she wanted to meet later. Tapping out a response for a rain check, she explained her sister was in town, sent it and turned the phone off. No distractions allowed. She found a hair elastic, wound it around her unruly mane of hair, and went back to the kitchen.

It was tidy, but empty. What a sweet girl Annette was. Gabrielle carried her stack of books to the kitchen table, sank onto a chair, and got to work.

She looked up from a thick volume where she'd been taking notes on the influence of traditions in culture, when a key rattled in the lock. Glancing at the clock in horror she realised it was nearly twelve. She hadn't moved from the same spot for over three hours. If they didn't go for lunch now, the restaurant would close until dinner service at seven tonight. And she'd promised.

Slamming the book shut, she gathered her papers and shoved them into her book bag before dashing straight to the bathroom. She flipped on the shower while she undressed, then stepped under the steamy water and lifted her face to it, feeling the needles of hot water wash away the stress of upcoming finals. The afternoon would be a welcome respite. Maybe she'd even take Annette to meet Andrew. Although introducing her to a new male friend might revive unpleasant questions concerning Lyam and his sudden disappearance.

She shampooed, conditioned, and washed in record

time, then wrapped herself in a huge white towel and brushed her teeth. Flying out of the bathroom, she waved at Annette, who reclined on the sofa paging through a fashion magazine.

"I'll be ready in ten minutes," she called, slamming her bedroom door behind her. A dress was what she needed. They were always the quickest outfits to put together. Her armoire door crashed into a chair as she flung it aside. The whole standing closet rocked unsteady for a moment, and she heard something heavy topple from behind it. Gabrielle groaned in frustration, but there was no time to worry about it. She began scraping hangers back and forth on the rail.

The blue dress? No, it had a small coffee stain she couldn't get out but she couldn't bear to part with it until giving it one last scrub. How about the yellow sundress with blue flowers that tied on the shoulders? Too summery. The green one! Perfect.

Yanking it off the hanger, she flung the boho style dress across the bed and dropped her towel. Moments later she stood in front of her mirror to assess the effect. This particular maxi dress always made her feel stylish yet comfortable. It was made of three long tiers of cottony green fabric covered in a pale pink rose print that gathered at the waist. The long sleeves were puffed at the shoulder and ended at the wrist in a huge bell shape. Long, silky ties allowed the wearer to fasten the V-neck tight at the neck, but she left them undone. She paired it with fancy flat sandals, a choker necklace, her hoop earrings, and a large floppy straw hat that matched a purse she found shoved in the back of her closet.

Her long dark hair fell in wet curls to her waist, but there was no time to dry it now. Sunshine would have to do that job for her. She added lip gloss, a touch of mascara, slipped her cell phone and wallet into the new purse, and dashed through the salon.

"*Je suis prêt!*" she announced, picking up a sweater in case it turned chilly.

Lazily, Annette consulted her watch, closed the magazine, and rose to follow her. "That was fast. I'm impressed. And the good news is that I think your purse is large enough to fit your hammer should you wish to be prepared for another late-night terrorist attack."

Both women broke into a fit of giggles as they exited the apartment. Pointedly, Gabrielle refused to look at the front of her door.

Chez Hélène was bustling with customers, but the proprietress, who knew Gabrielle well, met them with a hug and *les bisous*, kisses, on each cheek. Then, she found them a little table on the raised patio. The façade of the restaurant was picturesque. Painted a light shade of robin's egg blue, it stood out among all other shops on the street with low-hanging swaths of purple wisteria decorating the front. Gabrielle breathed deeply, closing her eyes to enjoy the powdery, delicate scent. It was reminiscent of lilacs, but sweeter.

Busy waiters wove between tables balancing trays over their heads as the warm glow of springtime sunshine bathed them in its glow. Hélène bustled around in a blue dress that rivalled the bright colour of her storefront and perfectly matched her welcoming eyes. Her dark hair was braided and had been wound around itself to create a fat bun at the back of her head. She hummed a tuneless song through generous lips painted a deep red. The rather eccentric lady stood out from the typical, sixty-plus and conservatively dressed women of Paris. She disappeared inside the building, then burst from the doorway bearing a loaded tray, pausing at their table to set two rose-coloured drinks in small, fluted glasses before them.

"*Kir Royal!*" Annette said with pleasure. "*Merci beaucoup.*"

The lady nodded cheerily at them. "*Vous avez choisi?*" she asked. They ordered and the owner continued on her way.

Annette snatched up her drink and held it out to make a toast. "To the end of school for Gabby," she said, clinking glasses with a tinkling laugh. "How did Hélène know to bring these?"

"Sometimes I come here after a long day and order one. I suppose she takes it for granted now." Gabrielle took a sip of her ruby-red drink and lifted it to the light, considering the contents. Crème de Cassis and champagne, what a flavorful and pretty combination.

Her cell phone beeped. It was only a reminder she'd set for herself. But her mind immediately went to thoughts of Andrew and that she had given him her phone number the night before. Hesitantly she said, "There's someone I'd like you to meet after this, if you don't mind." She looked searchingly at her sister.

"A man?"

Gabrielle twirled the tiny glass in her fingers, watching the liquid roll back and forth, admiring how it sparkled in the sunshine. She nodded. Without looking, she knew Annette's eyebrows were shooting up with interest. She added, "He's just a friend."

"That's what they all say." Annette said dryly. "What happened to Lyam? You know we're all curious. One minute you were a couple and then, *poof*, he was gone."

"I can't discuss it." Gabrielle sighed and lifted the glass for a revitalising drink. She'd known this would happen. Why had she been so foolish as to even mention Andrew? It was inevitable that Annette would be curious and ask for answers about Lyam. But Annette would be staying at least a week. She couldn't very well ignore Andrew until then. She looked directly at her sister. "Do you want to hear about my friend? Then you can decide if you want to meet this man."

"Of course. I always want to know the people in your life."

While they waited for their lunch, Gabrielle told the story of how she had helped Andrew, explained about the wine shop, their dinner out, and how he had caught the thief in the métro. She omitted the kiss and handholding. That was something she couldn't quite believe she had allowed to happen, and certainly didn't feel like discussing the situation with her little sister. It was probably for the best that Annette had arrived. Her presence would prevent any further closeness with Andrew. She wasn't sure of her feelings in that area. It was too soon after Lyam, anyway.

Annette listened with rapt attention, her chin resting in her hands as she leaned on the table. "Superman, hey?" Her eyes had widened at that part of the story. "I'd really like to meet him now. Are we going there soon?"

She leapt back as a server interrupted them with the usual basket of crunchy baguette and fresh spring salads made with baby arugula, asparagus, cucumber, sugar snap peas, artichoke hearts, thinly slice radishes, and mint. It had been drizzled with the special dressing made by Madame Hélène herself, and was delicious.

"I have never had a better salad anywhere else," Gabrielle speared a forkful and transported it to her mouth with a sigh. "When we are done, I will take you to Caviste de Tremblay."

They ate in leisurely silence. The restaurant was alive with the sound of laughter, the clinking of glasses, and a chorus of chirping birds in nearby trees. It was a perfect spring day in Paris.

"*Comment vont la mère et le père?*" Gabrielle asked, as they finished with a coffee. She thought of her parents every day and often wondered how they were. Each one led such a busy life. Her father was a doctor and her mother an X-ray technician working long hours at the local hospital.

"They are fine. Nothing changes. They work too hard, but it is what they like to do." Annette shrugged expressively.

"And you? What have you done with your art lately?"

"I'm always doing something to further my passion. I just finished taking a series of classes on the great impressionists." She smiled distractedly. "I can only dream of being as good as them one day."

"You have all the talent in the family," Gabrielle patted her sister's hand indulgently. "I'm proud of you."

"Merci." Annette placed her espresso cup into the saucer and straightened. "Are we ready? I am anxious to meet this brawny man from the Canadian Prairies."

Chapter Six

After introductions were made, they picked their way through bottles and dismantled shelves on a tour of the shop, deciding it would be a perfect afternoon to visit Montmartre. Annette watched with great interest as Andrew settled his large hat upon his head. She winked at Gabrielle. Clearly this man was a curiosity.

The métro ride was uneventful, for which Gabrielle was glad. There were no robberies, pickpocketing, or other signs of mayhem that might stir their companion to feats of heroism today. Soon they were stepping onto the street from having traversed the lower levels of the Anvers métro station.

Andrew looked around appreciatively as they began the climb to the Église du Sacré-Cœur, or the Church of the Sacred Heart, as Annette told him. The cobblestone streets were dotted with colourful shops and cafes, all busy with locals and tourists. People sat at bistro tables along sidewalk cafes, enjoying the warmth of the afternoon and the sounds of spring.

Gabrielle admired the quaint shops with their eclectic offering of merchandise. There were antiques for sale, women's hosiery, art, ice cream, modern footwear with 1800s style, and souvenir shops. *Boulangeries*, their windows bursting with sandwiches and the tantalizing aroma of freshly baked breads swirled out open doors. There was something to tempt everyone.

Eventually, they crossed another street and stopped at the gates. Andrew gazed up in awe. They had arrived at the foot of the stairs leading to the Sacré-Cœur and feasted their eyes on the brilliant white church perched at the top of the steep hill. A multitude of steps was the price to pay in order to reach it.

"That's amazing," he murmured.

Rather than taking a route straight up the center of the broad hill on which the basilica was situated, Gabrielle led them through the gates and to the side where flowers grew in a profusion of colour along an old curved path. Daffodils sprouted from grassy areas beside the crumbling stone steps, while tulips and gloxinias had been planted in beds beyond, sheltered beneath age-old trees whose trunks were covered in masses of ivy.

"What's that thing?" Andrew asked, pointing at two small rail cars that had just passed one another on their journey up and down the hill.

"*Un funiculaire*. You 'ave never seen one?" Annette was surprised.

Shaking his head, Andrew stared in fascination as people, standing stiffly inside the tiny railway car, rode blithely up the steep grade. "It's a glorified elevator of sorts," he said, half to himself. "Amazing." He turned his attention back to the majestic basilica. "It looks old."

"They started to build the church in 1875, but it wasn't

completed until 1914," Gabrielle puffed, as they paused halfway up. "So, the building isn't all that old."

"It's impressive," Andrew breathed, taking off his hat to wipe his brow. The sleeves of his charcoal gray button-up shirt were rolled as high as they'd go. Gabrielle eyed his jeans wondering if he was the sort of man who would ever wear anything else. She couldn't imagine him in a pair of shorts, or tan khakis, or sandals—forget it.

"I didn't think it would take so much effort to get here." He grinned, interrupting her thoughts. "Ready to continue?"

"I'm not." Red-faced and sprawled on a park bench, Annette looked exhausted. "Go on ahead, save yourselves." She lifted a weary hand, then let it drop to her lap. "I think I'll just wither and die right 'ere. The vultures will come clean my bones and you can shove me into the Catacombs later."

"You didn't tell me your sister was an actress?" Andrew said to Gabrielle with a lopsided grin. "That was quite a theatrical performance."

She laughed. "Come." She beckoned to Annette. "We're almost there. You cannot stop now." With a groan, Annette dragged herself upright and they continued to the top where there was a viewing deck. She plopped onto a stone bench to catch her breath and pulled out her phone. Gabrielle smiled indulgently and moved to the edge of the platform where Andrew had gone in order to gaze at the city.

Paris spread out at their feet. The air was still and muggy in the blazing sun, but the panoramic view was magnificent. They allowed the weight of the moment to settle on them in silence. Far in the distance, almost looking like a toy, the Eiffel Tower stood against the light blue of the sky.

"There's so much to see and do in this place," Andrew shook his head, marvelling at it. "It's almost overwhelming."

"Wait for the crowds of summer before you talk about overwhelming," Gabrielle said as they turned away. "You 'ave no idea how busy it can be. That's why it's nice to come 'ere now." There were tourists wandering about, snapping pictures, and generally enjoying the lovely spring day. Though it was nothing like she'd seen during the warmest months of the year. She remembered reading somewhere that the Basilica saw ten million visitors each year. She believed it.

They crossed a cobblestone road in front of the church and took in the grandeur of the iconic monument. The stark, white edifice was almost blinding in the midday sun.

"The architecture is wonderful," Andrew marvelled, lifting his phone to take a picture. "Let's all get in the shot, okay?" Motioning to Annette, he put his arm around Gabrielle and drew her to his side as he positioned the phone, moving it back and forth in order to frame all three of them. When the younger woman joined them, he snapped three photos in quick succession.

Gabrielle felt a thrill at his touch. Her face reddened, but she schooled her features and bent down, pretending her strappy sandals needed tightening. She didn't want either Andrew or Annette to guess how his proximity affected her. He'd made no attempt to hold her hand, for which she was also grateful. She didn't need unnecessary questions from Annette later.

This morning she had decided it was important to her that she and Andrew keep their relationship as friends only. When he dropped his arm and turned to look up at the four massive domes of the church, she straightened, pushed her hair away from her face and took a deep breath.

"Shall we continue?" she asked. "The streets in this area are very pretty and I'm sure you would like to see *Place du Tertre*."

"I might," Andrew said, with a lift of his eyebrows. "If I knew what the heck it was." His voice took on a fake friendliness and he reached out a massive hand as though to shake hers. "The name's Andrew. Have we met? Guess I haven't properly introduced myself, but I'm new around here and don't speak French."

Annette giggled. "He got you good, *ma sœur*," she teased, poking her sister in the ribs. "One point for the 'andsome cowboy and zero for the pretty French girl who confuses easily."

Gabrielle's faced flushed again, but she joined in the laughter with good grace as they set off along the road running along one side of the basilica. "*Désolé*. I try to introduce a few French words into the conversation so that you get used to them. But I forget you 'ave no idea what they mean unless I translate."

She swept an arm in the general direction they were headed. "*Place du Tertre*, roughly translated into English, means square of the mound, or hill. A square, of course, is a public area where people meet. In this case it is one of the most famous of squares in all Paris, because of the artists that gather there."

"I always enjoy strolling through it." Annette jumped into the conversation, her tone warming to the subject of artistic expression. "During the Belle Époque, which was the golden age of France, beginning in the 1880s, there were many significant artists living there. Montmartre was like a separate village back then. Of course…" she side-stepped a small child and his dripping ice cream cone, "the painters weren't important then. They struggled to make a living with their art."

"Would I know any of the names?" Andrew asked.

"*Oui*." Annette lifted a hand and began to tick off fingers as she went through a list. "Vincent van Gogh, Henri de Toulouse-Lautrec, and Pablo Picasso were a few."

Andrew looked suitably impressed. Gabrielle watched his face while he listened attentively to what Annette was saying. For all his teasing and smiles, there were shadows under his eyes and his face looked drawn. The walk through his uncle's life and memories was taking a toll on him. She resisted a sudden urge to link her arm through his.

"This area became popular. Well-known for its cabarets which I am sure you will also have 'eard of…Moulin Rouge?"

Annette paused to glance at him as they navigated a group of tourists who stood in a milling throng outside a souvenir shop fingering scarves, keychains, and postcards from racks that spilled into the street.

"Yeah sure. Like the movie."

She shrugged. "*Oui*, I suppose. With more real life situations and much less singing."

Now it was Andrew's turn to laugh. "Good point," he said, still chuckling. "Please tell me more."

Annette continued with her tale. Both she and Gabrielle were oblivious to the admiring stares they were receiving from men along the way.

"There isn't much more to tell unless I were to get into the detailed stories of each artist who played a part in the formation of this area. 'Owever, it is still quite an artistic place and always a favourite of mine to visit when I am in Paris. One 'undred and forty spaces, of only one square metre, are allocated to artists each year, which they may use on alternate days. This way, many artists are allowed access. Although the competition for those spots is extreme. In the end, they set up their easels, each of them offering something unique for visitors. People can 'ave their portraits drawn, caricatures created, or silhouettes prepared as they wait. It is quite entertaining to watch."

"I'm anxious to see it," said Andrew. "There's some historical point of interest around every corner in this city." He leaned into Gabrielle as they walked, nudging her with an arm. "You okay? Are you thinking of your studies and wishing you were home? We don't have to stay, you know."

Even that brief contact had sent her heart racing and she pointedly put more distance between them. "No, I'm fine. It's good to get away from the books for a while."

"She studied all morning," Annette announced. She made the words sound distasteful, as though Gabrielle had been caught rifling through the neighbour's garbage, or butchering hogs on Main Street. "If I do not visit 'er, she would never come out of 'er apartment."

"Oh," said Andrew with widening eyes. "That's odd. She comes to see me."

"*Vraiment?*" Annette squealed, forgetting to speak English. "I mean, really? That's interesting."

"You know I'm here, right? Listening to you two talk," Gabrielle huffed. She passed them and took the lead, rounding the corner.

Place du Tertre opened before them. Trees, filling out with leaves and softly blowing in a slight breeze, thrust through small patches of soil in the cobblestone square. They arched over the tent-like awnings that housed the artists. Old-fashioned streetlamps, spaced at regular intervals, would later add a late-night ambiance.

Slowly, they paced through the maze of vendors and visitors that filled the square and passed along the narrow lane that surrounded it. On the far side, restaurants spilled into the center area and servers darted across the street carrying large trays of steaming food. They navigated the swarms of visitors much faster than she expected. She wondered how many collisions took place each day.

Remembering a story her father had once told her, Gabrielle slowed her pace and fell into step beside Andrew to share it. "There is a legend that the first Parisian Bistro was founded 'ere. Early in the 19th century Russian forces occupied Paris. It was after Napoleon surrendered in a battle I cannot recall at the moment. Anyway, the soldiers who stayed 'ere would call out, 'Bistro!' to the servers of that time, urging them to 'urry up with their drinks. The word 'bistro' means 'quickly' in Russian. Soon, the name caught on and the word bistro, meaning a restaurant that serves quick, delicious meals, was born."

"I 'aven't 'eard 'im tell that story," Annette exclaimed, looking around at all the restaurants. "I'm sure they do good business in the summer. It's busy now."

After making one full circuit of the square, Gabrielle led them down Rue Norvins, a street narrower than the last. It was surprising the number of people that sauntered from side to side, eating pastries or spooning ice cream from cups. Gabrielle had always loved this street. It felt like a glimpse into what Paris might have looked like, centuries past. Wordlessly, she led them, dodging small children, prams, and people who would stop in their tracks without notice to point at something that caught their eye.

With a sigh of relief, she darted to the right down Rue des Saules. As a group they slowed their pace.

"You are taking us to La Maison Rose, *n'est ce pas?*"

Annette asked, jogging a little to come alongside her sister. Without waiting for an answer, she turned to Andrew. "It is a pretty pink 'ouse that became a restaurant on the corner of a winding cobblestone street." She plucked at Gabrielle's arm. "Am I right? That is where we are going?"

"*Oui*," Gabrielle said shortly. "Do you know any other facts about it?"

"I know that people have bought coffee there for over one hundred years," she said triumphantly. "And that it was a boarding 'ouse a long time ago where writers and artists could eat cheaply."

"*Tres bien*," Gabrielle congratulated her. "But I am surprised you do not know the long 'istory of La Maison Rose. It involves Picasso. The story is too long to tell now, but the famous artist spent much time there, along with others—"

"All this talk of artists has me wishing for a blank canvas and some paint," Andrew broke in to say, "but the only thing I've ever painted was the side of a barn and the tailgate of my old pickup truck. I don't think that counts."

Both girls giggled with him until Annette sobered and asked, "What is a…tail gate? And what is it that your truck picks up, *exactement?*"

Then, they all laughed in earnest. Gabrielle found the situation funny, yet she had no idea what the man was talking about either. *A tail gate?* But she would not allow him to think she was ignorant of the knowledge, so she kept quiet.

However, before Andrew could answer Annette's question, they arrived. Stopping on the opposite street corner, they gazed at the pretty little house with its pale pink walls. The name had been written in large script across the front in green to match the wooden shutters and seating. Potted herbs and flowers perched precariously on the sills in front of the latticed windows. It was charming.

"Shall we 'ave *un café?*" Annette asked.

"*Oui,*" said Andrew with obvious pride at using the lone French word.

Choosing one of the tiny, folding tables, Andrew borrowed an extra chair from an empty spot. He waited until the girls were seated on either end before sitting, half of him blocking the sidewalk. Almost immediately, a young girl appeared from inside. Her shoulder-length blonde hair was tied back with an elastic. She wore a simple green and yellow patterned skirt with a bright lemon-coloured t-shirt and carried a washcloth which she used to wipe down the table next to them. After straightening the one remaining chair, she asked them what they would like to drink.

"*Bonjour mademoiselle. Trois café, s'il vous plait,*" Gabrielle said quickly. "Do you want sugar or milk?" she asked Andrew. When he shook his head she turned back to the girl. "*Avec du sucre pour moi.*"

They sat in the sunshine, sipping their drinks in silence apart from the frantic yapping of a small dog. The creature sounded desperate and in trouble. Gabrielle looked around for the animal, but couldn't see it anywhere.

Suddenly, Andrew lurched to his feet, the table went flying and coffee splashed across his pant legs. His cup fell, smashing into a thousand pieces. Without a word he flung off his hat and raced across the street, his cowboy boots slipping on the cobblestones. Gabrielle and Annette leaped up behind him. Whirling around, they gasped with horror at the sight they beheld.

The barking they'd heard was coming from the fourth floor of a nearby building. A small black dog dangled by a leash from a window high in the sky. It swung back and forth, short legs pedalling pitifully in the air. The dog's terrified yelps slowed as the tightening collar around its neck began to asphyxiate him. He had moments to live if that.

Andrew lunged at a railing on the second level of the building, his fingers stretching to gain purchase. Miraculously, he caught hold and swung himself high, his knees and the toes of his boots scrabbling against the brick. He worked himself up with grasping fingers until he stood precariously on the thin ledge. A drainpipe ran down the center of the façade and he slithered along the shelf until he could leap out, his hands and feet snaking around the pipe. Then he began to worm his way up to where the little dog had gone still. The poor creature's head lopped over to one side. Its body dangled from the cord as great gagging sounds were ripped from its throat.

Andrew leaned sideways, almost perpendicular to the drainpipe he held in one powerful hand. He leaped again, his boots scratching against the red brick wall of the house as he clawed his way across some trailing vines and snagged the wrought iron railings of the third story window. Again he swung, hauling himself upright, his boots teetering on top of the barrier as he raised himself above the protruding lip of the fourth floor.

The dog sagged from the leash beside him, its swaying body banging against Andrew's shoulder. The pitiful beast's ragged gagging for air had ceased. Andrew's hand reached into a back pocket and pulled something out, flicking it open. Gabrielle watched as he reached above his head, gripping the crumbling old ledge with one hand as he stretched skyward with the other and began to saw at the rope that held the dog.

Moments later the dog dropped, free from the leash, but

now plummeting to certain death below. If it wasn't dead already!

But Andrew's hands changed places in the blink of an eye. He now gripped the wall with the other hand and his free arm snaked out and snatched the little dog in mid-air.

A cheer went up around her. Dazed and shocked, tears ran down Gabrielle's face and a sob of joy broke from her lips. She looked around to see a crowd of people hugging one another—applauding, whistling, crying, and shouting praises for the brave man. A few people rushed forward to take the little dog from Andrew as he manoeuvred downward. He hung from the lowest window to hand the body of the dog to a tall man with bushy black hair and a handlebar moustache. Then, Andrew jumped to the ground, landing on all fours like a cat before hurrying to the people grouped around the dog.

Gabrielle grabbed Annette's cold hand. They ran to where Andrew stood, surrounded by people patting him on the back and shouting words of praise in a variety of languages. It didn't matter if he couldn't understand their words. The language of joy was universally the same.

When the crowd parted to let them through, she saw that Andrew once again held the little dog, minus the collar and breathing. Its head lay across Andrew's palms, heaving body supported by his arms and a tiny pink tongue weakly licking his hand as it gazed at him with liquid brown eyes.

A side door of the house burst open, slamming back on its hinges with a bang. An elderly man stepped onto the sidewalk with a cane wobbling in one hand. He tottered toward the crowd who respectfully moved to either side.

"*Mon lapin!*" he cried, tears streaming down his lined faced as he reached for the shaggy little dog. By now, the dog had recovered enough that it lifted its head and whined.

Carefully Andrew shifted the weight of the little dog, so that it could be fondled by its master. The old man ruffled the fur on his dog's head and stroked his silky ears.

The man looked at Andrew, tears flowing unchecked down his face. "*Merci beaucoup Monsieur. Vous êtes un ange.*" He said something more in French, then lowered his face to the dog and nuzzled him. His tears made the dog's fur wet, and his gnarled hands held the dog's body gently. The man looked at Andrew and spoke in a voice shredded with emotion. "*Venez avec moi, s'il vous plaît.*"

There was no need for translation. Andrew appeared to know exactly what was being asked of him. With deliberation, the elderly man turned around and shuffled back to his door. Andrew followed closely behind carrying the small mound of fur.

Moments later he returned, grinning. The knees of his jeans had been torn, his shirt ripped and covered in red dust from the bricks. His hands were bleeding in several places, but Gabrielle had never seen him look so happy.

"Too bad I couldn't understand what he said," Andrew said, dusting off his clothes and smearing the blood from his cuts onto his jeans. "But I'm pretty sure the dog's name is Lapine." He shook his head. "Something like that anyway. Where's my hat?"

"He said you were an angel," Gabrielle said quietly. "And told you he had opened the top window for air, and leashed his dog for a walk before he became distracted with something else. The dog must have slipped through the window, and his leash caught hold." She sighed deeply. "The old man wasn't around to notice. He had gone down to his kitchen and only caught sight of the crowd toward the end when you climbed past a window."

Most of the crowd had dispersed by now, but a few

people still lingered. Hesitantly, they stepped forward again to tell Andrew how brave he was and to praise his ability to scale a building, particularly in leather boots. Some words were delivered in English, but Gabrielle and Annette translated the French for him to hear. He brushed it all aside with a broad grin and a wave.

"Mercy," he said, to everyone who spoke to him. Gabrielle felt too shaken to correct his pronunciation. He was a hero—again. Did it matter that he couldn't even say one word in French? No, it did not.

She linked arms with her sister who she could also feel trembling as they followed him back to La Maison Rose. They needed to collect his hat, and pay the bill for the smashed mug and discarded coffees.

But a man in a long white apron, who was sweeping up the broken china with an old straw broom, waved away their money. Instead, he grasped Andrew by the shoulders and kissed him on both cheeks.

"*Non, non monsieur! Pas d'argent. Vous sauvez le chien de notre client préféré. Merci beaucoup.*" He stooped, picked up Andrew's hat and rubbed it across his ample belly to clean it, his face wreathed in smiles.

Andrew accepted it with a nod of thanks, but looked to Gabrielle for clarification, puzzled at the long tirade of French he couldn't comprehend.

"He says, he won't take your money, because you saved the life of their favorite customer's dog. He is very grateful." Gabrielle thanked the man, who with further smiles, went back to his cleaning.

Andrew pushed his hat onto his head and ran exploratory fingers around the brim. "My hat seems to be okay," he said happily, his blue eyes crinkling at the corners. "Where shall we go now?"

"You really are Superman," said Annette in a barely audible voice. "Gabby told me what you 'ad done to help those people in the métro, but it was 'ard to believe until now." She shook her head. "The way you scaled that building was incredible."

Gabrielle felt tears prick her eyes once more. Pride surged in her chest for this man. He was like no one she'd ever known. Stepping to his side she threaded her arm through his and pulled him close. On the other side, Annette did the same. In this way the three of them continued down the street.

"Where are we going?" Andrew asked.

"I don't know where any of us are going," Gabrielle said cryptically. Her legs were still a bit wobbly. "I'm feeling a little muddled right now. Let's just walk and figure it out when we get there."

Chapter Seven

They retraced their steps back up Rue des Saules, the way they'd come not long before. Except when they came to the busier street, they turned to the right, rather than going back to the Artists' Square. The crowds thinned a little as they continued to wind their way down the hill, each of them lost in their own thoughts.

It was getting late, and the light began to change to the glow of late afternoon as the sun slipped behind the apartment buildings they passed. Gabrielle glanced at her phone; almost six o'clock. Soon they would have to think about heading home or eating out. She wasn't sure which would be best. The longer she was with this man, the more she liked him. Despite how wonderful he appeared, that felt both exciting and scary.

Branches, covered with sprays of white flowers gushed over a wrought iron fence atop a rock wall beside them as they came to an intersection. She pointed out their next move. Several more turns along the narrow cobblestone lane and they came to Place Émile Goudeau, another square shaded entirely by huge oak trees just beginning to turn green.

"Picasso lived here," Annette said suddenly, ending the silence.

"What? On a park bench?" Andrew looked at her in exaggerated surprise. "Are you saying the man was homeless?"

"No silly," she teased and then giggled, the uncomfortable tension was broken. "*Là-bas*, over there." She pointed. "The building with the green front that says Le Bateau Lavoir. It means, the laundry boat. Do you see it? Picasso rented a studio 'ere in 1904."

"I see it. You certainly know a lot about the art world." Andrew viewed her with interest.

"I should," Annette said with a sniff. "It will be my life's work." She stepped away from the pair and strolled toward the only exit from the square, down a flight of stairs at the center of a railing on the far side.

"Annette is an artist 'erself," Gabrielle explained, unlinking her arm from Andrew's brawny one. It felt awkward without Annette on the other side. "She 'as been accepted to a prestigious school called Beaux-Arts de Paris. We are very proud of 'er."

"That's amazing. I've never known an artist before," he said, sounding impressed.

Annette whirled around from where she stood at the railing. "*Alors*! And I 'ave never known a man such as yourself, who scales buildings to rescue the dog of an old man."

Andrew blushed. "I just react," he said, lifting his hands in a gesture of resignation. "It's the way I'm built. If I can help, that's what I do."

"I did not mean to embarrass you," Annette said,

hurrying over to place a hand on his arm. "You are a remarkable man, and I am glad we 'ave meet. Are all men from Canada like you?"

He chuckled. "Guess I can't answer for them. My father raised me and my brother to put others first."

With that the subject was closed. What could one add when faced with such gallantry? He was the polar opposite to Lyam and Gabrielle couldn't quite wrap her head around it. The man seemed too good to be true. Maybe he had some serious hidden flaw she hadn't spotted yet. She watched him surreptitiously from beneath her lashes.

"What did you use to cut the dog loose?" Gabrielle suddenly remembered the device from his back pocket.

"Oh that? It's a called a Leatherman. We always carry them on the farm, because they have so many tool attachments. I use three or four of them every day. I packed it into my checked luggage. Maybe I shouldn't have brought it on a trip to France, but you have to admit it came in pretty handy." He drew it out to show them, flicking a few of the attachments open for them to see.

"It's like a Swiss Army Knife," Annette said, reaching out to touch the tiny silver pliers lying on his palm.

"Yeah, I guess it is. Anyway," he said, snapping it shut, "I'm glad I had it."

They wandered down the steps and past a busy restaurant filled with chattering customers. Then strolled single file along a contracted sidewalk until they reached Rue des Abbesses.

They had only walked along the busy thoroughfare for a few minutes when Annette spoke. "*J'ai soif.*"

"What does that mean?" Andrew asked, unable to tear his eyes away from the activity about him. Cars honked, motorbikes whizzed past, and people bustled down the sidewalk carrying parcels of all descriptions.

Gabrielle considered the disparity between their two worlds, and what Andrew must be experiencing right now. He was likely feeling overwhelmed with the sheer magnitude of life in the city.

"It means she's thirsty," Gabrielle answered, already watching for somewhere they could stop to get a quick drink. "There is a small shop near the métro station?" She glanced at her pretty sister in her chic outfit and smiled. "Will plain water do, or would you like *de l'eau gazeuse?*"

"*Un soda, s'il te plait,*" Annette answered, switching her purse from one shoulder to the other. All three of them ducked into the confined space of a tiny store. Gabrielle made for the wall of drinks in an open air cooler. The space inside the shop was filled from floor to ceiling with canned goods, bottled pickles, condiments and other preserved foods, bread, laundry soap, shampoos, a few boxes of fresh vegetables and fruits, and even a shelf filled with wine. There was barely room to move around all the items for sale. Andrew peered at a shelf filled with snacks.

"Are you kidding me?" Gabrielle heard him mutter to himself. And then added, "I don't believe it," as he rustled through a few of the packages before choosing two. Moments later he joined them, chose a drink at random, and strode to the cash register to pay.

Out on the street, he clutched his bag of goodies protectively to his chest with a grin. "I got something for us all to share. Can we sit down for a while? Maybe on that bench?" He pointed at a green wooden bench near a children's carrousel ride that was situated next to the Abbesses métro station entrance.

They plunked themselves down and the women opened

their drinks, watching as Andrew mysteriously delved into his grocery sack and pulled out two small bags of potato chips. He waved them proudly in the air, the wrappers crinkling loudly.

"It was difficult to choose between all the ultra-delicious flavours I found," he said, sarcasm dripping from his tone. "But I managed to find two I just have to sample. I'll share them with you even though you probably grew up on…" He held up one package and read from the side, "Black Truffle, a taste sensation. And perhaps you often eat your fill of…" He raised the other and squinted at it, as he called out, "Oyster flavoured crisps." He made a face, but manfully ripped open the bag and offered it to the women before dipping a hand in himself. "I mean, really, with such options as truffle and oyster, how could you go wrong?" He grinned mischievously.

Narrowing his eyes, he popped several into his mouth and chewed consideringly. "Not quite as hateful as expected," he said, swallowing with only a slight shudder. "It gives a whole new meaning to the phrase, 'fish and chips.'"

Gabrielle and Annette laughed, the latter choking on a crumb and tipping most of a drink down her throat before she recovered.

"And what flavours do you enjoy in Canada?" Annette queried, checking her hair in a small compact mirror from her purse.

Andrew looked sheepish. "You got me. My favourites are ketchup and dill pickle."

"You're joking!" Annette sat back with a look of amusement on her face. "Ketchup? And you make fun of ours?"

They ate their fill of the snacks Andrew had provided. Gabrielle then swept the chip particles from her lap and made a small announcement.

"I want to show you, *Le mur des je t'aime*," she said, turning toward him as he rolled the bags into balls and fired them into a nearby trash receptacle.

Brushing crumbs off his mouth, he took another drink of his water. "The what?" A frown appeared between his eyes.

Annette chuckled before she said, "It is the, 'I Love You Wall.' It is just be'ind us, in that little fenced park.

Andrew swiveled around on the bench to look. "Looks like a cute garden." Removing his Stetson, he smoothed down his hair and placed the hat back on his head. "But again, what are you talking about? You French are well-known romantics, but what the heck is a love wall?"

Gabrielle stood up, placing hands on hips, regarded him sternly. "May I remind you Andrew, you also are 'alf French."

He laughed. "You may. And I'm proud of it! Let's see this wall of yours." Grinning, Andrew jumped to his feet still holding his bottled water. He bowed low, indicating that the women should walk ahead. But his smile fled as his attention was diverted to a spot across the street. His eyebrows knitted together, and his mouth thinned. Gabrielle followed his gaze, wondering what he'd seen to cause such concern, but only saw the usual crowds of a busy thoroughfare. Andrew rubbed his jawline thoughtfully and then turned away.

"Sorry," he said, with an attempt to return to his good humour. "Or should I say *dess-holy*?"

"If you're trying to apologize by using the French word, *désolé*," Annette said dryly, "you failed."

Laughing, they sauntered toward the open gate of the fenced Jehan-Rictus Square, where the 'I Love You Wall' was housed. It was close and they quickly passed through the gate, immediately enjoying the solitude it afforded despite its location just off a popular shopping street.

It was a pretty place with wide paved walkways, hedges, low laurels, leafy bushes, and lush beds of spring flowers. Fruit trees also bloomed, the waves of a sweet perfume wafting through the air. Gabrielle took a deep breath, listening as Annette, sounding a little like a tourist guide, continued her explanation.

"*Le Mur des Je t'aime*, is a wall which was created by two artists as an 'omage to lovers. It is covered with 612, black lava tiles inscribed with the words, '*I love you*' in 312 different languages. It is quite remarkable that the couple collected the phrase in each language by speaking to people in embassies, asking strangers and neighbours until hundreds of them were accumulated. Obviously, they didn't add all of them to the wall." She shrugged as they drew to a halt in front of the wall and stared at it. "Only the ones considered the most beautiful were used. It commemorates the international language of love, as all 192 countries of the United Nations are represented."

"Wow," Andrew said. A young couple held hands in front of the wall, their mouths repeating the sacred words in their own language before they sealed the promise with a kiss and moved along the path.

Gabrielle sighed. She had been here with Lyam once, but he had considered it a waste of time and beneath his dignity to declare his love for her in front of a wall. It didn't matter to him that she had considered it quite romantic. Another couple walked toward them, arm in arm. Annette wandered away to sit on one of the many benches provided in the garden.

She felt, rather than saw, Andrew's eyes rest on her, but she didn't meet his gaze. It would be a long time before she put her trust in someone again. Lyam had crushed something inside her. Still, she felt a surge of longing rise in her heart as she walked closer to see how many of the words she could understand. One day she hoped to find a man with whom to share these sacred words of love. Someone who didn't think they were foolish.

"This is beautiful," said Andrew's awed voice.

Gabrielle whirled around. "It is?"

"Of course," he said, reaching out a hand to caress the stone. "I'll bet a lot of marriage proposals are made here."

It wasn't meant as a question, but she answered it anyway. "*Oui*, I 'ave seen proposals, engagement photo shoots, and even a quick marriage performed."

"You come here quite often then?"

"My parents first brought me…" her words trailed as a memory came to mind of her father and mother whispering words of undying love as the two girls perched on a bench and watched. That was what she wanted. A marriage based on love, respect, and acceptance of one another's differences.

She looked up, realizing he'd been waiting for her to finish. "Sorry," she said, flashing him a smile. "Just reliving an 'appy time. Yes, I come 'ere once in a while. I suppose it's an eternal, 'uman desire to be loved and it makes me glad to see so many lovers, young and old, come here to profess it." Feeling as though she were becoming too maudlin, Gabrielle changed the subject. "We should probably go 'ome now, yes? We cannot eat out all the time and I 'ave plenty of work waiting for me."

Andrew shook his head as though to clear it of his own memories. "Sure," he said, offering nothing more in the way of conversation. "Thanks for bringing me here today. I can tell it's a special place for you. But you're right, I have a lot to do as well. I want to start painting tomorrow and I've set a shop opening date for the Friday after this. How do you think I should advertise it?"

Gabrielle waved to her sister and the three of them made their way out of the lovely little garden, and back down the winding stairs into the métro Abbesses. They were seated across from one another on the train when she replied.

"I think opening the shop quickly is fantastic, but you won't need to do much in the way of advertising. Put a large sign up in the front window announcing the date and time, and the local people will come. It may not be busy right away, but I feel certain your uncle had a devoted clientele. Once they learn you are 'is nephew and that you intend to carry on in the tradition of your uncle, they will return. And…" she looked directly into his clear blue eyes, "I will be there to 'elp you speak to them that first day."

"Mercy!" Andrew said, the grin on his face almost reaching ear to ear. "You're the best friend a foreign guy could ever have. Thanks."

When an elderly lady boarded the train at their next stop, Andrew hopped up to offer her his chair. As the woman thanked him and tiredly fell into the seat with a groan, piling several bags onto her lap, he moved to the center of the car. Catching Gabrielle's eye over the heads of nearby passengers, he pulled the brim of his hat low in a silent salute. Annette dug an elbow into Gabrielle's side and hissed at her.

"*Il tombe amoureux de toi.*"

Gabrielle shook her head vigorously. "*Non,*" she disagreed. Andrew was a friend, nothing more. Yes, he was grateful for her help and that made sense. But Annette's declaration that he was falling in love with her was outrageous and not to be entertained. To prove it, she ignored him all the way to their métro stop.

As they climbed to street level and began the familiar walk to their respective homes, Andrew kept turning to stare thoughtfully behind them.

"Are you looking for something?" Annette finally asked, craning her neck to see if she could spot what he was searching for.

In answer, Andrew threw back his shoulders and spoke determinedly. "I'm walking you to your door tonight." He raised a silencing hand as Gabrielle opened her mouth to protest. "No arguments," he said with emphasis. "Think of it as doing me a favour, not you. I'll sleep better tonight knowing you're both safely inside, with the door locked behind you."

Gabrielle narrowed her eyes. She peered at him, trying to decide what was prompting this display of masculine protection, but he wouldn't respond to her probing gaze. Very well, she decided if that was what he wanted to do, she wouldn't stop him.

Evening was falling and the shadows were growing long. Gabrielle's stomach began to growl. A handful of potato chips wasn't very filling, and it had been a long time since lunch. Annette chattered to Andrew as they walked, filling him in on her upcoming year of studies and showing him the way to the apartment. Though Gabrielle only listened with half an ear. She was planning out dinner for the two of them and wondering if she had enough eggs for a cheese omelet.

"Sorry to interrupt," Andrew said tersely, doing just that. Annette had been describing the Belliveau Estate in Provence where she and Gabrielle had spent summer holidays since they were children. Both women stopped abruptly. Andrew took an arm of each, almost propelling them forcibly along the quiet street.

"What are you doing?" Gabrielle said with annoyance, trying to pull her arm away.

"I'll explain when we get there," Andrew said in a low, tense voice. "But could we walk faster? It's important."

Something in his tone caused both women to quicken their pace without further question. The trio fairly raced along the final stretch of street until reaching Gabrielle's apartment block. Long before they arrived, she readied herself to input the code. Her fingers flew across the keypad and the latch clicked open. Andrew threw his weight against it and the two women almost fell into the foyer.

Behind them, Andrew snapped the door shut and leaned against it. Letting out a sigh he yanked the hat from his head and ran a hand through his sandy hair.

"I'd like to speak to your sister alone for a moment if you don't mind, Annette," he said with a smile. "She can fill you in later, if she wants."

"*D'accord*," Annette said doubtfully, looking at Andrew with suspicion. "I want to know what's going on when you come up, Gabby," she said pointedly. She held out a hand for the keys that Gabrielle jangled in one hand and marched stiffly up the stairs.

When she was safely out of earshot, Andrew took a deep breath. "I don't want to alarm you, or her, but I think we've been followed for most of the day."

Gabrielle took a step back. Coming in contact with the mailboxes, she sagged against them, feeling her heart race. "You do?" Her legs felt weak, unable to support her and she swayed before catching herself. Andrew had to be wrong. Who would follow them? "What makes you think this?"

He sighed. "It might be a coincidence, but...naw," he

shook his head. "It's no coincidence." Absently, he turned his hat around and around in his hands. "I noticed a man up at that big white church we first went to today. Can't think of the name."

"Sacré-Cœur."

"Yeah, that's it. Anyway, I didn't think much of it at the time. There were lots of people around. It's a busy place." He stepped closer to her, and she could see the worry in his eyes.

"The guy is tall, a heavyset man. I'd say in his early forties, with thick black hair and a goatee. He stands out in a crowd. Anyway, I noticed him again when we were sitting outside that little pink café. He walked past. Still, that wasn't a big deal," Andrew shoved his hands in his pockets and then withdrew them to wave around as he talked. "A lot of people walked by. But then I saw him again when we were sitting on that park bench having a drink. That's when I really began to take note. He was hanging around across the street, leaning against a lamppost and reading a newspaper."

He paused and she realised she was holding her breath, scanning her memory banks for heavyset men with goatees.

"I remember thinking that a tourist wouldn't do that," Andrew continued. "Read a newspaper, I mean. Plus, he was alone which also seemed unusual." Andrew shifted uneasily and began to pace. "I stared at him for a while, and he lowered the newspaper to look directly at us. As soon as he saw me watching him, he lifted the paper again. That incident shocked me, but I still couldn't quite believe someone would be purposely tailing us, so I tried to forget about it."

"And...?" Gabrielle said weakly. "You saw him again?"

"Yes." Andrew stopped in front of her. "Look, I don't mean to worry you, but I'm concerned."

"Where was he?" she asked tonelessly. Her worst fears were coming true.

Andrew resumed his pacing. "He wasn't on the train, and believe me, I looked. I felt as though I was dreaming stuff up. But I didn't see him, and I began to relax—until we were walking along the street just now." He raked another hand through his hair, this time half of it sticking straight up on his head.

"I caught sight of him not far from here, in a small car. I don't know how he knew where to find us, but it was definitely him. I'm sure of it. Do you have any idea why someone would be doing this?"

Gabrielle stared at the floor, flattening both palms against the cool metal of the mailboxes at her back and leaned forward. Her hair tumbled over her face. Lyam was mixed up in this. She just knew it. He hadn't tried to contact her since that fateful day when she'd called the police and told them what she'd learned and where he'd been that night.

She also recalled her fears from the night before and knew she'd been right. Someone had been out there watching her. But why?

Andrew came to a stop directly in front of her. "I want to help, but I'm not sure how. Can I take you to talk to the police?"

She took a deep, shuddering breath. "I will alert them, *oui*, but I'm sure they cannot do anything about a stalker unless an attempt has been made to physically harm me." She searched his concerned eyes. "They will tell me to go 'ome. Nothing can be done."

He nodded in acknowledgement. "But this isn't just

random is it?" he asked. "You're the most beautiful woman I've ever seen. But this seems more sinister than someone stalking you, because of your looks." He bent down to look full into her face. "You know more about it than you're telling me, don't you?"

"Per'aps," she said evasively, "I'm not sure. But if it's what I think it is, I don't want to include you in my troubles."

Andrew spread his arms wide. "Too late," he said. "I'm already included. That guy, whoever he is, knows that I know about him." He rubbed the stubble on his chin. "Do you have classes tomorrow?"

She nodded.

"What time?"

Gabrielle hitched her purse into a different position. "I should go upstairs," she said, avoiding his question and his gaze. "Annette will wonder where I am."

He crossed his arms in front of him and planted his feet.

"I don't want to involve you any more than I already 'ave," she insisted, pasting what she hoped was an unconcerned smile on her lips. She leaned past him to push an automatic release button for the heavy oaken door. "I'll text you okay." The door buzzed and clicked open. "Thank you for going with us this afternoon, and for walking us home."

She pulled the door open, ensuring she was hidden behind it. Andrew's revelations had unnerved her, but she was trying not to let him see just how badly.

Andrew took the door from her and placed his booted foot against it to hold it wide. "Fine," he said. "You don't want to talk about it and that's your right, but we're friends…I don't take that lightly. So, if you don't tell me what time you're leaving for class in the morning, I'll be here by six o'clock, sitting on the curb, waiting for you." A slow smile crept across his face. "You wouldn't want to deprive a cowboy of his sleep, now would you?"

Rolling her eyes, but acknowledging she'd feel a whole lot better if he was with her, she divulged the requested information.

"I will leave 'ere by nine."

"Great," he said, stepping through the doorway. "Don't go anywhere without me." The door clanged shut behind him.

Gabrielle raced up the stairs as though fifty heavyset men with goatees were after her, only slowing when she drew near the top floor. Should she tell her sister the truth concerning Lyam? She wasn't positive he was the reason for this sudden drama. After all, why would Lyam send someone to stalk her? Was it time that the family knew what he'd done? But knowing why the man deserved prison wouldn't make any difference now. She'd be filling Annette with fear needlessly.

And what of Andrew. Yes, they were friends, but he didn't deserve to be dragged into the middle of some late-night crime drama. She didn't want him placed in a position where he'd be forced to defend her.

Of course, the message on her door was tied in, but how? And if this was some crony of Lyam's, what did he want? Revenge? To report to Lyam on her whereabouts? Maybe just to frighten her? No. From the message, it appeared he wanted something. But what? Gabrielle flicked her hair over slumped shoulders and rubbed her throbbing head. She didn't know the answers to any of those questions.

Back and forth she went, arguing first one way and then the other. By the time she'd let herself into the apartment and locked the door, she'd decided.

She would protect them all. She'd say nothing to Annette, leave for university earlier than what she'd said, make up some reason why she couldn't visit Andrew's shop, and stay home as much as possible.

It was all she could do. Lyam and his friends were dangerous men who would stop at nothing to achieve their goal. And somehow she knew that goal involved her.

Chapter Eight

Gabrielle tiptoed past a sleeping Annette the next morning, deciding to go without breakfast lest she awaken her sister. A quick glance out her window told her it was overcast and dull. So, she'd slipped on a pair of jeans, a light pink hoodie, and her trainers before running a comb through her long hair, brushing her teeth, and frowning at herself in the mirror.

It wasn't nice of her to sneak out before Andrew would have a chance to arrive and walk her to class, but she couldn't make him a bigger part of this than was necessary. No one should be mixed up in Lyam's mess. Including her, but it was too late for that. She scribbled a note to Annette, asking her to stay in for the day and telling her she'd be home around two. Then, she grabbed her book bag, headed to the door for a jacket, and let herself out, locking the door behind her.

She paused at the top of the stairs to check her phone messages, and to determine the time. It was a little after seven. It wouldn't take long to get to school. She'd be quite early for her ten o'clock class. However, there was a café on her way that she enjoyed where a lengthy stop for a croissant and a *café au lait* would be perfect. She hurried downstairs.

The door clicked open and tentatively she edged outside, scanning her surroundings, her heart beating erratically.

"Going somewhere?" asked a drawling voice.

Her bag dropped to the pavement, and she lunged back, fear clutching at her chest.

A figure wearing a large, black cowboy hat untangled himself from the crouched position he'd been in and came to stand in front of her. "I've read the body language of enough obstinate animals to know what they plan to do next. Yours told me you'd bolt before I could get here." Andrew spoke easily, but there wasn't even a hint of a smile around his usually grinning mouth. "So, I came early. Looks like I was right, too." He tipped the hat back on his head and crossed powerful arms over his chest, awaiting her explanation.

Gabrielle opened and closed her mouth, fishlike. Her heartbeat was slowing, but the rush of adrenalin left her feeling weak. She reached for her bag, straightened, and lifted her chin.

"And I said I didn't want to include you." She knew her words sounded ungrateful and snippy. But how could she keep him out of this situation if he was continually playing the chivalrous card? "Maybe the whole incident was nothing," she continued in a more subdued tone. "Simple coincidence."

"You can deny it and believe whatever you want," he said, a determined edge to his voice. "I know what I saw and I'm not letting anything happen to you. So..." he grinned, but it was more wolfish than pleasant before he said, "You can walk beside me or I follow you ten paces behind, but one way or another I'm coming with you."

"I see," she said, barely above a whisper.

"Look…" Andrew's tone softened. He stepped forward and grasped her shoulders, just as he had done the night before. "I realise you're trying to think of me, but I can handle myself. I'll tell you about it sometime. Anyway, I'm not worried for my safety one bit. My concern is for you. I understand we haven't known each other long, but I—I mean…you're my only friend in this huge city and you went out of your way to help me when you didn't have a clue who I was. Consider this a little repayment, okay?" He placed a gentle finger under her chin and tipped her face up to search her eyes.

If Gabrielle felt weak before, she felt it doubly now. Was he going to kiss her? She swayed and Andrew's grasp tightened. She licked her lips and forced her stiffened cheeks to bend into a smile.

"*D'accord*," she said. "For today you may walk with me. I was going to 'ave a light *petit-déjeuner* at a café near the university. Would you care to join me?"

"I would," he said, his good humour returning. He straightened his hat, crooked an arm, patted her hand as she threaded her arm through, and rested it on the sleeve of his leather coat. "How very kind of you to invite me, *mademoiselle*."

"You said that *tres bien*," she noted and chuckled, feeling better already. They began walking toward the familiar métro station at a leisurely pace. "Per'aps, when you pick me up later…" she glanced up at his rugged profile, "I assume you intend to meet me after school?" He nodded emphatically. She smiled to herself and continued. "Then, we must go to a bookshop I know of where we can buy a book on wine and a simple one on learning the language for you. *Oui?*"

"*Oui*," he affirmed.

As they made their way along *la rue*, her eyes darted to and fro, looking for the man Andrew had described. "Have you seen him yet this morning?" she ventured in an undertone.

"Nope," he said with a jaunty lilt to his voice. "But if I do, I intend to question him."

"Question him!" Gabrielle pulled her hand free and stopped short. "You are going to stop him—to talk! You can't do that."

"Why not?" he asked reasonably. "I'd like to know what he's up to."

Her brain was working feverishly. Why not indeed? What was she supposed to say that wouldn't create more questions? If he was in cahoots with Lyam, the man might be armed and most certainly dangerous.

"I—I just think you should stay out of it," she said miserably, moving the book bag into a more comfortable position and wrapping her arms around her waist.

"Can't do that. Sorry. It's not my style. Mom always said confronting problems was the best option. Running from them never works, because they have a nasty way of finding you."

"Your mother sounds like a wise woman, but this situation might be different. In the first place, it really isn't your problem."

"I'm making it my problem," he said with a determined nod of his head. "And she definitely *is* a wise woman." Andrew's voice cracked. "I miss her," he looked sideways at Gabrielle. "But I FaceTimed her and Dad last night. She's planning to come for a visit in May. Wants to see what I've done with Uncle Olivier's shop and to offer her help in getting it running smoothly again. She said it provided him with a good living all these years."

"I'm sure it did. The apartment your uncle and aunt shared was opulent. What I saw of it looked like the centerfold from a magazine dedicated to lavish Parisian homes."

He chuckled. "That's what Mom said too. She did more in their upstairs living space than I thought. I walked through it again yesterday morning and discovered that every trace of Olivier and Clarisse's life together had been obliterated. All of their clothes are gone, personal items removed, and even pictures were taken off the walls, except for two that mom couldn't bear to part with. She said he'd asked her to prepare the house for its new owner." He shrugged. "Guess that would be me."

Gabrielle could feel sadness emanating from him and changed the subject. "What will you do today?"

He turned his dazzling blue eyes upon her and held out his hand meaningfully. When she moved closer and took it he answered. "I plan to see you safely to school, then go back to the apartment at ten, for your sister. We made a plan, when you weren't around, to paint and put up the shelves I re-built. After all, if you're being threatened by this guy then she must be too, and I'd like to keep her close."

He looked as though he'd like to ask questions, but said nothing more. He clamped his free hand on top of his hat to hold it in place, as a blast of air hit them from the métro stairwell. Still hand in hand, they descended and made their way below street level to wait for the next train.

It wasn't far from the Étienne Marcel to the coffee shop between Odéan métro stop and the University of Paris-Descartes. Although Andrew was silent as they boarded the train and were pressed amongst so many others, Gabrielle knew he was keeping a sharp eye on everyone around them. Because of his height, he gazed over almost everyone's head. While he attracted curious stares, due to his hat, for the most part, people ignored them.

The train squealed to a halt and more people pushed on, causing Gabrielle to be squished between a well-dressed woman with a carefully coiffed updo, a man wearing a teal business suit, and Andrew. He loomed protectively over her, lifting his arms to rest against the wall of the train on either side of her head. The cowboy was unaware of the emotions that stirred in every fibre of her being as he was pressed ever closer by the encroaching crowd.

The train lurched away. She leaned her face against the smooth leather of his jacket and breathed in the scent of his spicy cologne, feeling his muscles tauten as they swayed around a bend. This man was a safe haven for her, after only a few days of knowing him. How could that be? A long breath escaped her lips as his warmth spread through her bones. She fought the urge to slide her arms around him and hold on tight for the rest of time, or perhaps to ride the rails in just this position forever. She smiled at her fanciful notion and relaxed for what felt like the first time since learning of her pursuer.

It was noisy and chaotic inside the car amid the rhythmic howl of the rails outside as their train hurtled toward Odéon, the next stop. But in no time at all they arrived and made their way into the bright morning sun on Boulevard Saint-Germain.

"You can't possibly be headed there for your coffee?" Andrew pointed to their left where a huge sign proclaimed the name of Starbucks. "Doesn't seem very French to me."

"No," she stated with a laugh. "Some people protested

when the chain store opened in Paris…but…" she continued, shrugging, "they went ahead anyway and are always filled with customers. Per'aps it is frequented mainly by tourists as opposed to the French. I don't know. Personally, I like the bistro across the boulevard. Follow me."

Watching for a lull in traffic, Gabrielle darted across the street. She laughed while waiting for him on the other side as cars flew past with their horns blaring. He paused for a decent interval before striking out, and then strode purposely toward her, eyes riveted on her face. She remonstrated with herself for not avoiding this intimacy. It was exactly what she *didn't* want to happen—more closeness, shared time, and enjoyment of one another's company. How would it end? She needed to put distance between them, not fall in love with the man.

As soon as she thought the words, she sobered. Was that what she was doing? Falling in love. She couldn't! It was too soon. She hadn't thought she could ever allow herself to feel that way again. And to complicate everything she had Lyam rearing up from her past. She sighed deeply as Andrew reached her side.

"You okay?" he asked. "Your face just went through some crazy transformations. Did you see him?" He whirled around to scan the other side of the street.

"No, no," she assured him. "I was thinking of all I need to accomplish today." She peered at her cell phone, buying herself time to set her features back to normal.

The bistro she led him to, Germaine, was cute. A pale blue awning offered shade to people perched on matching rattan chairs surrounding tiny round tables. Tucked between a tobacco store and the arch to Cour du Commerce Saint-André, it was unassuming and quaint.

"Is this it?" asked Andrew, pointing at the tiny café.

"What's down there?" He shifted direction to indicate the narrow alley.

In answer, Gabrielle stepped sideways and lifted a hand to shade her eyes from the bright sunlight as she motioned that he come with her to look. "It's a lovely little passageway, Cour du Commerce Saint-André dating from 1776. If you look along it you will see that the original cobblestones have been preserved. We could walk down it another day, since it is like strolling back in time to the Paris that existed before Baron Haussmann created the grand boulevards and massive urban change we see today." She stepped out of the way, as a group of chattering teenagers came through at top speed with no sign of breaking rank.

"It houses many small, and interesting boutiques as well as the famous Le Procope. Do you know of it?"

Andrew shook his head. "Tell me."

"It is said to 'ave been the very first café opened in Paris. Created in 1686 it was a gathering place for literary agents and the theatre company of Molière. Later, in the eighteenth-century, other renowned persons met there." Juggling her book bag, she lifted a hand and began to count on her fingers. "Voltaire, Rousseau, Diderot, Napoleon Bonaparte, Victor Hugo, and even Benjamin Franklin ate inside the hallowed walls."

"Impressive, mademoiselle tour guide. How do you know so much?"

She felt the familiar lump of fear and disbelief rise into her throat. "My last boyfriend gave tours of museums, primarily of prized artworks. Plus, I am interested in such things." But she didn't want to encourage more questions along that line of thinking. "So," she forced a false brightness into her tone, "shall we sit *dehors ou dedans*?" Without offering a translation, she waited while his brain struggled to make sense of the words.

"Wow. It's hard to make that sort of decision," Andrew mused, stroking his chin thoughtfully. "While duh-or certainly has its benefits, I'd have to say that duh-don is a strong contender." He looked at her, blue eyes dancing with mischief. "Maybe if you told me what in the heck you're talking about, it would be easier to judge?"

She giggled, forcing her dark thoughts away. "I couldn't resist. Besides, you'll never learn the language if I don't use the occasional French word. I asked if you would like to sit outside or inside."

She could almost see him digesting the information as he blinked several times and then swallowed.

A young girl with a high ponytail, and short black dress stood just inside the door of Germaine, swinging a platter. She looked at them enquiringly.

"Go tell 'er what we want," Gabrielle urged, giving him a little shove.

"But I don't have a clue what I want!" Andrew resisted, leaning against her hands, and turning a frightened face to beseech her. "I mean, I know what I want…" he paused, ever-so-slightly and glanced at her before he said, "but I can't say it in French. You tell her."

Had he meant to insinuate something? Blushing, she ignored it.

"What's this?" she said in mock horror, clapping a hand to her mouth. "Superman is afraid of a little girl, whose greatest weapon is a serving tray? Inconceivable!"

Sheepishly, Andrew raised his hands, looking at each one in turn. "Guess I left my tights and cape back at Uncle Olivier's shop." He leaned closer and whispered, "Tell me what to say and I'll do my best. We want a table for two, right? And outside would be nice."

"*Une table pour deux, dehors,*" Gabrielle whispered. She then took a step back and waited. Would he have the nerve?

Andrew squared his shoulders. "I'm goin' in," he declared, with a firm set to his jaw. "Never let it be said Superman backed down from a fight, or a little girl in pigtails."

Gabrielle chuckled as he marched forward to speak. She couldn't hear what he said, but he accompanied it with much gesticulation in her direction. Suddenly the girl bent over double, laughing hysterically. Gabrielle closed her eyes. What had he said? She was afraid to find out as it appeared to have something to do with her. The girl, straightening with effort, stood with hands on hips, wiping tears from her eyes as both she and Andrew turned to stare in her direction. Gabrielle lifted a hand to smooth her hair, feeling as though something was awry with her appearance.

Finally, with a face the same colour as his bright red t-shirt, Andrew waved her over. Giggling, the server led them to an outside table near the latticed windows of the bistro and waited for their order.

"*Deux cafés au lait, et deux pains au chocolat, s'il vous plaît,*" Gabrielle said, waiting to speak to Andrew until the girl left.

The server winked at Andrew before scurrying away.

"What just happened?" Gabrielle demanded suspiciously.

"I was afraid you'd ask," he said, taking off his hat and brushing imaginary dust from the brim. "Turns out the server's English is really good and as soon as I said bun-jure she knew I was lost. Then, when I asked to sit with, 'da hoore'…" his voice trailed off. "You can imagine what that sounded like."

"What!" Gabrielle shrieked, recoiling in her seat. "You told her I was a whore?" People at nearby tables paused with food midway to their mouths to gape at this loud exclamation. Ducking her head and lowering her voice, Gabrielle hissed, "You told her I was a whore?"

"Not exactly," he fidgeted on his seat, looking everywhere but at her. "Uh…I mean, yes, but not intentionally. I tried to tell her we wanted to sit outside, but I…uh, messed it up."

"*Mon Dieu*! What next?" she spluttered. "You are not safe to leave alone."

"I agree," he announced, bending to set his hat under his chair. "I shouldn't go anywhere without your supervision. Anyway, you don't need to worry," he hastened to assure her, looking up with a sickly attempt at a grin. "As soon as I realised she spoke English, I told her you were my friend who was struggling to teach me French. She understood…eventually…after she caught her breath."

The incongruity of the situation caused a peal of laughter to burst from Gabrielle's own throat. Andrew looked guilty, but hopeful.

"Does that mean I'm forgiven?" The server reappeared with two tiny cups of coffee and croissants which she thumped onto the table before placing a hand over her smirking mouth and hurrying away.

Gabrielle lifted her drink and took a sip before answering. "You are forgiven," she managed, trying to ignore all the stares she was receiving. Pulling her cell phone from her book bag she checked the time. "Fabulous. Not even nine o'clock and I 'ave been publicly labelled a prostitute. Oh well…" she broke off a piece of her pastry and lifted it in silent salute. "Everyone 'as to eat breakfast. Even women of the night. *Bon appétit*."

The sun felt warm on her shoulders and a slight breeze had cleared away most of the cloud cover from earlier. It was going to be another lovely day. As snippets of conversations echoed around them, they passed an enjoyable half hour over a typical Parisian breakfast. A coffee and pastry were what she was accustomed to, but Gabrielle noticed Andrew picking up crumbs with his fingers and popping them into his mouth.

"Would you like to order something more?" she asked, wondering what he ate back home. Hot cereal? Bacon, eggs, and toast? Sausages and pancakes? Or perhaps all of the above. She imagined he'd need a hearty breakfast to work as he did on the Canadian Prairies. He likely wrestled with cattle, drove heavy machinery, and tossed bales of hay on a regular basis. These thoughts painted an appealing image.

"Gabby!" he waved a hand in front of her face. "Are you in there? I don't want anything more to eat. I just asked if you think we should go now? I mean, it's almost nine o'clock and time for me to pick you up at your apartment."

With a jolt she came back to Earth and stared at him. "Oh," she said with some surprise, "you are 'aving another dig at me, because I tried to sneak away. It's deserved and I apologize." She glanced at her phone. "But you're right. It's almost nine and I should be on my way to class. However, please allow me to pay. Bodyguards must be offered something in compensation."

After she settled the bill, he thanked her, and they wandered back onto the street, quickly angling over to Rue de l'Ecole de Médecine. Soon they left the bustle of business behind. The sidewalk grew wider and the buildings on either side became somber and studious looking.

"*Merci beaucoup* for walking me safely to my destination,"

she said, stopping in front of the huge double doors. "I'm sure I will be fine from 'ere."

"You promised to take me shopping for books later," he reminded her. "I'm counting on it. That kind of fun doesn't come around too often, and I don't want to miss it."

"You're teasing me again," she said with narrowed eyes. "Very well, meet me 'ere at three. If you can find it again," she added with a hint of mockery.

"*Touche!*" he laughed. Waving, he turned on his heel and strode away.

She watched him till he was out of sight, taking note of several women who turned to follow his progress, as she was doing. It wasn't just because of the hat either. For a woman that was supposed to be putting distance between herself and this man, she was failing. Failing utterly. She sighed, pushed open the door, and went inside.

It was after three when she stepped onto the street looking for Andrew. She'd sat through today's two classes, taken notes, and studied in the campus library. She yawned. Sleep had proved difficult these last few weeks, but last night was awful. She'd tossed and turned until almost 2 am.

With pleasure she spied Andrew detach himself from the wall across the street and stride toward her. She noticed he'd left the leather jacket behind, he only wore his blue jeans, boots, and red t-shirt. Waving, she started out to meet him. That particular shade of crimson he wore, had always been her favourite colour which, she told herself, was why she was so drawn to it now.

"Hi," he said, doing an abrupt turn and falling into step beside her. "Come here often?"

Despite herself she chuckled. "Is that 'ow you meet girls in Canada?"

"Figured I'd give it a try," he drawled. "How about this one?" Quickly he stepped in front of her and cleared his throat. "May I carry your books, *mademoiselle*?" He bowed low, tucking one arm to his waist, and flinging the other high behind him in a flourish. His hat tumbled onto the cement, catching a wayward breeze it rolled away before he caught it and rammed it back on his head.

"Your delivery is lacking, but I think your 'eart's in the right place...so yes," she said with a laugh. "You may carry my books." Unlooping the bag from across her shoulders, she handed it over. He slung the bag over his neck. Suddenly it looked small and the strap too short.

"Thank you," he said gravely. "I'll work on my approach."

"Are you okay?" she asked, as he shifted the bag several times. Finally, he dragged it back over his head and hung it off his shoulder instead.

"Yeah, I'm great. The sun is shining. Your sister and I got all the painting done." His face beamed with happiness. "I haven't seen that guy's ugly face all day. And I'm walking with the prettiest girl in the whole of France. Things couldn't be better."

"*C'est incroyable*! I am so 'appy for you. Is that where Annette is now?"

"Yep. She wanted to finish up some trim, so I told her we'd be right back. After a trip to the bookstore, that is."

Gabrielle touched his arm to get his attention, looked him in the eye, and enunciated distinctly, "*La librairie.*" She thought it was as good a time as any for a new word to be learned, and an excellent way to bypass his remark concerning her looks.

"The library?" he said, looking confused. "I thought you said I was buying books, not borrowing them."

She rolled her eyes. "*La librairie*, is French for the bookstore."

"Ahh, I see." Andrew walked in silence for a few moments. "No. On second thought, I don't see. Then what do you call a library? *La bookstore?*" He laughed at his own joke, alone, and then coughed. "Sorry. What do you call the library then?"

Giving him a severe look, Gabrielle again spoke clearly. "*La bibliothèque.*"

Immediately, Andrew tried to repeat it, but everything jumbled up in his mouth. "La ba-by-tech," he said, pausing after each syllable. He raised a hand as though to ward off a blow. "Go easy on me. I am but a simple man, unused to these fine Parisian ways of yours."

"*C'est vrai*," she said with a groan. "We had best hurry and per'aps buy every book in the store on learning the French language. You are going to need some 'elp."

"Naw. I don't need help. I have you," he stated. His blue eyes twinkled down at her, and her heart leapt.

The bookstore she had in mind was on Boulevard Saint-Germain, not far from the university. A bell tinkled as she pushed open the door and an older man straightened from a table of books he was arranging. The lighting was soft as though welcoming the customer into the pages of well-loved books filled with old friends and glorious adventures.

"*Bonjour*," the proprietor said, taking off his glasses and giving them a polish from a handkerchief in his breast pocket. "*Est-ce que je peux vous aider?*"

"*Bonjour Monsieur*," Gabrielle said. She went on to ask if he had any beginner books on learning French for English speakers, and for entering the world of French wine.

"*Oui, mademoiselle.*" The man shuffled around an extensive rack of postcards depicting the Eiffel Tower and Arc de Triomphe, and between two aisles that stretched to the ceiling with books. At the end of it, down low on the wall he pointed to a shelf that held what they were looking for. Bending, he pulled one out and handed it to her.

"*Voila,*" he said, inclining his head graciously. "*C'est le mieux pour un débutant.*" He looked meaningfully at Andrew.

"*Merci.*" Gabrielle took it from the man and handed it back to Andrew. "He said it's the best book for beginners."

The owner beckoned with a finger, gnarled from the ravages of arthritis. She followed him again to a section of books higher up and further along the same wall. He jabbed at a row of books, but made no attempt to choose one for her this time.

With a nod of gratitude, she leaned in to peruse a selection of glossy, beautifully illustrated books covering information on a wide range of wines. Unfortunately, they were all written in French.

"This isn't going to 'elp you," she said sorrowfully. "You'll 'ave to look a few books up on the internet and order online. Until then I will do all I can to educate you." She craned her neck around the corner to see where the storekeeper had gone, then looked back at Andrew with a playful smirk.

"Per'aps I could write up a few flash cards in a believable sequence. Then, instead of speaking to your customers, you could simply hold up a card that says, 'Ello, my name is Andrew.' Then, 'The price of this wine is__.'" And the last card could wish the customer a good day and thank them for their patronage. It would be much safer than actually speaking to them. What do you think?"

"I'll show you what I think," he growled. Andrew made

a swipe for her, but she jumped nimbly out of his reach. Laughing, she hurried to the cash desk where he joined her, clutching his book and giving her a look that plainly said, 'Just you wait till we're out of here.'

Andrew paid with due decorum, accepted the paper carrier bag, and thanked the man with a bold, "Mercy bow-coop." Afterwards he marched stiffly to the exit to open the door for Gabrielle.

Once outside, however, he glowered at her in mock anger. "Flash cards, hey? I suppose you think you're pretty funny?"

"Actually," she said coquettishly, "I do."

This time, when Andrew snaked a long arm out, he caught her around the waist and pulled her roughly to him. Laughing, she slammed into his chest, her hands flying forward to push him away. Except as their faces came close, and their eyes locked, the merriment ceased. Of their own volition, her hands slid gently up his chest to cup his face, and her fingers glided over the smooth skin of his shaven cheeks to pull his face closer. When their lips touched she felt as though she might melt with the rush of emotion that flooded over her. Nothing else mattered. She forgot where she was and what she was doing.

"*Excusez moi, mademoiselle!*" barked an irritated voice.

Gabrielle felt someone pushing her aside. Andrew pulled her closer, out of the person's way. Shaking her head, she broke free of the embrace, feeling woozy, as though she'd had too much wine. She staggered. Coming to her senses she saw two plump, white-haired ladies dragging their two-wheeled shopping carts home from the grocery store, each of them turning to glare at her for such a public display of indecency.

"*Désolé mesdames!*" she called after them, but they only

snorted as they scuffled on in their long coats and headscarves despite the warmth of the day.

She didn't dare look at Andrew. What had she been thinking? She'd flirted shamelessly with him after promising herself she'd begin pulling away from their friendship. Now, here she was kissing the man on a busy street. She swiped a hand across her forehead, pushing back the mane of hair that sometimes allowed her to hide from the world.

Andrew stood next to her, his arm still touching hers and his breathing rapid. "Come on," he said, clearly sensing her regret. "Let's get you home. We'll stop to pick up Annette and I'll see you both to your door. It's been a long day."

The trip back to Caviste de Tremblay was uneventful. After what had just taken place, neither of them said much. Gabrielle found Annette with her hair tightly pulled into a ponytail, tapping the lids onto several paint cans she'd been using. Her jogging pants and t-shirt were splattered with the efforts of her labour.

"It looks good, *n'est-ce pas?*" She stood up, roller in hand to survey the shop with Gabrielle.

It did indeed look good. Thanks to a tall ladder, Andrew and Annette had been able to refresh the ceiling with a light cream colour, and new lighting had been erected which added vibrancy to the space. On the walls, a pale grey-blue had been used and the shelves were strewn about the room to dry, having been given a revitalising coat of chocolate brown.

"Thanks to Annette, I'm much further along than anticipated," Andrew said proudly, hands on hips as he surveyed the room. "I think Uncle Olivier would be pleased."

"Several of the local people from the neighbourhood stopped by to ask what we were doing today," Annette said, scratching her nose and leaving a long line of cream coloured paint behind. "I was able to tell them who Andrew was and that he was opening for business next week. They appeared happy with the news and said they would tell their friends."

"That's wonderful," Gabrielle said. Really, it was coming together faster than she ever would have guessed.

As though reading her mind, Andrew spoke. "It's because of you two," he said simply. "I could never have done this alone. I can't thank you enough." He turned away, walking to the far end of the store to turn off the lights. "Now, I'll walk you home and we'll all get a good night's sleep. Tomorrow I'll raise the shelves and start filling them."

"Could you use some help?" Annette sounded eager.

"I'd love it." He smiled at her, but his eyes shifted past the younger woman to rest on Gabrielle with a haunted look in their depths. "What time is class tomorrow?"

"It is getting close to finals," she lifted one shoulder and let it drop. "There are not so many classes after this, but my first exam is two days from now, Friday afternoon. I'll stay at the apartment and study tomorrow."

For a moment, Andrew looked disappointed, but he corrected himself immediately, reaching for his hat to walk them home.

"Really, you don't need to do this," she protested.

"Why not?" asked Annette. "I think 'e is showing us a taste of old-world courtesy. No one has ever walked me home—until now." She grinned up at Andrew and sighed. "It 'as been a productive day for you and gives me something to do, besides shop while Gabby is working." She walked out the door with Gabrielle close behind. Raising her arm, she rubbed the glass with her elbow.

"These windows are going to need cleaning too," she remarked happily. "I can do that tomorrow."

Gabrielle was pleased her sister had found a purpose during her visit and glad Andrew's store was progressing so well, but the last thing she wanted was to encourage more togetherness. She paused, waiting while Andrew locked up. Nothing was going as it ought to. She should have put a stop to this as she promised herself she would, before now. She stole a look at the broad-shouldered man at her side, her heart was singing to its own tune and ignoring her.

When they reached the apartment, Andrew left them at the door. She lifted subtle hands in question, and he shook his head slightly to indicate he hadn't seen the man. She felt her body relax. Maybe the whole incident had been blown out of proportion. It could happen. There were so many visitors to the City of Lights that it wouldn't be unusual for someone to appear on your radar twice and at popular sights. But driving a car near her home, directly after seeing him in a completely different area? Not likely. That didn't fit the scenario of coincidence, but she kept trying to convince herself otherwise.

"*Bonne soirée*," Annette said, giving Andrew a quick peck on both cheeks and disappearing inside.

"Good night," Andrew called after her. He turned to Gabrielle. "So, maybe I won't see you tomorrow, hey?"

She shook her head with a rueful smile. "No. I must study." She made no move to offer him the same farewell as her sister had done; *les bisous*, the kisses which were so much a part of French life. It felt far too risky.

Instead, she laid a hand on his arm. "Thank you so

much for caring about us and going out of your way to ensure we are safe. Still..." she paused and lifted an arm to indicate the world around her before she said, "everything seems perfectly fine today. Per'aps yesterday was pure coincidence."

"Perhaps," he agreed doubtfully. "But I don't think so." He moved away from the door and raised a hand. "Anyway, if you're staying home tomorrow you should be fine. Just, please let me know if you want to come over or go out...I'll go with you."

She nodded, having no intention of doing so. What was her body language telling him now? Did he know?

"I'll come around in the morning to collect Annette. Goodnight, gorgeous Gabrielle," he said, his voice dropping to a low timbre. "I hope to see you soon."

She gave him an answering wave and went inside.

Inside the apartment, she and Annette prepared a simple evening meal of salad and sat in front of mindless television. Annette was thoroughly engrossed in the plot, but Gabrielle couldn't concentrate on the program. All Gabrielle could think of was the feel of Andrew's lips on hers and the warmth and sense of rightness in his embrace. Was she losing her mind? How could these feelings be so strong after such a short time? It had only been five days since she met him. She lifted her fingers to her mouth. They still tingled with awareness of the man. And desire.

Shaking herself, she leapt to her feet, thinking she'd prepare her notes and books on the table for tomorrow so she could get an early start. But she needed a pen and highlighter first. *Where were they? Ah right, in the depths of her old purse that hung by the door.*

Glancing at Annette, who had stretched out on the sofa the second she left, Gabrielle walked to the entryway and dug an arm deep into her purse, searching for what she needed. Instead, her hand came upon the letter she'd forgotten to open.

She fished it from her bag, letting the purse drop unheeded to the floor as she studied the handwriting. The familiar icy tendril of dread clutched at her heart. Yet, it wasn't Lyam's scrawl, she was sure of it. Turning the envelope over in her hands she slit it open and pulled a plain sheet of folded paper into the light. Unaccountably, her fingers trembled, but she wasn't sure why. It was just a letter, after all. Maybe it was from her mother, or a friend, or even for some odd, obscure reason to do with school. Although it wasn't anyone's penmanship she recognised.

She leaned against the door, feeling as though her legs wouldn't support her as she unfolded it. Her eyes scanned the contents before it slid, fluttering to the floor. Then, galvanized into action, she rushed to the balcony windows and pulled them shut with a bang, ensuring the locks were on. Despite the warmth of the room, she yanked the heavy drapes shut. Next, she hurried to the window in her bedroom and then jogged to the kitchen, securing the locks each time, ripping the heavy outer curtains over the thin sheers to close out the night. Panting, she dropped onto a kitchen chair. She would not let fear overtake her. The last thing she wanted was to scare Annette, but she felt a cold terror take hold of her body. She felt chilled to the marrow. Telling herself to take deep breaths, she willed her heart to stop its wild racing before moving back to the door where she stooped to pick the letter up and read the contents again.

Lyam left a painting in your apartment. I want it. You have till 3 pm this Tuesday to find it and give it to me outside your door. He's rotting in jail because of you and your big mouth. Involve the police again and people you care about will suffer. I'm watching every move you make. If I don't get what I want, you'll pay.

Today was Wednesday.

In neglecting to read the letter when it had arrived, she'd missed the deadline given to her to produce a painting she knew nothing about. No wonder someone had been following her. But she didn't have the painting! Lyam had left nothing here. He'd never even given her a birthday present. What could this person mean? She crumpled the paper and hurled it across the room.

Gabrielle wracked her brain, trying to remember any friends Lyam had ever introduced her to, any family he'd mentioned, or the names of those he'd been in partnership with. A heavyset man with black hair and a goatee… nothing came to her.

Her brain felt fuzzy and her mind frantic. Pleading tiredness, she went to her bedroom. With the TV blaring in the next room, she quietly paced for what felt like hours. This letter mainly threatened her, but ignoring it meant she had endangered people she cared about too. All because of trying to do the right thing. Should she have simply broken up with Lyam and turned a blind eye to his wrongdoings? No. She couldn't have lived with herself. But now her family was in danger. And her friends. Where was this painting?

A sudden vision of Andrew flew into her thoughts. If this person was watching her, seeking revenge as they said, they would know about Andrew's shop. Perhaps they were watching as she held his hand—kissed him. She groaned. Why had she gotten involved with this innocent man? Now she had to worry about him as well as everyone she spoke to. Should she leave Paris? Go into hiding somewhere?

She had already informed the police she thought she

was being followed. That much could not be undone. They'd been interested too since at least one member of Lyam's gang had never been found. But did she reveal this further development and then fear what might happen to those she loved? Who knew how far this threat would be taken? Did they want her dead? Maybe Lyam had directed one of his cronies in crime to seek revenge and punish her for reporting his despicable crimes and pinpointing where the police could find him.

Wearing herself out with nervous exhaustion, she finally threw herself into bed around 3 am, still fully clothed. She knew she would do whatever it took to keep those around her safe. That meant Andrew too. She would refuse to see him again. It was the only way to keep him from harm. Annette must return home to Toulouse.

Apart from that, there was no other solution. She would have to face this alone.

Chapter Nine

Gabrielle groaned and rolled over. Her hips ached and groggily she wondered why. She ran a hand down her thigh, feeling the rough fabric of her jeans and was jolted into wakefulness. Sitting straight up in bed, she remembered— the letter. Tossing the blanket aside she leapt to her feet, staggering a little with the force of immediate fear that gripped her. She scrabbled through the bedding in search of her phone. She knew she'd had it in her hand last night. There! She flipped it on and looked at the time.

It was ten in the morning! Frantically she raced for her bedroom door and flung it against the wall in her haste to find her sister. But the bed had been returned to its other life as a sofa and the cushions were arranged prettily.

"Annette!" Gabrielle bounded into the kitchen, skidding against the table in her headlong rush. Damn! Her sister was gone already. Off to Andrew's shop where they'd both be under constant surveillance and subject to danger. She felt as though there were eyes everywhere. Just because they hadn't noticed that man yesterday, didn't mean he wasn't near. He could be lurking in the shadows, prowling behind buildings, or hunkered low in a vehicle, waiting to pounce.

Tapping her phone to life once again she rang her sister's number, falling into a chair at the sound of Annette's cheery voice.

"'Allo, *bonjour*."

"Annette! Are you alright? Is Andrew there? Did anyone follow you this morning?"

There was a puzzled silence on the other end and then Annette's voice, low with concern, spoke. "He's here, of course. Andrew came to get me about half an hour ago. But you were still asleep, so I didn't wake you." She drew a breath. "Are you alright? You sound terrified."

"I—I...don't ask. Look don't leave the shop alright. Stay there with Andrew and tell him to watch for that man. He'll know what I'm talking about."

"Gabby, you're scaring me," Annette's voice rose with agitation. "Are you okay? I want to come to you."

"No!" Gabrielle tried vainly to calm herself, to take a breath and speak normally. "I'm fine. Just stay with Andrew and tell him what I said. Do I have your word?"

"*Oui*," came the quavering reply. "I will tell him."

"I love you." Gabrielle ended the call and stood to pace once more. She would contact Commissaire Chevalier. He was the detective that led the investigation before, and she trusted him. The police needed to know she had received a threat, and that there was still a piece of missing art, supposedly with her. She rummaged in her purse for the number she'd written on a crumpled bit of paper in case she'd ever needed him again. Smoothing it on the table, she leaned forward, holding her head in her hands. This was too much.

With shaking fingers, she ran a hand through her

tousled hair and took a moment to breathe before making the call. She didn't want to sound like a babbling lunatic. She needed to be taken seriously.

Picking up her phone, Gabrielle closed her eyes and checked the paper before entering the first three numbers with trembling fingers. But before she could enter more, there was a knock. Gripping her phone in one hand, she crept silently to the door and squinted through the tiny hole at the top.

Her landlady? That was strange, but not unwarranted. Madame Moreau stood outside, shuffling a number of papers in her hand. Reaching out, she knocked again. True, the woman looked agitated, but then again, she often did. With an apartment building nearly full of students, she always said she was, '*s'enfuir*' or run off her feet.

With trepidation, Gabrielle slid the top bolt across and lifted the latch. Finally, she snapped the main dead bolt and reached for the tiny lock on the handle, but there was no need. With a crashing sound of splintering wood, the door flew back, knocking her back and slamming against the wall. The landlady came flying through the opening to land heavily on the tiled floor.

Tears streamed down her withered cheeks, the woman raised herself on shaking arms, sobbing an apology as a man burst through the door behind her and slammed it back in place, wedging it with one of Gabrielle's boots to keep it shut.

"Quit yer whinin' hag," the man growled in a thick British accent. He took a kick at the woman's extended legs. Poor Madame Moreau curled away from him, edging herself into a corner, great wracking sobs breaking from her body.

The intruder was big and burly with black hair and a

goatee. Gabrielle had known it would be him. The only distinguishing characteristic Andrew had failed to see from a distance was a livid red scar that ran from the corner of his eye to halfway down his cheek. It looked recent too. Menacingly, he stepped into the room, towering over her, but Gabrielle stood her ground. Now that her fears had finally come to confront her, she faced them without flinching.

He leered at Gabrielle from her toes up to her face. "So many times, I asked him what 'e wanted yeh fer," he sneered. "S'ppose I can see what 'e wanted," the man laughed nastily. Taking several steps, he stopped right in front of her, reaching out to roughly seize one of her breasts. She recoiled. His hot, reeking breath assailed her like a cess pool, and he grabbed her roughly by the shoulders, lifted her, and shook her like a doll. Her cell phone clattered to the floor. Malcom lifted a huge boot and smashed it into little pieces.

"I want that paintin' see. Where is it? I know ye have it. Lyam said it was 'ere and I told ye to bring it to me, but instead you went gallivantin' off with your friends."

"I'm not saying a word until you let me go." Gabrielle managed to stay calm, her brain feeling as though it had been rattled loose.

He dropped her to the floor. Cursing, he lifted a huge, meaty hand and smacked her across the face, causing her to spin helplessly across the entry and smash her head into the kitchen table. Madame screamed.

"Where is it?" he thundered, striding across the room to pick her up and shake her again. Gabrielle couldn't think. A blazing pain had erupted over her left eye and when she tried to push her hair away, to see what this giant of a man was going to do next, a warm sticky mess met her fingertips.

Her eye was rapidly swelling shut. Groggily she pulled her hand away and squinted at it. Blood.

"I don't know," she slurred. With another shake, he tossed her away again. This time she slammed into a wall and crumpled.

"He was yer boyfriend, wasn't 'e?" the man bawled. "If 'e says it's 'ere, then it's 'ere."

He began a systematic search, ripping out drawers, ransacking cupboards, and flinging the contents across the room. Gabrielle heard the sound of her dishes breaking, her precious trinkets, and pictures from family trips smashing on the floor. She mourned the loss. Hot tears escaped her eyes regardless of the swelling and mingled with the blood that trickled down her face.

Dimly, with her one good eye, she watched her landlady try to crawl for the door, but the madman screamed an oath. In two strides he was on her, grabbed her by the back of her dress and dragged the woman back before hurling her through the air to land in a crumpled heap beside Gabrielle. One leg was bent at an unnatural angle.

Swearing again, the man snatched up the toaster and with one deft move he ripped the cord from it. Then it was the kettle's turn. Marching to where they lay, he rolled Madame Moreau onto her face with the toe of his boot and then wrenched her arms back to wind the plastic cord tightly around her wrists. He dropped her to the floor where she landed with a painful yelp, hitting her head on the sturdy leg of Gabrielle's free-standing cupboard. The landlady didn't move.

It was Gabrielle's turn next. She felt his hand flip her over and then her arms were nearly yanked from their sockets as he snapped them behind her and bound them tight.

He moved from the kitchen into the salon. Furniture scraped across the floor and personal objects tipped over, slamming against the floor. She heard the rending of wallpaper and plaster and knew the paintings that were hers had been torn from the wall as he searched for the one he wanted. More cursing ensued.

The sounds grew further away. Either he was in her bedroom, or she was close to passing out. Her head was a throbbing, hazy cloud of pain and she felt herself slipping in and out of consciousness. Her arm ached and every time she tried to ease it into a better position, a stabbing shock went through her shoulder. What could she do to fight back? Nothing. All she prayed now was that he would find what he wanted and leave.

The muffled sounds of banging continued as he dismantled her bedroom. Growls of fury interspaced with bouts of livid swearing. She wondered what the painting was and why Lyam hadn't just told him where to find it?

Summoning all her energy, she tried to turn her head to see if Madame Moreau was alive. But even her good eye was blurry now. She couldn't tell. The pool of blood continued to grow as it dripped rhythmically from her head onto the floor.

There was a huge crash followed closely by a shout of exultation. The only thing that would have made that much noise was her armoire. She wasn't sure where the painting could possibly have been, but he must have found it. His heavy tread echoed through the tiny apartment. He kicked her belongings aside with a sickening crunch as, triumphantly, he charged back into the kitchen.

He stopped short. All that Gabrielle could see were his enormous boots a breath away from her face.

"Yer old man's a doctor ain't 'e?" he yelled, nudging her

side with the toe of his boot. She didn't respond. Partly because she couldn't, and partly because she wanted him to think she was unconscious.

"Ye don't 'ave to tell me. I knows 'bout all yer family and all yer friends. No one's safe from Malcom." He chuckled proudly. "I'm thinkin' this lousy paintin's not the only way to make a little coin in this town." Crouching down on his haunches, he continued speaking to himself. "I'll bet 'e'd pay handsomely to get 'is pretty wee daughter back."

Appearing to come to a decision, Malcom slid beefy arms beneath Gabrielle's knees and back, and lifted. She flopped unresistingly against his protruding stomach, her head lolling. Her mind told her to resist, and she fought feebly against the man. But he only laughed at her weak attempts.

"There ain't nothin' you can do to escape me," he boasted. He tucked the painting between her body and his own. Making his way to the door, he kicked it open and marched through, slamming Gabrielle's feet painfully against the frame. She was past caring. The overwhelming agony of her head had consumed her.

Getting downstairs was a little tricky. Malcom stopped and shifted Gabrielle, like a sack of flour, to flop over his shoulder. In this ghastly way, they descended the stairs. She hadn't thought the pain could get worse. However, when all the blood rushed to her head, and she was slammed up and down with every heavy clump of Malcom's boots, she knew it was not only possible, but a sure thing.

The time it took to navigate the steps felt interminable. Finally, they reached the bottom and groggily she wondered how the man proposed to carry her, bleeding and battered, onto a main street and stuff her into a car. He had to have some sort of vehicle waiting outside. He couldn't possibly stroll through the streets of Paris with an injured woman slung over his back with her hands secured by a length of electric cord, could he? She opened her good eye a crack.

But he didn't pass through the heavy double doors. He didn't go outside at all. Instead, Malcom ducked beneath the low-hanging staircase and strode down a short flight of stairs to where the corridor narrowed. They came to a door Gabrielle had never noticed before. He kicked it open with a bang. It appeared to be some sort of tiny storage room that smelled damp and musty. The room was bare apart from a tall stack of dusty crates in one corner and some discarded appliances in another. He locked up from the inside and moved toward the boxes.

There was only one, dirty window built below street level. A small measure of light managed to filter through the grime. Malcom crossed the room in three strides and threw her down on some filthy rags in a corner. Her head snapped back and hit the wall. She stifled a gasp and knew only darkness.

Somehow Gabrielle woke. Her head was one big blazing, throbbing mass of pain and her body felt as though she'd been thrown down a flight of stairs. That assessment wasn't wrong. She thought of Madame Moreau. Had the woman been killed by that monstrous man? She prayed not. Groaning on the inside, too afraid to make a sound lest it garnered the attention of Malcom, she shifted positions slightly and tried to ease the pain in her shoulder.

She lay in darkness apart from a flashlight that wobbled to and fro as Malcom studied the painting, his breath raspy.

How long had she been unconscious? Hours? Days? No, the monster across the room wouldn't have sat here for days. His efforts were bent on escape and greed.

For a moment, she lay perfectly still, then, little by little she rolled, the long electric cord trailing across her. The gash above her eye was still oozing blood, but most of it had dried over her swollen eye, down her cheek, and matted in her hair. She didn't think anything was broken, although she wasn't positive about her shoulder. Her body must be a mass of bruises. She considered whether she could get up and make a run for it.

No.

Like an enormous cat, Malcom was on his feet and at her side in seconds, beaming the flashlight into her face.

"So, ye've opened yer eyes. Well…" he laughed cruelly and then said, "one of 'em anyhow." Roughly, he grasped her arm and yanked upward. "Let's see if ye can stand. We need to git movin'."

He stuffed the light into a back pocket and pulled her to her feet. She teetered, dangerously close to falling over. The man steadied her, the stench of sweat as he lifted his arms acted very much like smelling salts. She reared back then winced, closing her eyes, and willing herself not to be sick. The pain was agonizing.

"Aww come on, it ain't bleedin' much now. Move it." He pushed her forward. Gabrielle stumbled, feeling as though she was going to fall. Instinctively, she tried to lift her bound arms to catch herself, but the electric cord wound around her feet and threw off what little balance she had. She toppled forward.

Malcom caught hold of her bad arm again and dragged her to the door. She tripped, faltering, and falling on her knees that scraped painfully on the uneven cement. He held her arms with both hands in a vise-like grip and leaned down, getting close to her face, so flecks of spittle pelted her as he hissed instructions.

"I'm not tyin' up yer legs, but ye ain't gonna run cause I'm right here behind ye. Now that I 'ave da paintin', don't need ye anymore. So, I could just as soon kill ye as look at ye." With jerky movements, Malcom showed her another length of cord, coiled and then stuck it in another pants' pocket. "If I don't get no reward for yer safe return—I don't care if yer dead or alive." He leaned back, a satisfied smirk on his face. "Now, there's a car outside, see, and we's gonna get into it without a struggle or ye might find yerself with a broken neck to match that eye a yers. Ye got it?"

She nodded. She didn't think she could speak anyway. Her throat felt dry as dust. From around his neck, he pulled a vile smelling bandana and forced it into her mouth before fastening it securely behind her head.

The taste caused her to gag. Sweat, dirt, and some nameless cheap cologne spread throughout her mouth, and she choked, coughing and spluttering.

His hand closed around her throat. "Shuddup!" he snarled.

He yanked open the door and craned his neck around it, listening for any signs of life. He then moved away from her, no doubt checking to see if anyone was lurking along the corkscrew staircase that led six flights above.

Gabrielle wondered where Annette was. What would she have thought when she got back to find the apartment torn apart and Madame Moreau badly injured or dead on the floor? Her sister would have called the police. Maybe Andrew was with her? She hoped so. Annette shouldn't be alone. All of that must have taken place while she was passed out in a musty corner. And now the building was silent.

Oh, how she wished she had Andrew at her side. The morning's events would have gone much differently if Superman had been with her.

She wondered if she could muster up the courage to break away and run for the outside door. Only she knew her injuries wouldn't allow her to dodge past the big man and she didn't have enough time to escape while the safety mechanism that released the door whirred to life. She sagged against the wall, her head pounding. All she could do was maintain—to survive.

The monster loomed out of the darkness before her and although she knew he was there, the sight of him frightened her badly. She tried to swallow the lump in her throat, but the dirty rag sucked up every bit of saliva she had.

Malcom pushed her out the door and grasped her arms in his vice-like grip, the painting tucked under one beefy arm. He manoeuvred her around the staircase and up to the big double doors where he flattened her between his huge body and the oak door while he stretched his arm out to punch the release button.

The door clicked open, and Malcom pulled it carefully toward himself. He paused, still inside the building. His head cocked to one side, listening, waiting, and watching before he ventured into the open.

Gabrielle's knees buckled. She would have fallen if he hadn't thrown an arm around her waist to hold her up. He shook her angrily, as if threats of bodily harm would serve to strengthen her failing legs. But she was too weak. Half dragging her, Malcom eased his bulk out of the door. He stopped again, lifting his face like a bloodhound to test the air.

Looking satisfied, he shuffled forward, hitching her onto his hip to take most of her weight himself. They were on the sidewalk now and Malcom took several strides toward a line of parked vehicles. Something jangled and a set of keys glinted in his hand. He aimed them toward the cars. She heard an answering beep as one unlocked.

If he got her in a car and took her away from this place she feared she'd never live to see it again. Lifting one leg, with every ounce of strength she could muster, she raised her foot and thrust downward, stomping on his toes as hard as she could.

"Yow!" he bellowed in rage, momentarily slackening his grip. Gabrielle slid toward the ground, but caught herself. She took a couple of faltering steps before her feet tangled and she fell.

It was then that something erupted from the shadows across the street. Pounding footsteps caused Malcom to startle violently before he reached down to grab his quarry. She pushed herself just out of reach. But before he could follow her, he was hit from behind and knocked to the pavement. He expelled a loud, "Oof" as he went down.

Gabrielle came up on her good arm, pushing herself into a seated position as she watched this mysterious figure attack her assailant.

Hauling Malcom up by the collar of his jacket, the other man drew back a fist and hit him hard. Malcom staggered backward, but the man was built like a solid wall. He caught his balance almost immediately, ducking to evade the advance of his attacker and throwing his own volley of punches. Back and forth they went, each one grunting, straining, panting, and landing punch after punch. Striking the face, the stomach, and the back, each one sounding painful and life-altering.

Suddenly, the shadow man slipped on something that crunched under his feet. The painting, Gabrielle thought hazily. Losing his stride, he stumbled back, and Malcom was on him like mud on a stick, taking the advantage, pounding him over and over until the man tumbled to the pavement.

Wheeling around, Malcom picked up the painting and lunged for her. She rolled, trying to scramble away, but it was futile. She was no match for the powerful man. He snagged the electric cord that trailed along the pavement behind her as she tried to crawl out of reach and yanked, ripping her toward him. A muffled groan of misery escaped her lips.

Dragging her by her bound wrists, he marched for the car. Gabrielle scraped over the rough sidewalk behind him, the sensitive skin on her stomach and chest feeling as though it were ripping away. Malcom halted beside a small car and began reeling her in like he was landing a marlin. He flung wide the door, picked her up, and shoved her inside, uncaring that again he had slammed her head, this time against the roof of the vehicle.

Gabrielle rolled weakly on the seat, struggling to keep her one eye open. Her heart filled with paralyzing fear as she watched Malcom round the front of the vehicle. And then, in the spotlight of lights that were flicking on in homes all along the street, she saw the shadow man rise. He raised an arm over his head, twirling his clenched fist in the air. She heard the whine of something fly through the air and could just make out a blur of movement. It was some sinuous, snakelike creature, unleashed by the tall stranger who stood, arm outstretched at the other end.

Whatever it was, it dropped over the head of her abductor. Like a coiled python it snared the massive man, pinning his arms to his sides just below the shoulders. He hollered, cursing as he wheeled in search of the source before turning back on his heels to charge at the one who dared to oppose him. But the man at the other end was already on the move.

Both his hands grasped the rope and jerked it back in a sharp, powerful move. Using his body, the man flung himself against the cord, tightening its command over Gabrielle's persecutor. The big man screamed with rage.

Then the shadowy figure ran at Malcom, bringing the rope with him. Yanking it again he brought the big man stumbling to the sidewalk where he toppled to his stomach like a felled tree. The shadow man dropped a knee onto Malcom's beefy posterior and reached for his hands, yanking them behind him as he writhed, yelled, and fought.

But it made no difference.

Knotting the rope through, around, and back, the shadowy man secured the bull of a man's hands before turning to grasp one of Malcom's legs. Fast as greased lightning, he bent it toward the man's head. Shrieks of profanity erupted from the goateed giant along with cries of pain. Undeterred, the shadow man's hands worked quickly to wind the rope around Malcom's ankle, pulling everything together in one big knot before he threw his hands in the air.

It was a strange thing to do, Gabrielle thought. Almost as though he was participating in a timed event.

Gabrielle saw it all happen with blurred disbelief, wondering if her eyes were playing tricks. But now the shadowy man was walking over to her, opening the door, and looking in.

Andrew.

He reached out a gentle hand and eased the filthy kerchief from her mouth, cupping her throbbing head in his large hands.

"Oh, my poor…sweetheart," he said, his voice breaking with concern. Carefully, he untied her hands and tossed the cord away, then slid gentle hands beneath her and lifted. He took infinite care to remove her from the vehicle without further harm. Straightening, he cradled her in his arms, pulling her close. "I thought we'd lost you."

Chapter Ten

People joined them on the street, aroused from their slumber by the racket outside their windows, and informed Gabrielle that the police had been called. Although her voice was barely above a whisper, Gabrielle managed to briefly convey what had happened, since the majority of people didn't speak English. A few were concerned that the wrong man was tied up and thrashing on the ground. One woman stepped forward, a nurse. She insisted that Gabrielle come inside her home to sit down and be doctored.

Andrew helped her walk inside, then stood stoic and alone on the doorstep, refusing to leave Gabrielle even for a moment. A small crowd gathered uneasily around Malcom, guarding the furious man even though Houdini himself could not have escaped his fetters.

The nurse, who had introduced herself as Marie, seated a shivering Gabrielle by the door and ran to fetch a blanket for her shoulders. Then, the lady brought a basin of warm water, a soft washcloth, towel, and bandages to bathe and cover

Gabrielle's wounds. She worked silently. Gabrielle was grateful for it, feeling the traumatic effects of shock setting in. She was unable to speak. Too many of her own questions needed answers before she could respond to the queries of others.

"The cut is not as bad as it looks," Maria said cheerfully, bandaging the wound on Gabrielle's forehead. "But I think you should be checked for concussion." The nurse stepped back, cocking her head to one side and regarding her patient with a practised eye. "'Ead wounds always bleed profusely. Fortunately, it won't need stitches and the scar should disappear after it 'eals. We wouldn't want anything to mar your beautiful face." The woman smiled. "Your shoulder needs to be checked as well."

Gabrielle tried to return the smile, but it felt very lopsided. Her whole body ached. "Do—do you 'ave any pain medication?" she croaked. "A-and water. My 'ead-dd…" Groggily she lifted a hand to her forehead and closed her eyes.

"*Bien sûr.*" Marie hurried to the nearby kitchen and came back with a bottle of pills and some water. "You must be parched." Kindly she offered two tablets on her palm and steadied the glass as Gabrielle held it with shaking hands to take a drink. Water ran down her chin, dribbling onto her pink sweatshirt.

Marie set the glass down and took Gabrielle's hands in her own, rolling back her sleeves to examine the angry red wounds on her wrists. "Ooh la la," she said, shaking her head. "You 'ave been through so much." Setting to work, the kind woman cleaned and added a soothing ointment to the welts before wrapping them with gauze. "You need to see a doctor and then rest," she said with concern. "I 'ave seen you in this neighbourhood. Do you live nearby?"

"Y-yes, I live 'ere, but no…I can't go 'ome." Gabrielle shuddered. "'E-e destroyed it."

"It will all work out," Marie said reassuringly, her face breaking into a wreath of lines as she smiled again. "Your 'usband will take care of you. I witnessed the last moments of the fight from my bedroom window. It was impressive." She rolled her eyes, lifted a hand, and fanned it in front of her face. "'E is 'ot, that one."

"'E is not my 'usband," Gabrielle managed to say. Despite her condition, laughter bubbled up inside her at the description, but quickly turned to tears. Heaving sobs rose in her chest until she could not contain them. Every muscle in her body leapt with pain, but still she could not stem the flow. She bent low over the chair, wracked with sobbing as though her heart were breaking. Maria rose to pull a few tissues from a box on her kitchen counter. She pressed them into Gabrielle's hand.

The door was flung open, and Andrew charged into the room. "Is she alright?" he demanded of Marie. Sliding to his knees before Gabrielle, he pulled her gently into his arms.

"It is a reaction to all that 'as 'appened to her," Marie explained. "She will be fine."

Gabrielle melted into him, his warmth and strength cocooning her better than the coziest blanket ever could. He held her close, breathing reassurances into her ear and stroking her hair.

"You're safe now," he murmured. "The police have taken him away."

She stiffened. "But…where—where is—is Annette. And —and my poor…the lady…Madame Moreau?"

Those were her only concerns. She needed to know her dear sister, and the woman who had been hurt by that monstrous man were alright. Gabrielle tried to pull away. She wanted to look into Andrew's face to hear the news she feared, but she couldn't stop crying long enough to do it.

"It's okay," he whispered. "Annette is safe at my uncle and aunt's home. She was worried sick and wanted to stay here with me, but I wouldn't let her." His face tightened. "Madame Moreau is in hospital with a concussion and a broken leg, but she will recover."

Gabrielle broke into fresh tears of relief, draping herself over the shoulder of this wonderful man who had saved her life. A variety of emotions flooded her being. Her weeping continued unabated. In the background, Maria quietly retired to another room, allowing them privacy.

"Honey," he said, stroking her back. "I was so scared when you were missing. But now you're safe and I'm not going anywhere. Just cry as long as you need to."

Her heart swelled. Andrew's words of caring had a calming effect. After a few last, gulping breaths, her weeping ceased. A long sigh escaped her lips and Andrew cupped the back of her head. His closeness was like a balm to her soul.

"*Merci de m'avoir sauvé*," she whispered, pressing her mouth to the soft skin of his neck. She felt his body become rigid. "Thank you for rescuing me."

"I would have gone to the ends of the Earth to save you," he said into her hair, his voice low.

Andrew slowly pulled back to search her face. Gabrielle knew she probably had never looked worse, but she felt beautiful in his eyes.

After thanking Maria for her care, they exited her home. After all, it was 2 am and everyone needed some sleep. Andrew picked her up in a bridal carry, transporting her across the threshold and onto the cement stairs outside as though she weighed nothing more than a feather.

The streetlamps cast strange shadows on a few people that still lingered outside discussing the exciting events of the past two hours. They broke into a subdued applause when Andrew appeared.

"You cannot 'elp it, can you," Gabrielle said in wonderment, her head resting against his chest. "Everywhere you go you become some sort of hero." She worked hard to pronounce *hero* in a Canadian accent.

He acknowledged the congratulations of the assembly with an embarrassed nod. Speaking just to her, out the side of his mouth, he said, "Why don't you ask one of these fine people if they have a car and would be willing to give us a ride to a hospital? And yes, you're going to see a doctor. I won't listen to any arguments. Then we'll get you back to Uncle Olivier's home."

Two young women, both students, introduced themselves as Chloe and Nicole. They offered their services at Gabrielle's slurred request. They also insisted they would wait and bring her and Andrew home afterward. Gabrielle thanked them with much gratitude. The headache medication was already taking hold. She wasn't sure what Marie had given her, but the pain had subsided considerably. She was starting to feel more groggy than anything.

"We share...*un appartement*," said Chloe, in broken English as she led them to her tiny car. "There." She pointed to a window just above the fight scene. "I was doing some study and 'eard the noise. *Tu étais formidable*." She unlocked the doors and held the back one open for Andrew to help Gabrielle inside.

After getting her settled, Andrew turned to accept his rope from another of the bystanders. The man handed it over with a reverential smile. On impulse Gabrielle cleared her throat and called out in French to the group who had trooped along to see them off.

"This man, who caught the criminal tonight, and saved my life, is Andrew Filmore," she said as loudly as she could. "He is from Canada and is the new owner of Caviste de Tremblay on Rue Saint-Denis. The shop will be opening next Friday, and he would appreciate so much if you would come to his opening and tell everyone you know to do the same."

The effort to raise her voice exhausted her and she flopped back against the seat. Despite the circumstances, the people outside offered him good wishes and promises to do as she had asked, she felt pleased she had thought of it in spite of everything. After all, if Superman couldn't draw a crowd, who could?

As they motored down the street toward the nearest emergency room. Regardless of the pain in her shoulder, Gabrielle leaned against him, soaking up his strength. What a horrible day it had been. Now that she was safe, Gabrielle fought to stay awake. Yet, she had a burning question that needed to be asked.

"When I was being dragged away, you appeared. Where did you come from?" she mumbled. "And why were you there so late at night?"

She could only see flashes of his profile as they passed by streetlights, in the darkness of the car. His became grim and she imagined his jaw setting in an angry line as he spoke.

"The minute you ended your call with Annette, we left the shop. I knew something was terribly wrong. So did she. We arrived at the apartment to find the place ransacked, your landlady unconscious on the floor, and you gone." His voice cracked with remembered torment. "I nearly lost my mind," he said, shaking his head in agitation. "Annette called the police and an ambulance for Madame…whatever her name is, and I started searching for clues as to where you might have been taken."

"You did not think the police would want to do that?"

"I wasn't thinking about much, other than how to get you back," he said without regret. "Anyway, I found a scrap of paper under a pile of rubble in the kitchen that had the number of a detective on it and…"

She interrupted quietly. "Commissaire Chevalier 'elped me the last time."

"Yeah, well, I'd like to hear about that 'last time.' Anyhow, Annette contacted him, and he came too. Wouldn't divulge a lot about what he knew. None of them did really." She felt him shrug. "But I knew a few things they didn't either. I described the man I'd seen following us and I gave them a threatening letter I found crumpled up on your bedroom floor."

"*Merci*," she squeezed his hand. "Still, why would you think the man would return to my apartment? That would be a 'long shot,' as they say in crime dramas. Clearly, the police didn't consider it. And 'e didn't leave with me after ripping apart my apartment. I was thrown into a storage room on the ground floor."

"I didn't think he'd return." He pulled her closer and planted a kiss on her forehead. "I just couldn't leave. I sat in a doorway across the street, so I could watch the building. I'm not sure why. Guess I fell asleep though since I didn't hear him until he yelled. I imagine that was something you did?"

She chuckled a little at the remembrance. "I stomped on 'is toes. I thought I was going to be killed if I didn't do something to escape."

"I'm sure glad you did. The sound woke me up. Without that, he might have gotten away with you." She felt him shudder.

How lucky she was to have gained the friendship of this man. She thought of something else. "But you 'ad some sort of rope?" She left the question hanging. Now that the pain in her head had lessened, she was remembering a few things.

He laughed. "Yes, a rope. Calf roping," he said cryptically. "I'm pretty good at lassoing calves and tying up three of their legs in a few seconds flat. The cord for that is usually pretty short though. I had to get creative with this baby." He patted the coiled rope on the seat beside him. "I've won a few awards for steer wrestling too," he continued matter-of-factly. "I used to compete in rodeos all summer long. When I found a length of rope in Uncle's back room, I decided it wouldn't hurt to take it along. It's not exactly a lasso, but it worked well enough. While I was sitting across the street I made a noose. A good rope can always come in handy."

Gabrielle had no response. Before tonight she would have said she didn't see how a length of rope with a hangman's knot at one end would ever be considered useful. Now, she was convinced of the opposite. Still, she had only read of rodeos in books or seen them portrayed in movies. Trying to envision Andrew wrestling a huge, horned animal made her head hurt. It defied description. So, she stopped.

"We 'ave arrived," called Chloe, the driver, pulling the little car up to a set of large double doors.

The next hour passed in a blur for Gabrielle. She was seen almost immediately by a doctor and wheeled away for a CAT scan. Andrew, against his wishes, was told to wait in a room outside. Everyone just assumed he was her husband and Gabrielle didn't bother to disabuse them of the idea.

Finally, she was told there was no concussion and that the nurse had done an excellent job of doctoring her wounds. Her arm was badly sprained and bruised. Gabrielle was released with strict instructions to rest for the next few days, keep her head elevated, and avoid stress.

That would be easier now that Malcom was in custody. Although her first psychology exam was tomorrow. She couldn't fail the course now. Merely thinking about it caused her anxiety.

The moment she appeared at the doorway of the examination room, Andrew was on his feet and at her side. Thanking the doctor and nurses for their care, she shuffled outside with his help to the waiting car where the girls were happily texting. Vaguely, she wondered who they'd be talking to in the middle of the night, but they were young, probably only about Annette's age. Andrew tapped on the window. Nicole, the passenger, jumped and unlocked the doors with a big grin. Gabrielle was settled inside next to Andrew, and they were off once more.

The trip to Andrew's wine shop was swift and spent in silence as the young driver handily wheeled the car through empty streets to pull up by the curb in front of Caviste de Tremblay. Stopping the engine, Chloe and Nicole both hopped out of the car and came to say their goodbyes.

"Thank you very much for the ride," Andrew said, after helping Gabrielle out of the car. "Can I give you some money for your help?" He looped the rope over his arm and reached for his wallet.

A torrent of outraged French met with his query and even though it hurt, Gabrielle laughed, then winced with pain as she loosely translated. "They both wish to tell you an emphatic, NO!"

"*Merci beaucoup*," she told the girls, swaying slightly. Andrew gently steadied her.

She exchanged *la bise*, the French equivalent of a hug, with each girl and awkwardly, so did Andrew.

"*Alors, c'est son caviste?*" Chloe asked, with a pointed nod toward the shop.

"*Oui*," Gabrielle answered. She was happy they were asking whether the shop belonged to Andrew. Clearly, he had made an impression on quite a few people this night and on several different age-groups. She proceeded, in French, to tell the girls to spread the word about Caviste de Tremblay opening, and that it was to be run by the hero of the neighbourhood.

They nodded vigorously, their teeth gleaming white in the darkness. As Chloe turned away, Nicole leaned toward Gabrielle to whisper. "*Gardez cet homme. Il est fabuleux.*" Then, with a wave to Andrew, she hopped back in the car and the girls roared away.

Andrew kept an arm around Gabrielle as they walked to the door leading to the upstairs suite. "What were you talking about?" he asked. "I wouldn't ask, but something about how Nicole looked at me as she spoke just now made me curious."

Lost in her own thoughts about the man she was with, Gabrielle didn't answer for a few moments. "…They asked if this was your shop and I told them it was."

She wasn't sure why she didn't fully answer his question. Part of her wanted to keep the young Nicole's final remark to herself. Twice this night, two women of varying ages, had commented on Andrew. She wanted to think about what they had said. However, at the moment she was too tired to do anything but sleep.

"I see." Andrew dug into a jeans' pocket for his keys and opened the door, flipping on the muted light at the top of the stairs. He took Gabrielle's arm and ushered her through, closing and locking it behind him.

She lifted a tentative foot to the first stair, gripping the railing with a clenched hand.

"Don't be ridiculous. You're not walking up there." Andrew swept her off her feet and into his arms. His eyes locked on hers as he made her a promise. "I won't let anything bad happen to you, ever again."

She rested a sleepy head against his shoulder, wondering how he could be so sure. That had sounded like a lifetime commitment, and they were only friends. "*D'accord,*" she mumbled as he began to climb.

Without warning, the door on the landing above them slammed open and a wild-eyed Annette leapt onto the platform.

"*Gabby! Tu es en sécurité!*" she screeched. She rushed toward them taking two steps at a time, in danger of toppling over and bringing them all to a crashing heap. The young woman lunged at her sister with tears of joy streaming down her face.

Andrew stopped, resting Gabrielle on his bent leg as the two women hugged and kissed.

"Yes, I'm safe. Now, let's get into the apartment. I am very tired," Gabrielle rested a loving hand on her sister's wet cheek.

Annette shot Andrew a worried look, but scampered up the stairs ahead of them to hold the door wide.

"What happened? You are 'urt!" Annette said, the second they were inside. "I 'ave been so worried about you!"

"I believe it, because I was worried about you too," said Gabrielle in a gravelly voice. Andrew didn't set her down. Instead, he made for the hallway, calling back to Annette as he strode purposefully for the bedrooms.

"I think we'd better save questions for tomorrow," he said firmly. "We all need some sleep. Especially your sister."

Reluctantly, Annette fell silent, but followed to flip on the light as he carried Gabrielle into an opulent bedroom and laid her on a sky blue, satin bedspread.

"Maybe you could help her get undressed and comfortable?" he said, straightening and looking at Annette. "I'll see you both in the morning. I'm going back down to the shop for the night." Swiftly, he bent over Gabrielle, took her face in both hands, and lightly kissed her forehead. Then, turning on his heel he was gone.

"*Bonne nuit*," Annette said bemusedly.

As they heard the apartment door close, Annette leaned closer. "I told you he was falling in love with you. I'll do my best to be patient to hear what happened. For now though, I am just grateful you're with me. I love you Gabby." She kissed her sister and began to gently peel away the soiled jeans and hoodie.

Gabrielle felt unable to utter another word. Lifting a weary hand in farewell, long after Andrew was actually gone, she let it drop onto the silky material. She could barely keep her eyes open. Dimly she felt Annette help her out of her clothes and tug a large t-shirt over her shoulders. Her back and chest hurt where she'd been dragged, but even that didn't prevent her from dropping off to sleep moments later.

Yet the last thought in her mind was what the young girl, Nicole, had said in French, just before she left in her car.

"Keep that man. He is fabulous."

Chapter Eleven

Gabrielle rolled over in bed, throwing out a hand to reach for her alarm clock. When it wasn't there, and she met with another satiny smooth pillow instead of her night table, she remembered. Her eyes flew open. Immediately she was aware of how her body ached and lifted tentative fingers to touch her eye. It was still swollen, but less so.

She breathed a sigh of relief. Malcom was incarcerated and the reign of fear that had followed her since Lyam's capture, was over. Thanks to Andrew.

The bedroom door silently swung inward and there stood Annette. "You're awake!" She hurried over next to the bed, looking down at her sister, her eyes once again, filling with tears.

"Hey, I'm safe now," Gabrielle said softly. "No more crying." She reached for her sister and Annette came closer to give her a gentle hug. "What time is it? I'm ravenous."

Hastily Annette wiped the moisture away with her fingers and stepped back to smile tremulously. "I'm sure you are. It's 3 p.m. and I doubt if you ate anything yesterday.

Can I bring you a croissant? Baguette and jam? Some toast?"

Gabrielle reared upright and then fell back, gasping with the pain. "It's three! But I had an exam this morning!" Her stomach clenched. These exams were the culmination of everything she'd worked toward for the last four years. She couldn't miss one.

"Gabby...It's okay," Annette said soothingly. "I called your school to explain and they understood. It's been rescheduled."

"*Merci*." She reached a hand toward her sister who grasped it with a loving smile.

"No problem. Now, about that breakfast…"

"First I'd like to have a shower, and then a coffee and toast would be wonderful. But I'll come to the kitchen." She sighed, luxuriating in the cozy bed, and wondering if she really wanted to leave it. A sudden thought crossed her mind. "I don't have anything to wear!"

Annette pointed across the room to a chaise lounge of the same sky blue colour as the bedspread, where a small mound of clothes had been laid out.

"While you slept, I went to the apartment to tidy up a little and bring you a few clothes. Do you need help getting up or bathing?" Annette's brow furrowed with concern.

Gabrielle relaxed into her pillow. "That's wonderful, thank you, sweetie. No help is necessary. I'll be out soon." Not looking convinced, Annette nonetheless left, closing the door behind her.

For a few minutes, Gabrielle stared up into the gauzy white material of a canopy that was suspended from the ceiling over her head and tucked behind the headboard on either side. The walls were painted a pale, dove-grey and curtains of white with a sprinkle of tiny blue flowers billowed in a spring breeze at two long windows. On either side, ornate, dark-grey frames held the silhouettes of trees and other plants.

A large bureau, painted white with soft grey accented swirls, sat solidly at the far end of the room beneath a beautiful antique mirror. Beside it, was a door that Gabrielle presumed led to the bathroom. A matching armoire elegantly graced the wall opposite the windows and a stack of rectangular wicker trunks were arranged artistically near the chaise.

It was the most beautiful room Gabrielle had ever seen, and admitted to herself, she had seen quite a few gorgeous rooms at the family estate in Provence.

But, enough procrastinating, she must rise.

It took her longer than she thought it would to ease out of the soft bed. She sat on the edge, curling her toes into the soft pile of the cream-coloured carpet and admiring her surroundings once more.

On the night table beside her was a lamp, several books, and two framed pictures. She reached for the closest. It was a black and white wedding picture, aged by the passage of time, but she knew at once it was a photo of Olivier and his bride, Clarisse. They stood facing one another in a garden, holding hands and laughing at something only they two understood. The essence of love fairly jumped from the frame, causing tears to spring into Gabrielle's eyes. She brushed their happy faces with a finger and set it back down.

The other picture was again of them, but far more recent. It looked to be a re-enactment of the first photo, only the garden behind them was now alive with colour and their faces were older and lined with years. What emanated from the simple photo, however, had not aged or diminished in any way. It was true love. They gazed at one another with such emotion expressed in their faces that Gabrielle felt as though she were peeking into their very private world.

She set the photo down and looked again at the room, knowing it had been theirs and feeling the love of sixty years envelop her. Closing her eyes, she allowed the emotion to wash over and around her. She knew why Andrew couldn't bring himself to stay in this house. He too could feel the echoes of the past. It was a desecration of sorts to invade this beautiful space.

Yet here she was.

Rising, she shuffled to the pile of clothes and selected a favorite old track suit from the pile. It was a faded red that had seen better days, but it was comfortable and warm, the perfect thing to wear while recuperating. She sorted through several more items until she found lacy wisps of underwear and some socks before she slowly carried everything into the bathroom.

It too, was large and opulent. The soft grey walls had been painted throughout and light flooded the room from a wide window that overlooked the backyard. She stepped toward it to admire the washstand that had been refinished in shades of pale blues and grey surrounding a bouquet of pink roses. A washbowl with an antique-looking faucet with matching knobs graced the top and Gabrielle leaned over them, pulling back matching curtains to peer outside.

Just as she guessed, it was the same garden as in the pictures with the exact configuration of trees and flowerbeds, but overgrown. She sighed and moved to a modern shower installed in the corner opposite a white, old-fashioned, claw foot bathtub. Turning on the water, she looked for a towel and found a stack of them on a tall shelf by the door.

She stepped into the hot spray, gasping as it hit her wounds, but lifted her face to the water, feeling it strip away the grime inflicted on her by that terrible man and his fists.

Fifteen minutes later, dressed and feeling more like herself, she made her way to the kitchen. She would need Annette's help to re-bandage the abrasions, but that could wait. The aroma of brewing coffee and toasted bread drew her like a magnet.

Annette and Andrew both sat at one end of a long table, waiting for her. The kitchen was long, white, modern, and scrupulously clean. As she entered they both jumped to their feet and hurried toward her.

"It's okay," she laughed, waving them away. "I don't need help. I'm feeling much improved." She sank into a chair and reached for the cup Annette slid toward her. She looked at Andrew, who had dark circles under his bright blue eyes.

"Cornflower blue," she said absently, then giggled when both her companions looked up as though she'd lost her mind.

"Are you sure you're okay?" Andrew asked, reaching out a hand to take hers. He frowned, appearing concerned, and she hastened to assure them both.

"Yes—yes, I'm good. It's just…cornflower blue is the accent colour of the bedroom you put me in and it's the same colour as your eyes."

He laughed self-consciously. "Same as Mom and Uncle Olivier, I believe. At least that's what I remember of him."

"That would be why your aunt had the room painted that colour," she announced, as though solving a great mystery. Reaching for a plate and the toast, she grabbed a knife and began slathering butter and jam across several slices at once.

"I am 'appy to see this ordeal 'as not affected your appetite," Annette said. "Can I ask questions now?" She looked inquiringly at them. "We don't have a lot of time, because Andrew says Detective Chevalier will be arriving at 4 pm. He needs to speak with you as soon as possible."

"*Bien sûr.*" Gabrielle cut a triangle of toast and stuffed it into her mouth, rolling her eyes at how good it tasted. She had expected immediate questions. The whole story would have to be told several times she was sure.

Between bites and sips of coffee, she relayed the awful events of the previous day. Annette and Andrew were horrified all over again, but she felt quite detached from it now. It was as though someone else had lived through that terror.

"I would like to know what all of this 'as to do with Lyam?" Annette added to the tail end of the story. "And why would 'e 'ave a valuable painting secreted in your apartment?" She sat back and crossed her arms.

Gabrielle pushed the plate away and dabbed at her mouth with a paper napkin. Lifting her cup, she glanced inside and then turned it upside-down to show it was empty. "*S'il te plaît?*" she asked her sister.

As Annette bustled a few steps away to boil the kettle and rinse out the coffee press, Gabrielle began.

"Lyam and I met at a gallery opening, last May. It featured contemporary art as well as a few exhibition pieces by well-known artists of the early 1900s. Lyam told me 'e owned an antique shop and was a tour guide who specialized in taking people through art galleries that displayed great works of art. After the show, 'e asked me to dinner, and we found we 'ad much in common. At least, I thought we did at the time." She stared into space, recalling that fateful evening. "But Lyam was a narcissist of the worst sort. Self-absorbed and never interested in me as a person, only in what I could provide for 'im—an 'ideout and an alibi."

"Over the next two months we grew close, at least, that is what I 'ad thought." She fussed with crumbs on the table, keeping her eyes fixed in one place as she told the story she'd been so reluctant to tell before. "But I started to notice 'is strange idiosyncrasies. He was seldom available in the evening and gave vague reasons for where 'e was going. 'Out with friends,' was all I was told. Yet I did not ever meet one of these people, nor did I ever 'ear a name. Not even of a family member. In retrospect, I realize 'e did not want me to know anything about 'im that could be traced…" She sighed heavily and continued.

"In an age of cell phones and instant access to the internet, 'e chose to use an old style of flip phone. Archaic for a thirty-year-old man," she mused, understanding it now. "I was not allowed to touch 'is phone. The only time I did was when it slipped between the cushions of my sofa…Lyam, 'e was furious, warning me to never touch it again no matter what 'appened." Annette reappeared with the coffee and Gabrielle took a sip before continuing with her tale. Andrew sat in stony silence, hands folded across his stomach, long, jean-clad legs stretched out in front of him as he contemplated the floor.

"He 'ad plenty of money. Always cash. We would go to some extravagant restaurants and attended many fabulous shows. But only on certain nights. Other nights I was told not to contact 'im for any reason. 'E would get very stressed while talking to me about it. Consequently, I left it alone. I was so busy with my own studies, you see, I accepted it. Ugh…I was such a fool." She shook her head angrily.

Looking back on it all now, she did feel like a fool for being duped by the man. If only she had recognized the signs and not been so wrapped up in her education or overwhelmed by his expensive, carefree lifestyle.

"Anyway, one night Lyam appeared at my door and fell asleep on my sofa after telling me 'e felt ill and couldn't return to 'is own place. But where 'ad 'e been all evening I wondered? 'E 'ad arrived around midnight with a duffle bag that made a strange clattering sound when 'e set it on top of my book bag. It was odd."

Annette rose and took the seat beside her sister, lightly rubbing her back in a supportive gesture. Gabrielle took a deep breath and forged on.

"I 'ad been studying when 'e arrived and wasn't about to stop. 'Owever, I needed a book from my bag. Since 'e was dead to the world, I lifted 'is bag to get to mine." She plucked at lint on the leg of her pants, feeling as agitated as she had then. "It was unzipped, and a strange, golden statue fell out. The tiny image of a cat, similar to one I 'ad read about in the campus newspaper the day before. It 'ad been on loan to the Louvre along with several other priceless artifacts which were part of an exhibit of Egyptian antiquities. But it 'ad been stolen." She stood and began to pace back and forth across the kitchen, knowing her audience was as shocked as she had been.

"I was scared. I looked further into the bag and discovered a golden mask wrapped in cloth along with a note listing future dates and other museums. I pushed them back into his bag and went to my computer. What I found sent chills down my spine. There 'ad been six major thefts in the city over the last few months. Paintings, statues, carvings…" she flung an encompassing arm wide. "I found the same article I 'ad read, and others, some with pictures of the artifacts that 'ad been taken. Two of them were exactly the images of what I 'ad just uncovered in my apartment."

"*Mon Dieu!*" Annette had come straight up off her chair and Andrew hit his fist into his other hand.

"He was making you an accessory to his crimes just by being there," he said. She nodded.

"Reading the article further, I noticed that the nights they 'ad been stolen corresponded exactly with nights I remembered Lyam 'ad been unavailable, busy, or out with his supposed friends…the nights I was not to call or text. The police were baffled. The lead detective, Commissaire Chevalier, felt two to three people were responsible for all six robberies and that the artifacts were being sold on the black market, moved at night by individual members of this gang. And suddenly, I realized the leader of the gang was sleeping on my *canapé*."

She flopped back in her chair and ran trembling hands through her damp hair, re-living the revelations of that time and the frantic thoughts that had accompanied them.

"What did you do?" Annette breathed.

"I took my phone, crept onto my balcony, and called the police." She shrugged and raised her hands helplessly. "I told them what was 'appening. Then I waited for them to arrive." She took a gulp of her coffee and willed herself to relax. After all, it was in the past and the gang was caught.

"Chevalier spoke to me after it was all over. They 'ad Lyam and all the proof they needed to convict 'im. Unfortunately, 'is accomplice was not found. I 'elped Chevalier all I could, but I did not know that at some point Lyam must have 'idden a painting in my apartment." She stared sightlessly into her empty coffee cup before setting it down with a thump. "And that's where Malcom comes in."

"Malcom?" said Annette.

"The man from yesterday who barged into my 'ome," she said shortly.

In the silence that followed, Andrew spoke. "Does the name, Chagall, mean anything to you?" Andrew looked at each woman in turn.

"*Bien sûr!*" Annette cried, jumping to her feet. "*Pourquoi?*"

"She means to say, of course, why?" Gabrielle translated, feeling tired again. Going through the whole story had taxed her limited energy.

"Because, only the frame was damaged in the scuffle between me and your kidnapper. When your investigator friend looked at this painting you're talking about, the artist's name on the bottom was Chagall. I'd never heard of him, so I didn't think much of it. But you," he motioned toward Annette, "would probably know a lot more."

"I do," she answered, enunciating carefully. "Marc Chagall was a French-Russian artist who painted surrealist images before they were made popular by others. But that is not all 'e did. This man was involved in theatre and costume design, mastered the difficult art of stained glass, and learned lithography. At least one of 'is paintings sold for more than $28 million dollars US."

"Well," said Andrew dryly, "that would explain why Malcom was so desperate to get his hands on it. It doesn't explain what the heck lithography is, but…" he said quickly, holding up a preventative hand as Annette opened her mouth to explain, "that's a story that can be told another time."

"I would like one more thing to be explained," said Annette with a little sniff toward Andrew for halting the discourse on her favourite subject. "Why didn't you tell us this before?" She stared at her sister. "Why go through all of that alone and not talk to your family?"

Gabrielle rubbed her forehead. Her headache was

returning. "You're right. I should 'ave talked to you. I didn't, because I knew the people Lyam was involved with were dangerous. And when I found they wanted something they thought I 'ad, I didn't want to endanger any of you. I thought I could deal with it alone." She lifted her shoulders in the classic shrug she was known for. "You showed up at my door despite my best efforts."

"But…" interjected Annette, waving a hand at the man sitting next to her, "so did Superman and it's thanks to him that you're sitting here with us now."

Gabrielle didn't need her sister's reminder to know exactly how much she owed to her friend, the cowboy from Canada. She reached for his hand and squeezed it tight. "I'll never be able to thank you enough," she said, recalling a few of the things he'd told her last night. She could have sworn he'd promised to keep her from harm for the rest of his life. No. That couldn't be right. Her brain was muddled and her hearing questionable. Many words had been spoken last night and most of them were terrible.

"I'm the one who's grateful," he said. "I'd still be riding the Paris Métro if not for you." He squeezed Gabrielle's hand back and then let go. "Which reminds me, I'd better get back to work. I have a grand opening in a week and the work won't complete itself. You get some rest now. Okay?"

"Per'aps I could help y—" Andrew stood and placed a finger on Gabrielle's lips, preventing another word.

"No. And, no books either. Besides, Annette has offered to help me today."

"I did," her sister agreed with a grin. "Give me a few moments to clean up the kitchen and I will be down."

Andrew strode to the archway and looked back with a wave. "Commissaire Chevalier will be here any minute. I'll send him up when he arrives. If you need me you know where to look." Then, winking at Gabrielle, he left.

Annette followed him and poked her head back around the corner after making sure he'd left. "I have something to tell you, now that he's gone," she said with an air of mystery that Gabrielle found amusing. "I think we should keep it a secret and surprise him." She paused a moment for the full effect of her words to sink in.

"I checked Le Parisien digital newspaper this morning and there is an 'uge story on how Andrew Filmore, of Caviste de Tremblay, took down one of the most wanted criminals in Paris! Can you believe it?" her lowered voice rose in intensity until she was nearly shrieking. "It's all about the art thieves and how one of them eluded the police for months until a cowboy from Canada lassoed him on the street, averted a kidnapping, and recovered a stolen painting by the renowned artist, Marc Chagall."

Gabrielle's mouth hung open. Reporters must have interviewed the people that were on the street last night. And they remembered Andrew from what she'd said.

"There are eyewitness accounts and even one grainy-looking picture that someone must have taken under a streetlight where Andrew's talking with the police. Do you see what this means?" Annette was almost jumping up and down by this point. "The whole city will know about Andrew's wine shop! And about how he's a hero, saving you and a piece of priceless French art! This is the best advertising anyone ever had!"

Chapter Twelve

The following Friday dawned fair and clear. Gabrielle turned from the small bedroom window in her dear little apartment to admire her chic new outfit in the mirror Annette had purchased to replace what Malcom had destroyed. Annette had also chosen the perfect dress for her to wear for Andrew's opening day. No one could ask for a better sister. Tilting her head to one side, she lifted the chiffon skirt and let it swish back into place around her legs.

It was a rich, cherry-red mini dress with a full skirt, ruched bust, a smocked waist, and square neckline that showed off her beautiful hourglass figure. The flowing lantern sleeves were the icing on the cake and did double duty by covering the remainder of her bruising. With a sigh of happiness, she added a gold locket her parents had given her for her eighteenth birthday and some dangly gold hoops.

She'd spent more time than usual on her makeup, finishing off with an extra coat of mascara and matching red lipstick to compliment her glossy mane of black hair.

Regardless of the scab over her eye, and a few remaining bruises to her face, she knew she'd never looked better and admitted it was entirely for Andrew's sake that she did it.

He and Annette wouldn't allow her to see the finishing touches to the shop until it was ready for the world. She was excited to discover what miracles had been wrought.

The first four days of her recovery had been spent in the beautiful home above the shop. The three of them had spent some lovely times talking and getting to know one another better in between Andrew and Annette renovating.

However, Gabrielle begged to go home and had slowly puttered about, putting things to rights in her apartment with Annette's help in the evenings. Many of her dishes, her mirror, and other breakables had needed to be replaced. Overall, she counted herself as lucky. Things could have ended much worse.

Even Madame Moreau had sent a message upstairs with her niece, who was staying with the older lady during her own recovery. The woman knocked loudly on Gabrielle's door. For a second, her heart had leapt into her throat, remembering the last time that had happened. However, she wouldn't let such fears overwhelm her, and opened it to find a little wisp of a woman holding a box of chocolates and wishing Gabrielle, 'All the best.' It had meant a lot and Gabrielle determined to pay the lady a visit once the opening day of Caviste de Tremblay was behind her.

Andrew still knew nothing of his city-wide fame. There was no reason for him to look at a French newspaper. Although he revealed to Gabrielle that he'd been asked to pose for a picture with several ladies at the local Monoprix grocery store, something which he puzzled over, he was none the wiser.

She glanced at her clock where it resided on her night

table. It was 10:30 am already! The opening was only a half hour away. Grabbing her purse, she slipped on her wedge sandals and hurried out the door, locked up, and made her way downstairs. She planned to take her time as she walked in the warm April sunshine. Birds twittered in the branches of young oak trees planted along the street and poppies bobbed their heads in greeting as she passed beneath their window boxes, humming a tune.

It was almost 11 o'clock when she drew close to the shop. She heard the buzz of voices before seeing who made the noise. Turning the last corner, she saw cars jamming the street on both sides. Masses of people were milling about in chattering groups on the sidewalks and out into the street. A long, snaking line of customers waited eagerly to get inside the doors. There was a small van with a satellite dish perched on its roof blocking traffic. Two men were talking with a camera mounted on a tripod just outside the store.

Could it be true?

Quickening her pace, Gabrielle wove through the crowd, ignoring the looks of appreciation she received from men. She sought the appreciation of only one.

It wasn't easy to break through the tight throngs of well-wishers, people curious to see the 'Canadian Cowboy' as he'd been dubbed by the newspaper, and anxious would-be customers. She had to explain several times that she was working at the shop today before people would let her skip past the line and head straight for the door.

She rapped sharply on the glass, leaning close and cupping her hands around her eyes to look inside and let them know it was her. Eventually, she was rewarded with the sight of a harried Annette rushing toward her and waving. Her sister unlocked the door and Gabrielle slipped inside with people pushing behind her in an effort to enter the shop early.

"It's amazing," her sister said, her eyes widening in shock as she looked outside. "There's probably another fifty outside since I last checked. It's a good thing I convinced him to order more wine. He'll be sold out today."

With a smug look of satisfaction, she turned and led the way to the back room. "Oh, by the way, Andrew still doesn't know about the reporters, the cameras, or all the people out there. He's been in the cellar all morning, arranging the latest shipment of wine. It's going to be quite a shock." She reached for a bottle that was slightly askew and set it squarely on the shelf.

The pink floral mini dress she wore had a full skirt, but the material was heavier than Gabrielle's and was flocked with a lacy white print. A pretty bow hung from the ruffled round neck and the little cap sleeves were gathered into a flounce that matched the bottom of the skirt. She wore flat white sandals in preparation of the busy day ahead.

Gabrielle smiled. When her little sister moved to Paris this fall, to begin her formal art education, she would enjoy having her nearby. Perhaps even living with her, although you never knew what might happen in the space of a few months, she mused as she looked for Andrew.

She stopped, gaping at the shop around her. She hadn't even noticed the fantastic changes that had been made. The walls shone with a coat of fresh paint and new, stainless steel track lights had been erected down the full length of the space. It was bright and welcoming. Gone was the dark, dingy look from before. New shelves ran from floor to ceiling down either of the walls with long spaces at regular intervals. The spot at the center points of the openings allowed for a special display of wine to be spotlighted.

Sparkling bottles filled each shelf, organized according to region, colour, and type.

Down the middle of the room were the display crates that Andrew had made. They were filled with raffia and loaded with glistening bottles of less expensive wines. Trailing pots of ivy hung from a couple of end shelves adding life and greenery to the store while a chalkboard highlighting today's specials was propped in a corner over a half barrel of wines especially brought in from her family's estate, Chateau de Belliveau.

The floor had been cleaned, varnished, and polished to a high sheen. Uncle Olivier's cash desk had been totally revamped, yet without altering his original design. It was amazing. Gabrielle felt an immense pride in the shop that Andrew and her sister had created.

The man himself appeared. He straightened up from behind the desk with another wooden box of clinking bottles in his arms.

"It's you!" he cried. Hurriedly setting it down, he brushed dusty hands down the length of his pants, then realized what he'd done and smacked his legs to remove the grime. "I suppose you can take the man out of the country, but you can't take the country out of the man," he joked.

He had combed his unruly hair, shaved, and even at this distance she could smell the faint spice of his aftershave. Locking eyes, she moved toward him and lifted her arms to share *le bise*. "It is a day of celebration," she announced.

Moving out from behind the counter, they greeted one another and then he shoved one hand in his pocket, stepping back and looking at her as if asking for her approval. She was startled, stopping short to stare at his attire. The omnipresent blue jeans were gone, replaced by cream-coloured chinos and dressy brown leather loafers. A salmon-pink button up shirt with the sleeves rolled over his strong forearms, completed the ensemble. He looked the part of a casual, but elegantly dressed Parisian.

The words of the young Nicole floated through her mind as Gabrielle stared at him, trying to keep her jaw from dropping.

'Hang on to that man. He's fantastic.'

"I—I think you look fabulous," she stammered at last.

"No," he said, taking in her dress with glowing eyes. "If anyone looks fabulous it's you. I've never seen anyone so beautiful."

"It's nice that you like what one another is wearing," interrupted Annette. "But we should 'urry. There are people outside, all clamouring for the doors to open."

"Oh right! Sorry." Andrew jumped back, tucking, then untucking his new shirt. "Wish I didn't feel like such a fool," he mumbled, turning away, and reaching for the box of bottles.

Gabrielle leapt after him. "You feel like a fool? Why?" she asked. "Is it because of the language barrier?"

"No," he growled. "The clothes. I look like an idiot in this outfit. Your sister got it, thinking it would help me to fit in with my surroundings for the grand opening. But clothes don't make the man, as my mother always says, and I'm longing for my jeans." Hefting the box into his arms he set off through the store to place the bottles in a cupboard, then straightened and turned to Annette and Gabrielle. He still hadn't so much as glanced out the window to see the throngs of people waiting for him. "Ready?" he said with a grin, pulling at his collar.

"In five minutes we'll be ready, but we aren't yet," Gabrielle said firmly. Stepping forward, she grabbed

Andrew's arm and pulled him toward the back rooms. "You're coming with me."

"If you're going to kiss 'im would you make it fast?" Annette yelled after them. "People are starting to bang on the door."

Gabrielle didn't bother responding. Dragging a reluctant Andrew behind her, she made for his bedroom.

"What are you doing? Why did your sister say that? *Are* you going to kiss me?" he asked with an edge of both disbelief and hope in his voice.

"Don't be ridiculous," she said. She pushed him through the doorway, grabbed the handle, and barked out orders. "Take off those clothes and put yours on. 'At, jeans, belt, boots—the works. And don't come out until you do. People came 'ere to see the Canadian Cowboy whose strength and selfless concern for others 'ave made him a local legend. They don't want to see a cookie-cutter version of some well-dressed Parisian. They want to see you. Understand?"

Andrew came to attention and saluted. "*Oui Madame!*"

Lifting a hand, she blew him a kiss. "*Bien*," she said with a grin. "That's all you get for now."

After slamming the door, she marched back to the front of the store, joining Annette who had retired to a safe spot behind the cash desk. They stood together watching the restless crowd grow by the minute.

"It's amazing," Gabrielle breathed. She consulted her cell phone and expelled a long breath of air. "But it's past eleven now. Per'aps we should open the doors ourselves. What do you think?" She turned a worried face to Annette.

"They want to see 'im, not us." Annette pushed a strand of hair from her eyes. "What's 'e doing back there?"

A firm clomp of boots on a wooden floor told them he was on his way. They both turned to watch him duck through the door and stop, thumbs hooked through his belt loops, assuming a comical stance.

"Better?" he asked. Andrew had on his usual slim-fitting jeans, but today he wore a black, long-sleeved, button-up shirt that followed the lean lines of his flat stomach and broad chest. A belt, with a shiny silver buckle, was cinched at his waist, and his feet were encased in boots that had been buffed to a high sheen. His trademark Stetson was pulled low over his piercing blue eyes.

"Perfect," both women chimed in. They moved forward to hug him and plant a kiss on each cheek. He flushed with the attention.

"People are waiting for you," Annette said, urging him forward with a hand on his arm.

"Really? I can't imagine too many would turn out for the re-opening of a little-known wine shop that had fallen into disrepair." He smiled ruefully at Gabrielle and her sister, but allowed himself to be tugged along by Annette.

"Time to meet my adoring public," he quipped sarcastically, throwing back his shoulders.

But his footsteps faltered and came to an abrupt halt as Andrew neared the window. A cheer went up from the people closest to the polished glass. He whirled around to gape at his friends.

"What are all those people doing here?" he asked in amazement.

Gabrielle hurried to fling the door wide, and Annette pushed him again, moving him like an automaton toward the door.

The throng surged forward, engulfing him in a wave of humanity that pulled him into their midst, patted him on the shoulder, and shouted and whistled their appreciation. The photographer zoomed in, his assistant clearing a line of sight so he could get footage of the event. A couple of reporters snapped pictures, waiting for their chance to ask questions of the heroic man.

And Andrew, wide-eyed and dazed, nodded and smiled. For once he didn't say mercy, but pronounced his gratitude in perfectly accented French. "*Merci*," he said, over and over again.

The three of them sat behind the counter, exhausted but happy, on old wooden chairs brought forth from Uncle Olivier's back rooms. The shop door had, reluctantly, been closed and locked for the night. They surveyed the wreckage. Not that anything had been harmed, but a good portion of the store had been purchased in one day.

"Lucky thing you made me order more wine," Andrew said to Annette. "I thought it was a bit presumptuous at the time, but tomorrow morning I'm going to need it to fill the shelves."

She giggled. "You were so surprised."

He ran both hands through hair that had been compressed under a hat all day long. "Thank goodness you guys were there to translate and speak for me. Who knows what I would have told those reporters?"

It was Gabrielle's turn to chuckle, but she sobered quickly. "I was proud of you. You 'ave been in Paris less than two weeks and look at all you 'ave accomplished." She looked around the beautifully renovated store. "Your Uncle Olivier would be proud also."

Andrew blinked several times before answering. "I believe he would be. I could feel him here today." He rose to stand before them, clearing his throat.

"I want to thank you both from the bottom of my heart." He swept a hand around the store. "None of this would have been possible if not for your support and assistance. Heck, I don't know if I could have even stayed in Paris. But you both made such a difference in my life." He grinned and wiped his eyes. "For a start I wouldn't have been able to find my way out of the métro. Or buy food. To quote a famous artist I know, I might have ended up as a withered corpse, waiting for vultures to come clean my bones."

They laughed, the girls standing to join him in a group hug.

"And now," he said, bending low in a sweeping bow, "if I may have the pleasure of your company, Mademoiselle." He reached out to Gabrielle, taking her hand and kissing it. Lifting his head, he took a deep breath. "*J'ai une surprise pour toi à l'étage.*"

"Wh-what?" Gabrielle was astounded. He just spoke perfect French. "You 'ave a surprise for me? Upstairs?" She glanced at her sister who was bouncing with barely supressed glee.

"I taught him that," she blurted, then, flying at Gabrielle she hugged her tight. "Just so you know, I'm staying here," she announced, as though speaking a rehearsed line. "*À plus tard.*"

"*À plus tard,*" Gabrielle said robotically. "See you later." She was thoroughly overcome and allowed Andrew to gently lead her out the door and up the staircase to the beautiful home above the shop.

He opened the door and pushed it wide. She wandered in without him, not knowing what to expect, but noticing the perfume of cherry blossoms flooding her senses. Behind her, Andrew flicked a switch, and the soft glow of lamps revealed bouquets of the fragrant, pink and white flowers gracing every flat surface in the room.

"Oh!" she breathed. "It's beautiful. You brought the orchard to me." She went to the closest spray and buried her face in the petals, breathing deep.

Turning to Andrew she was startled to find him down on one knee. Her heart caught in her throat as he took her hands.

"I know we haven't known one another for very long. The last two weeks have been a whirlwind." He shook his head in disbelief. "But my parents met and married in a whirlwind too, and they've been together thirty-six years. Maybe you need more time before you're ready to be committed," he said, his handsome face flushed and earnest as he looked up at her. "But I can't contain how I feel, and I know it's the real thing."

He took a deep breath. "I love you, Gabrielle. You're my soulmate, my other half, and I can't imagine a life without you in it. In this home, built on generations of love, I ask you to marry me and stand at my side to share in the joy and the trials of life."

Gabrielle was speechless.

She stared at him, her long black hair tumbling forward, casting her face into shadow. It was sudden and unexpected. But she knew what her heart was telling her too.

"If you need time to think about it," Andrew said weakly, "I understand. Take as much time as you need. I just wanted you to know that I love you and I would wait for you forever."

She opened her mouth to speak, but said nothing. Her heart felt as though it would beat its way out of her chest as she looked into the adoring eyes of the man she loved.

"Yes," she whispered. Lightly, she tugged at his hands,

needing to feel the strength and warmth of his arms around her.

"Yes?" he repeated, getting to his feet, but not daring to come closer.

"Yes…I will marry you. Yes, I love you." Standing on tiptoe she pulled him down to her and lifted her face for the kiss that would seal their love forever.

Epilogue

Dry leaves swirled around their feet as Gabrielle and Andrew strolled, hand in hand, along the paths of Jardin des Plantes in the cool October breeze. Autumn had come early to France, and she shivered, wishing she'd worn her favourite green sweater under her jacket. Andrew slipped an arm around her waist, holding her close and dropping a kiss into the cloud of black hair that twined about her head.

"Do you want to go back?" he asked. She snuggled closer, drawing from the warmth of his love.

"No. You haven't had a break from the shop in ages. Besides, I love it here. It clears the mind."

"Still worrying about your latest client?" he asked with a frown.

Gabrielle smiled up at him. "No. I decided to leave those concerns at work, although that girl does present an interesting case."

"You'll help her," he said with confidence. "You always do."

They passed beneath the bare branches of the cherry

tree where they'd taken their first walk together. Andrew reached up, trailing an arm through the stiffened limbs. "Thanks," he said softly.

"You're talking to trees now, are you?" she teased.

"This one, yes. It was instrumental in convincing you to accept a guy like me. Now we're an old married couple of..." he lifted a hand and counted before he said, "two months, I felt a little gratitude was in order."

She giggled. "*Tu as raison.*"

"I know I'm right," he said, pulling her closer.

She'd been speaking in her native tongue more and more as the weeks had flown by. Andrew was improving all the time. It was amazing how far he'd come in such a short while. He'd even said his marriage vows in French, and had understood every word, or so he had assured her.

She reflected on all that had transpired since the grand opening of Caviste de Tremblay. Further stories in newspapers and on television had ensured that the little shop was thriving. It remained busy with satisfied customers, almost from the moment it opened till the minute it closed each day. The neighbourhood had accepted Andrew with open arms. Many of them told stories of his bravery to the far reaches of the city. They bragged of him, their local hero, which brought business from well outside their area.

Annette worked in the shop a few evenings each week, in between her studies at the prestigious school she was now attending. She'd taken over Gabrielle's apartment after their marriage and was happily ensconced in the *chambres parmi les étoiles*, as Gabrielle had always called it.

Andrew's mother, Sophie, had arrived, as she had promised him she would, soon after the grand opening. Gabrielle loved her. She was tall and sandy-haired, like her son, with bobbed hair greying at the temples and the same icy blue eyes as her son. The woman loved to laugh and had a wonderful sense of humor. In a short time, she became like a second mother to Gabrielle, and she was sorry to see the lady depart for Canada. But Sophie had returned soon after with Andrew's father in preparation for the wedding.

The rest of the family had all come for the late July nuptials. Gabrielle's parents arrived a week before in order to spend time with him and his parents. Andrew's brother Jayke stayed home to continue working the farm, but didn't miss the honour of being the best man on the wedding day itself.

Angelina and Julien were there with their two adorable children Celeste and Philippe. Elyse and Armand flew in from Florence, where they had been staying with friends, and Sarah and Raphaël drove in for the day. Long after the ceremony, Sarah made the announcement that she and her dark-eyed husband were expecting their first child. There were hugs, kisses, and tears all around. It couldn't have been more perfect when the day culminated with Andrew, playing his guitar and singing to his new bride his favourite Irish love song.

Gabrielle came back to the present with a thump as Andrew suddenly swung away from her and raced toward a line of tall trees. She called after him, wondering what in the world was happening now.

A shrill scream rent the air. Looking ahead along her husband's trajectory, she saw a child dangling from a high branch of a sturdy oak. Gabrielle broke into a run herself, a lump of fear forming in her throat as she witnessed a woman, presumably the child's mother, shriek as she rushed to the scene pushing a cumbersome baby stroller.

Andrew got there first. Raising his arms into the air, he shouted something and at that moment the youngster fell, dropping like a stone into his waiting arms. He went down onto his knees with the force of impact, but the little boy was unscathed. She watched as the mother threw herself first at her son, and then Andrew.

Gabrielle stopped. Panting and bent over double, she laughed until tears streamed from her eyes. It was to be expected. Andrew had rescued yet another wayward soul from a nasty fate. Love for him like she had never known possible consumed her. She walked toward him knowing every day would bring a new, and wonderful, exciting adventure.

After all, that was her husband—the Canadian cowboy. Otherwise known as Superman.

Next in the Chateau de Belliveau series

vinci-books.com/withlovefromparis

A family legacy on the line, a love story in the making.

In the breathtaking Rockies, Parisian fashionista Annette Dupont must protect her family's ranch from an unexpected danger. Drawn to her aloof but captivating neighbor, Jeff, Annette discovers love in the unlikeliest of places. As the danger intensifies, can she safeguard her heart and her family's legacy?

Turn the page for a free preview…

With Love From Paris: Chapter One

Tap-tap-tap.

With a small shriek of delight, Annette flew to her apartment door and threw it open, her heart racing. Gabrielle stood outside, leaning the extended handle of a small red suitcase against her hip, and shifting from one foot to the other.

"Ready to go?" Her eyebrows arched.

Annette's stomach dropped. She hated to disappoint her sister, but she was nowhere close to being ready. Grabbing Gabrielle's arm, she pulled her inside, the clattering of the suitcase echoing through the hallway. Today they would embark on their long-awaited journey to Canada. The trip was in celebration of Annette's four years of hard work towards her fine arts degree and she could hardly contain her excitement. Annette pushed the door closed behind them.

The small entry, that Gabrielle had kept scrupulously neat and tidy when this had been her apartment, was a testament to disorganization and clutter. She tripped on a jumble of Annette's boots, that were tossed in a heap beside the empty shoe rack, and pitched headlong toward a teetering trolley of art supplies. Just before impact, she righted herself by slamming the palm of her hand into the center of a dead fern.

She caught her breath and straightened. The brown fronds of the plant crumbled in her fingers, and she shook the remnants off distastefully as she glanced at Annette with a frown. An easel was set up in the kitchen, and tubes of paint, brushes and rags littered the table.

"Don't be upset. I know it's messy in here, and I should have packed yesterday, but I didn't have time." Ignoring the exaggerated sigh that issued from her sister's lips, Annette grasped Gabrielle's shoulders and kissed her cheeks, one after the other, four times in quick succession. "This might be a good time to remember," she suggested mischievously as she led the way through the salon, "that you love me."

She stepped aside as her sister entered the bedroom where an enormous, suitcase lay open nearly buried under piles of clothes. Gabrielle's sharp intake of breath was unmistakeable, and her eyes widened in horror.

"It's not as bad as it looks," Annette hastened to say.

"It's not…how?"

"I'm almost done," she said defensively, tucking a strand of curly chestnut hair behind one ear. "What time did you say our flight leaves?" She tucked the protruding leg of a favourite pair of trousers further into the bag.

"How can you *not* know this?" Gabrielle threw her hands in the air with exasperation. "We need to be on route to Charles de Gaulle airport in one hour. And at the rate you're moving…" she explained and waved at the cyclone of clothes spread over the coverlet, "we may need divine intervention to achieve it."

Annette giggled remorsefully and bent to grab a pair of lilac high heels from the closet behind her. She held them in the air, admiring the lavish satin bows over the toes and the long ribbons that would secure the fragile shoes to her ankles. The colour matched a dress she'd recently purchased, and she was looking forward to wearing the ensemble. Exams had concluded in May, and she'd treated herself to the outfit with a little of the money her father had sent as a graduation gift. It was an extravagance. Yet holding the shoes up in the light of the small bedroom window, she admired them without regret.

"You can't take those!" Gabrielle gasped, pointing at the shoes as though they were coiled rattlesnakes. "Put them down and step away from the closet. We're going to a ranch. Not New York City for a luxury stay at the Ritz." Gabrielle gestured at the gaping suitcase already full of brightly coloured clothes. "And this bag is too big. I didn't pay for checked luggage. Trade it for your carry-on, and pack less. They have washing machines in Canada, you know." Sarcasm lent an edge to her tone.

"Relax," Annette soothed. "I can downsize…maybe." With a sinking heart she surveyed the mound of clothes already overflowing from her bag and glanced at the closet where others she had planned to take, still hung. Despite all that she had removed, the wardrobe was still stuffed to overflowing. How could anyone be expected to make do with such a cramped space? Boxes filled with shoes, purses, and scarves were stacked underneath the full hangers and she stifled a groan of disappointment to think that Gabrielle would no doubt prevent her from taking any of her outfits' co-ordinating accessories that littered her dressing table.

She didn't want to annoy her sister, but packing was difficult. She had painstakingly curated so many outfits and loved each of them. After all, for the past several months she had eagerly anticipated this trip. Still holding the shoes, she flipped through a heap of garments on the bed and found the co-ordinating dress before folding it with care and laying it on top of the to-go pile. She added wistfully, "I have to take a few nice clothes, don't I? What if we go out for dinner somewhere? Or to a party?"

"Parties!" Gabrielle spluttered. Closing her eyes, she took a few deep breaths and appeared to be counting, then responded in an even tone. "If, by the remotest chance, we go out to dinner, we'll wear our very best jeans with a nice blouse." She tossed her signature braid of glossy black hair over her shoulder. "Honestly, you have no idea what it's like in Canada. It's not a resort, it's a working ranch." She sighed and shook her head. "We talked about this already. Andrew's mom owns a gorgeous piece of the rolling foothills near Canada's Rocky Mountains. But you're not going to sit inside the house staring at the scenery through a window. Or drink cocktails on the veranda while I gallop past on horseback. I want you to experience this week *with* me. It will be an adventure. That's the whole point in you going." Her voice rose in annoyance. Lifting a pastel-pink crop top from the piles of clothes already in the case, she examined it with deep disapproval.

Annette turned away to rummage through hangers in her closet, struggling to remain unperturbed. She chose another dress and whipped around to fling it on the heap. "But it's still a holiday, right? I want to be prepared." She folded her arms, knowing it was a losing battle as Gabrielle took another deep breath.

"Please listen to me, Annette. No one will be wearing dresses. You need to take a warm jacket, sweaters, jeans, boots, t-shirts, long-sleeved shirts, and maybe a couple of prettier blouses. It's June in Canada. Sophie said it might be cool, especially at night. And we'll be outside a lot." Despite the warmth of this beautiful morning in Paris, Gabrielle was a living example of what she was trying so hard to convey. She plucked at the sleeve of her light blue, hooded jacket with a white turtleneck peeking out the top, and leaned across the bed to catch her sister's eye.

"See," she said meaningfully indicating to her outfit. "These are the sorts of things I've packed. No party dresses or ball gowns in sight."

Annette sniffed. "Ugh, I suppose you'd be happy if I wore head-to-toe flannel. Or a shapeless, plaid sack that drapes to my ankles with a nice pair of rain boots underneath?" She lifted her hands in a pleading gesture. "Fashion is part of who I am." She looked down at what she was wearing for the flight. It had taken hours to pick her outfit: a form-fitting cream, off the shoulder long-sleeved t-shirt that exposed her bare midriff before her fashionably high-waisted, baggy blue jeans began. The ensemble was finished with a pair of short, chunky black leather boots. It was comfortable, but stylish and she knew it perfectly set off her shining halo of nearly waist-length hair. She twisted one of the gold hoop earrings she wore, and hesitated. Gabrielle would know what was best. She squinted at the heap of clothes she'd accumulated on the bed and began to rethink her choices.

"Fashion isn't going to impress a herd of cattle or amaze a pack of coyotes," Gabrielle continued to explain. "Be reasonable. I've been to Canada a few times now and it's not a beach holiday."

Although it hurt her to do so, Annette flipped the case over, dumping the contents onto her bed, and set it aside. "Fine. I believe you. Well then, help me to decide please.

But the dress and heels are going." Firmly, she set the lilac-coloured ensemble into a corner of the smaller bag, feeling her sister's displeasure but avoiding her gaze. Some things were worth fighting for. She straightened and waited expectantly.

Half an hour later, with the much smaller case rolling behind her, Annette locked the door, and tucked the keys into a zippered pocket of her purse. She slung it over her shoulder, and followed her sister out of the sturdy cream-coloured building in the Marais and onto the street below. The apartment had been Gabrielle's home when she'd attended university in Paris. Once she and Andrew married, it had passed to Annette. However, the small rooms were too perfect and orderly for her taste. She liked clutter and didn't allow a little dust to rule her life. Art and fashion were far more important.

Annette continued to refer to it as her *chambres parmi les étoiles*, or her rooms among the stars, as Gabrielle had done, due to its lofty position on the fifth floor. And she had lived happily in the apartment for the past four years as she studied art at the famous Beaux-Arts de Paris in Paris. The two women fell into step as they strode down the street toward the metro.

"You'll thank me for this when we get there," Gabrielle said with satisfaction. "And you'll never wear that purple dress, but if it makes you happy to drag it across two countries and an ocean—"

"It does," Annette interrupted resolutely. Just knowing it was tucked in her bag had cheered her immensely.

They continued the trek in silence until seating themselves on the train, at which point Annette's thoughts brightened a bit more. Gabrielle was right, it would be an adventure. She reached forward taking her sister's hand.

Squeezing it she said, "I'm sorry to be so much trouble. I should have asked for your advice yesterday. Packing on the morning of the trip was foolish."

Gabrielle squeezed back and smiled. "We're going to have a wonderful time. And maybe while we're there, we can help Andrew's mother. It's only been a year since her husband died. Running the ranch alone has been hard on her."

"Sophie, right? I remember her from your wedding."

"Yes, she was born in Bordeaux and grew up in the Dordogne. But fell in love with Mason, Andrew's father, when they were quite young." Gabrielle's face took on a faraway look. "They'd been married forty-three years when he died, and were still very much in love. I can't imagine what it feels like to lose someone like that..." Her voice trailed away. She stared out the window as the train burst from a tunnel into the bright morning sunshine. She twisted the diamonds on her left hand.

"You and Andrew shut the store and stayed with her for close to a month after he passed, yes? Do you think she'd come back to Paris? Perhaps she could sell the ranch now that her husband's gone, and leave those struggles behind."

"No." Gabrielle was emphatic. "The ranch has been her home for all those years. Besides, her youngest son Jayke lives in Canada. He moved to Vancouver two years ago, but he's home often. Andrew asked her if she wanted to sell and return to France. She refused."

"Well, I'm sure having us visit will be exciting for her and I'm willing to help in any way I can. Just not sure what an art student, fresh off the streets of Paris, and wearing a lovely mauve dress and heels could do. Maybe, I could try to rope a few steers. Although, it would probably help if I knew what those are." Annette watched her sister closely as she tried to lighten the mood.

Gabrielle laughed. "I love you, but you're crazy, you know that?"

In no time at all, they were disembarking at the airport and running through the usual stressful muddle to get through security and find their way to the correct gate. They plunked into two vacant seats, some distance from the loading area. Since the space was filled with throngs of people, most of them looking anxious and drawn. Annette gazed around her.

An older lady sat nearby, primly holding a blue plastic pet carrier on her knee, and staring with a fixed, slightly frazzled expression at the gate as though she was trying to will the airline attendants to allow her on board the plane an hour ahead of schedule. Annette knew why too. A cat yowled from within the confines of the cage, sounding as if it was being slowly strangled to death. It drew the stares of all those around her. Studiously, the woman ignored the din, pushing back in her seat to sit a little straighter.

Meanwhile, two young fathers bounced whimpering babies on opposite sides of the waiting area. One held a squirming toddler on his shoulder as he paced the aisle with the fractious child. While the other, his face red and perspiration glistening on his forehead, tried to offer his wailing baby a bottle of milk, to no avail. The child only batted the comforting drink away and renewed his howls of displeasure. Each person studiously ignored the restless crowd surrounding them and for good reason. Looking at the faces of her fellow passengers, Annette knew they were all thinking the same thing. "Please, oh please don't let them be sitting next to me."

She chuckled and turned her attention to Gabrielle who

was busy texting. "Sending a few last words of love to Andrew? Or telling him how to run the store in your absence?"

"That would never happen. Besides, I've already hidden notes around the house for him to find," Gabrielle said loftily. "If you must know, I'm sending a text to Sophie to inform her of our arrival time. Of course, it's only three in the morning over there. So, she won't get the message until we're flying over the Atlantic, but at least she'll be aware that all is well."

"Will she be picking us up?"

"Yes." Gabrielle looked dreamily out the massive airport windows, her wide green eyes getting a faraway look in their depths. "It's beautiful there. Quite unlike anything you've seen before. And the people that live and work on the ranch are so nice." She clasped her hands together. "I have a few favourite spots to show you, too. Hidden places that are only accessible by horseback."

Annette coughed. Hesitantly, she voiced a concern she'd had since this trip was first proposed. Brushing lint from the black bomber jacket she'd thrown on as they left the apartment, she mentioned casually, "You know I can't ride a horse, right?"

Gabrielle patted her hand. "Of course. But don't worry, I'll teach you."

"But what if I don't want to be taught?"

"You don't..." Gabrielle gaped at her, then smiled consolingly. "That's only your nerves talking. I promise you'll be fine once I saddle Lassie for you. She's elderly, doesn't like to move past a walk, and is quite safe for beginners."

"Is Lassie a big dog, or a horse?" Annette asked dryly, raising her eyebrow. "And, if you say horse, is she also toothless? I have no desire to be chomped on by those gigantic, horsy teeth." She shivered just thinking about it and clutched her rose-coloured Prada purse to her chest with fuchsia-tipped fingernails.

Her sister laughed out loud. "No. Not a dog, silly. And 'horsy teeth,' really? Do you think horses bite people for the sheer fun of it?"

"I don't know. Maybe," Annette answered doubtfully. "I don't want to take any chances. Is there a possibility I *could* just sit on the veranda and watch? Uh, I—I'm a little concerned about those coyotes you mentioned, too."

"Don't be ridiculous," Gabrielle began and then held up her hand as a boarding announcement was made for their flight. Automatically, people began leaping up and hurrying to form a queue. As though stuffing themselves into a cramped seat, before anyone else, was going to get them to their destination faster.

"We'll discuss it on the plane," Gabrielle said, standing and stretching. "Though first let's make one last trip to the toilet before we board."

Dutifully, Annette nodded. Together, dragging their luggage behind them, they hurried away.

Annette had been peering out the plane window for the last half hour, straining to see something below, to no avail. Heavy clouds obscured the land, and she wondered if it would be raining when they landed. As if reading her mind, the captain of the plane cleared his throat and interrupted the movie she was only half-watching, to make an announcement.

Well, that's too bad, she thought as he concluded. Apparently it *was* raining and only twelve degrees Celsius in Calgary. Although she hated to admit it, her sister had been right. She drew the edges of her faux leather bomber jacket together and zipped it as they descended through the heavy white mist and bumped onto the tarmac.

It was a large plane and their seats had been situated toward the back. So, it felt as if an eternity had passed before they were free of the mob and striding out the other side of passport control.

Gabrielle beamed at her as they turned the last corner and burst through double doors into a milling throng.

"See," she said with quiet triumph. She gestured toward the heavy-lidded, yawning people who loitered by the conveyer belt that would eventually bring them their checked luggage. "This is what we avoided." They walked past the crowd, dragging their smaller bags, and made their way toward the exit. "Isn't it wonderful? We're free to leave as we please."

"Yeah. Great," Annette mumbled, thinking of all the extra clothes she could have brought—especially an extra sweater. She shivered.

"That's odd." Gabrielle drew her phone from her purse and turned it on. "I'm sure Sophie said she'd meet us at door number ten, but I don't see her anywhere." They waited while her device flickered to life. Annette noticed an attractive man wearing a battered black cowboy hat standing near door number ten with a small cardboard sign in his hand.

The name *Tremblay* had been scrawled on the surface with a black marker. Annette elbowed her sister, who was craning her neck to see over the crowd.

"I don't think your mother-in-law is coming," she whispered. "That guy over there is holding a card with your name on it."

"What?" Gabrielle was only half listening. She raised herself onto her tiptoes and alternated between punching her phone and tipping her head one way and then the other in an effort to locate Sophie.

"That man in the big hat is staring at us. Now he's waving the paper with your name on it," she hissed again. "Do you recognize him?" Taking Gabrielle by the hand, she turned her sister to face the man. By this time, he was bearing down on them with a determined step and a face like a thundercloud.

"No," Gabrielle squeaked. But it was too late to say more as the man stopped in front of them and spoke.

"Gabrielle Tremblay?" he asked brusquely.

"*Oui*." Gabrielle answered in French, clearly taken aback.

"Sophie asked me to come get you," he said, touching the front of his hat in some semblance of a polite greeting which wasn't the slightest bit welcoming. He glowered at them both from beneath dark eyebrows. "Is that all of your luggage, or must we wait for more?" He scowled over the heads of the crowd to where the conveyer belt remained unmoving. "I'd like to get back home to see what's happening."

"No. We 'ave everything with us," Gabrielle switched back to English, but narrowed her eyes suspiciously as she peered at the man. "Who are you, may I ask? And where is Sophie? Is she alright? What do you mean you want to see what is 'appening back 'ome?"

The man turned his velvety brown eyes on Gabrielle and his face relaxed for a moment. "Uh, sorry," he said. "I should have explained everything immediately. Sophie sends her apologies, but something pretty serious happened on her ranch this morning. She couldn't get away. She was upset by it, but she's fine. My name is Jeff Douglas. I own the ranch adjoining your mother-in-law." He held out his hand and she took it, if dubiously. Their hands shook in greeting.

Annette studied him as he spoke to her sister. He was about six feet tall and slim, but powerfully built. At least, that was what she could tell from the breadth of his shoulders underneath the pale blue jean shirt he wore. The sleeves were rolled up as though he'd been working, and the metal snap buttons undone at the throat, exposing a dusting of hair on his chest. She assumed the hair on his head was the same colour, but she couldn't tell with it hidden beneath the large hat.

His face was handsome, if one liked that sort of rugged, outdoorsy look, however she didn't. His chiseled jawline and upper lip were covered in a couple days growth of beard. A leather belt with a large silver buckle sat at his waist holding rumpled jeans tightly to his narrow hips. The jeans looked as though they'd seen hard labour, with a hole ripped across the knee and several dark stains on his thighs. She assumed he'd wiped his hands on his clothes to rid them of some particularly unpleasant substance and shuddered. As if only noticing her for the first time, Jeff turned to look at her.

She was unprepared for the way his dark brown eyes swept over her from head to toe in a cool assessing way, appearing unimpressed. His face hardened once more, but he held out his hand anyway and grasped hers in a crushing grip.

"And you must be the sister," he noted. "Nice to meet you." But even as he said the words, he was already turning away. Annette felt oddly indignant at his dismissal. "I'll explain more once we're in my truck. Can I take your bags for you?" His eyes flicked from one woman to the other.

"No, thank you, and my name is not 'Sister.' It's Annette," she ground out the syllables. Really, five seconds after meeting this man she found him insufferable.

"Okay, Annette," he shrugged. "Whatever you say. Now, if you and Gabrielle could walk this way I'll take you to my truck and we can get out of here."

A comic sketch of the phrase, *walk this way*, in which the people walking behind the speaker adopted the mannerisms of the person they followed, caused her to giggle. She could imagine herself striding similar to him with her chest puffed out, taking giant steps, and exuding an overbearing air of command. He glared at her over his shoulder. Sighing, she realized he must have heard her laugh and taken umbrage.

Jetlag, she thought, shaking her head with surprise. It was causing her to become giddy and getting her in trouble.

Crossing a busy road in front of the airport, they entered a huge concrete parking garage, and she began to wish she'd taken him up on his offer. He was walking so fast that she struggled to keep pace. She glanced at her sister and knew Gabrielle was puffing too. Her blue jacket had been removed and slung over one arm. At least she'd worn sensible white trainers and wide-leg jeans which allowed her to move easier.

Perhaps her stylish chunky boots hadn't been such a great idea. Her left heel was already starting to throb. Ahead, Jeff used his key fob remote to unlock the doors of an enormous, four-door, black truck. Looking around them, Annette realized that almost every vehicle in the parking area was a similar looking truck. How strange. She'd never seen so many of them in one place before.

"I got a text from Sophie," Gabrielle whispered, falling

into step with Annette as she caught up. "She's very sorry she couldn't be here, but assures us we're in safe hands with Jeff. I was a little concerned until I heard from her."

Gabrielle flicked her long black braid over her shoulder, a trademark move, and hurried ahead when Jeff opened the back door of the vehicle and beckoned to them. He grabbed her bag and set it on the seat, pushing it to the far side. After thanking him, she straightened her purse on its long strap, stepped back, and smiled encouragingly at Annette.

Annette withheld comment on this latest revelation. She didn't get a good feeling about the man at all, and wasn't convinced his hands were all that safe. Nonetheless, she waited while he tossed her bag to join Gabrielle's on the seat and added her own thanks.

"Please make yourself comfortable," he said stiffly, as he held open the door for her to scramble inside the monstrous vehicle. She felt his hand on her elbow and felt like shaking it off. Instead, she allowed him to steady her since her rather clumsy boots caught on the chrome step.

"Thank you," she said with reluctance, and noticed him lift an eyebrow as he closed the door behind her.

She settled herself and searched for the seatbelt amongst the rubble of a hammer, a length of coiled rope, an old black and red checkered blanket that looked and smelled like it had been used to bed down a cow, and an odd-looking leather contraption that must be used to lead animals. Her mind was reeling with questions. What did this visit hold in store for her? Why was their hostess not meeting them? And who was this strange brooding man that had taken charge of their immediate destiny?

"Like I said earlier, Sophie asked me to pick you up," he explained, rattling a set of keys as he started the engine. A throaty roar echoed in the concrete parking garage. "Since she couldn't leave the ranch after what happened this morning." He reversed smoothly and they were on their way.

"I appreciate you coming to get us," Gabrielle said gravely. "And I'm so sorry Sophie is 'aving trouble. If we 'ad known…" She broke off with a concerned shake of her head. "Well, we most certainly would not 'ave come. Can you tell us what's 'appened?"

"It's been difficult for her," he said, gripping the wheel until his knuckles showed white. "But she's determined to run the ranch alone. Jayke could come home and help, but she won't hear of it. I don't think she's told him half of what's gone wrong. She doesn't want him to feel obligated." Clearly, he didn't agree with this reasoning.

"You mean there's more than what 'appened today?" Gabrielle turned to look at him, and then at Annette, her face registering shock.

He nodded, but said nothing.

It was only after he'd paid for parking and entered the stream of traffic on the busy highway, that he tilted his hat backward on his head, ran the back of his hand across his brow, and started to explain.

"I'm sure you're wondering what's going on," he began. "And I'll try to keep it simple since, according to Sophie, Annette has never been to Canada, or to a ranch before." He caught her gaze in the rear-view mirror, and she looked swiftly away.

"As you know, losing Malcom was really hard on her." He darted a glance at Gabrielle. "But she's a determined woman and was doing well, until about a month ago. It just seemed like everything went wrong. Machinery broke down, cattle unaccountably disappeared, and two of her most valued employees quit. She confided in me yesterday that she hadn't said anything about it for fear of worrying you and Andrew, or causing you to cancel your plans to come for a visit..." He paused to navigate a lane change.

"I'm so sorry to 'ear this," Gabrielle closed her eyes and took a deep breath. "It's true we did not know. Of course, we are aware it 'asn't been easy for her since Andrew's father died. But she's insisted she is okay. We 'ad no idea she was struggling."

Annette wondered if this was why Jeff appeared so unfriendly. Perhaps he thought their presence would add more stress on Sophie. It might be true, she thought ruefully, but how could they have possibly known what was happening on another continent. She stared out the window at the traffic, thinking how life could change in an instant, and wondering if she and Gabrielle could be of any help to their host. It might be best if they left as soon as possible, so as not to become a burden.

"Anyway..." he cleared his throat. "I'll leave it to Sophie to fill you in on the particulars, but the worst thing to happen, so far, occurred this morning. One of the ranch hands came to work early. He found a heifer dead and three others very sick. They had been brought in from pasture yesterday, very healthy, and put in a corral ready to be transported to a buyer in northern Alberta today. Those four animals were some of her best breeding stock and worth a lot of money, making their deaths a serious loss. No one could understand what had gone wrong, so the veterinarian was called. He came immediately and said it looked as though the cows had consumed some sort of toxic substance."

Gabrielle gasped. "Oh no...poor Sophie."

"I assume a heifer is some sort of cow?" Annette

remarked, but no one appeared to have heard her. She raised her voice. "Will the others live?"

Jeff shrugged. "We couldn't figure out how it happened, because the animals were fine the day before. They hadn't been given anything to eat, but some good hay. It wasn't until someone started the pump to fill a trough for the horses, that a strange odor was detected." He sighed heavily. "The water was turned off immediately. Fortunately, all other animals are out in pastures anyway, except of course, those four. Sophie's worried the well is somehow contaminated. She hauled the dead cow to the veterinary clinic for an autopsy and is having the water tested."

"If that is true, then it could easily 'ave killed a person?" Gabrielle gasped.

"Yes," he answered simply. "But it didn't, so that's some good news. But until the water has been cleared, no one can touch it." Jeff shrugged. "It could have been worse. Sophie called Public Health and they're sending someone out to test the water quality right away." He stopped for a traffic light and turned to look at Gabrielle. "She's a good lady. I just don't know why everything's been going wrong for her."

"There is no way we can 'elp I suppose?" Gabrielle asked, her brow furrowed with concern.

Jeff's voice softened. "No, there's nothing you can do, but it's nice of you to offer. She's had quite a day so far. She'll also have to call the buyer to explain that their deal she was counting on is off. She can't even be sure the other three cattle will live."

"Is Sophie in trouble financially?" Gabrielle asked quietly.

"That's for her to tell you," he said. "She confided a little in me, because our families have been close for years.

But I certainly don't claim to know every detail. Nor have I asked."

A nasty suspicion was forming in Annette's mind. Leaning forward to strain against the seatbelt, she rested an anxious hand on the console. Without pausing to phrase it in gentler words she blurted what she was thinking.

"We're not going to be staying with you, are we?"

She watched his reflection in the mirror and saw his lips tighten before he answered.

"Sorry for your luck," he said with a hard edge to his voice. "I know Sophie feels bad about the situation, but nothing else can be done." His narrowed eyes flicked up to hold her appalled stare.

"Yes. Until this gets sorted out, you'll be staying with me."

With Love From Paris: Chapter Two

What was it about people that rubbed you the wrong way upon sight? Annette slumped in her seat, coming to terms with the startling news that she and Gabrielle would be spending quality time with this...uh, person behind the wheel.

Of course, this situation they were in wasn't about *her* feelings or discomfort, she reminded herself, sitting up straight. Sophie was coping with some serious problems. It was understandable, but not pleasant to think they would have to stay with Jeff. She felt herself seethe with dislike for the man. Although, none of it was his fault, she grudgingly admitted. However, her feelings weren't entirely unwarranted. He'd been short and unfriendly, in fact bordering on rude since the moment he'd laid eyes on them.

Well, maybe not toward Gabrielle. But no one could be angry with Gabrielle. She was beautiful with a disposition to match. As the two occupants of the front seat continued to discuss the grim state of affairs on the ranch, Annette gazed admiringly at her sister from the seclusion of the back of the cab. Gabrielle's eyes were so brown they were almost black, her thick sweep of dark lashes fanned a porcelain complexion, and the natural ruby-red of her full lips was striking. All these attributes conspired to turn men's heads and always had since they were young.

Annette wasn't jealous. She was proud of her lovely sister. But sometimes it was hard to have a beautiful sister. She herself was plain and uninteresting by comparison. At least she didn't have to wear glasses any longer, since the laser eye surgery. Though it really didn't make much of a difference. Her sense of fashion, long curly hair, and artistic talents were the only assets she possessed. She thought of all her lovely clothes lying on the bed back home in Paris. What a shame they were left there without her. Never mind, she would comfort herself with knowledge of the pretty lilac outfit tucked away in her bag. At least it had made the trip.

She turned her thoughts to the rigid back of the man seated in front of her. What had she done to deserve his annoyance? It had been evident in his every word and gesture since the moment they met. Perhaps he was naturally unpleasant. She would avoid him...but that was going to be harder than it sounded, considering they were staying at his house.

Annette groaned inwardly. *Ugh!* This was not good. Not good at all.

The powerful beast of a truck ate up the kilometers with a low growl of its diesel engine. Before long they were out of the city and speeding toward the mountains on a busy highway. Ahead of them, a hazy blue ridge of mountains rose in the distance, just under a bank of cloud. The Rockies promised tranquility and beauty, Gabrielle had spoken so lovingly of them both. Annette edged as far to the center of the seat as she could, where she could get a better view, and wished she'd been able to bring her paints. The landscape was already inspiring her. She was glad to be finished with her studies. Despite that four years at Beaux-Arts de Paris had left her wanting to put her own artistic stamp on the world.

Jeff slowed, signalled right, and they turned onto a road covered in coarse, grey rock. Clouds of choking dust billowed behind them, but a storm swirled overhead. A few drops of rain began to hit the windscreen, promising to settle the dust.

Annette took in the rolling green hills that appeared to have no end. Occasionally she saw cattle grazing, but mostly nothing except vast open spaces bordered by the occasional barb-wire fence. Each field stretched like an adjoining, perfectly fitted carpet that disappeared over the hills.

The truck roared past fields of lush, emerald-green crops and tall fronds of sea-foam grass that rippled in the breeze like waves across the Mediterranean. She assumed it would be cut for feed, but wasn't entirely sure. She'd grown up in the city of Toulouse, in the southwest of France, and the only time she spent in the country was in passing through it on her way to somewhere else. The scenery was lovely though, and her heart lightened just from the sheer pleasure of looking at it.

The road carried along, for perhaps a half hour before they turned onto a narrower gravel track that led over a tall rise out of sight. Over the entrance a huge slab of weathered wood was suspended by chains from two stout logs that rose high in the air. On the wooden sign were carved the words, *Douglas Ranch*.

It was still a long, winding drive until they mounted a hill and looked across a sweeping valley to the buildings nestled against another rise. Seemingly, not far away, the fitful peaks of the Rocky Mountains disappeared into the looming clouds.

A massive log home drew the eye to where it backed into a stand of dark fir trees. It was two-storied and broad, with high windows that jutted to a peak in the center. Two verandas on the upper level, one on either side of the center peak, projected out from glass doors. She could see chairs for the occupants of those rooms to enjoy a fantastic view on warm summer nights. The lower veranda, on the bottom floor, ran the whole length of the structure.

A neatly trimmed expanse of lawn rolled gently down a rise at the front of the home, and bordering it was a stout, wooden-plank fence. Flowers bloomed in profusion from long boxes that hung along the fence. Small shrubs and what appeared to be perennials flourished just under the deck at the front.

On the right hand side behind the house, corrals could be seen built with metal poles. Each area was fitted with a brick-coloured shed to house animals during the harsh winters Gabrielle had told her about. Then, like a beacon, an enormous red barn rose in the background. And all of it was set against the ridge of towering, snow-capped peaks.

"Your home is beautiful, Jeff," Gabrielle noted. She twisted in her seat to see her sister's reaction. "Now you know why I wanted to bring you 'ere. Sophie's ranch is just as spectacular. Imagine living in this place."

"It's gorgeous and I am imagining it. I'd love to live here," Annette breathed, then suddenly realized what she'd said. "Uh, I mean..." she hastily corrected herself, "not specifically living here...with you. I meant this area...not this exact place." She could feel her face growing hot and fell back against the seat feeling stupid.

"I knew what you meant," Jeff said without even a trace

of humour. "My grandfather always called it his 'little patch of heaven' which sums it up about right. Although the buildings have changed quite a bit since his father first arrived here in the early 1900's, the land remains the same. It will always be part of who I am," he explained.

Maybe the man wasn't such a cold rock after all, she thought curiously, considering his last statement. Annette slid sideways to lean on the two suitcases beside her for a better view out the other window.

It didn't matter that grey clouds hung overhead. Somehow they only added to the magical ambiance of the scene. In any case, they had parted enough for her to see into the distance. Although the mountains looked close, due to their size, she was aware of the acres and acres of huge rolling hills between the ranch house and them. It was idyllic. Exhaling with rapture, she leaned forward and touched Gabrielle's arm.

"Thank you for bringing me to Canada," she breathed. "And thank you Jeff, for your…uh, generous 'ospitality." She stumbled over the correct English phrase to use in the end. Only realizing that the awkward moment made her words sound sarcastic rather than politely grateful, as she'd meant them.

Jeff stiffened. "You're…welcome," he responded in kind.

Annette's stomach curled. *Great.* She'd offended him again.

He stopped the truck in front of the house. In one fluid movement he jumped out and opened her door before striding around the other side to do the same for Gabrielle. He then busied himself with retrieving their luggage from the back seat.

Annette was glad he hadn't tried to help her climb

down. She would have felt worse than she did already, but it was too late to explain her error. Instead, she bypassed the step, and slid from her seat to the gravel driveway.

Rain was beginning in earnest now. A crack of thunder split the air, causing her to jump. Zipping up her jacket she followed the others up a flight of steps to underneath the roof of the deck. Jeff was already at the heavy wooden door with a suitcase in each hand. He tucked one bag under his arm, turned the door handle, and kicked it open wide.

"Why did you say it like that?" Gabrielle whispered in French. She frowned at her sister, as they followed their host inside.

Annette grimaced and shook her head, then quickly plastered a smile on her face as Jeff turned to look at them.

"I'll show you to your bedrooms right away," he declared, with a face devoid of emotion. "I'm sure it's been a long day for you both and you might want to wash your face or something." Still gripping their bags, he whirled away and set off across the large room toward a staircase in the far corner.

Gabrielle followed immediately, while Annette lingered to gape in awe at the living room. She'd only ever seen homes like this in photographs, or in movies, but never thought she'd stand in one. It looked as though everything in the room was made from monstrous, fawn-coloured logs, apart from one wall. Stones were inlaid to create a dramatic fireplace with a broad hearth and a good supply of kindling lying in wait.

Windows stretched up to the cathedral ceiling, following the triangular shape of the center peak and letting in natural light despite the darkness of the storm outside. Moving further into the room, she realized that the same sort of windows was mirrored on the other side of the home, offering a dazzling view of the mountains.

"*Oh la la,*" she marvelled. "*C'est magnifique.*"

"Coming?" her sister called, and Annette made her legs move in the direction of her voice, still trying to take in the surroundings. Of course, not quite everything was made of logs. She brushed past several plush leather sofas in a lovely caramel colour, a contemporary glass and metal coffee table that almost looked out of place, and an area rug in shades of burnt orange, browns, and cream that lent a cozy warmth to the room.

No deer heads adorned the walls, for which she was grateful. However, a complicated mass of antlers formed a strange light fixture that hung low overhead.

"Annette!"

With an exasperated sound, she dashed to the staircase, also made of beautifully polished poles, and took them two at a time to the next floor.

Gabrielle stood alone waiting for her. She spoke French, as they'd agreed to use English only when with non-French speakers. "Jeff has taken our bags into these two rooms," she said, pointing. "He said they're both the same, and I told him I'd take this one." She leaned in close and whispered again. "I'm hoping we won't have to bother him by staying long, so I wouldn't unpack." With this sage advice, Gabrielle shot her sister a smile and disappeared into the room she'd chosen.

Jeff emerged from the other bedroom with his brows furrowed. "I put your bag on a chair. I have a few chores to take care of. My housekeeper will prepare the evening meal. Her name is Mrs. Lewis," he said with great formality. "When you're ready feel free to go downstairs and make yourselves comfortable. Dinner will be at six." He pulled his hat, still glistening with raindrops, farther down on his head, and turning on his heel walked to the head of the stairs.

"I do appreciate all you're doing for us," she called faintly. He paused for the briefest of moments, then touched the brim of his hat in answer, and clomped downstairs.

Annette moved, rather robotically, to the room she'd been assigned. So much had happened since the morning. She yawned and her eyes felt heavy. She wondered if it would curb or prolong the problems of jetlag if she laid down for a nap.

Then she stepped into the room and snapped awake. If she had thought the downstairs was beautiful, this space was absolutely fantastic. Her room was built into the corner end of the house which meant she had windows on two walls—but what windows! A queen-sized bed sat against a whole wall of them, all looking out on the white peaked Rockies in the distance. Heavy brocade drapes of mossy green, sprinkled with pink roses, were pulled to either side. The material co-ordinated perfectly with the bedspread and pillow shams. A beautiful night table made from the fat knotted trunk of a tree had been varnished until it was glossy. On top of it sat an ornate lamp in the shape of an old-fashioned urn, also in a pretty shade of rose.

An arched door, tucked on the other side of the room must lead to a bathroom. She'd make use of that soon, but first to explore.

The other wall was the one she'd seen from the road with double glass doors leading to a sheltered sundeck outside, but the design wasn't rectangular and basic. They were gracefully rounded at the top and set into the heavy logs making her feel as though they led out of a Hobbit hole into some fantastic tale of magical proportions. She walked to them, drawn by the loveliness of the design, and stepped outside.

About twenty horses grazed in a pasture nearby and as she watched, they lifted their heads as if on cue to peer at something. Following their line of vision, she saw Jeff, wearing a long raincoat and rubber boots, walk toward the animals carrying a pail and some sort of harness. He set the pail to one side, looping the harness over one arm, and reached over the wooden rails to pat them as they trotted over to greet him. Then, he unlatched the gate and slid inside. He lifted the halter and fastened it over the head of one white horse. Deftly he manoeuvred the beast by itself out the gate before closing it behind him.

As the horse joined him, even from this distance she could see that it wasn't young. Its head hung low against the driving rain. The animal moved slowly beside him as Jeff picked up the bucket and headed off toward the barn. Tugging her purse from where it hung at her side, she dug around for her cell phone and turned it on. Annette lifted it, adjusted the settings a little, and took several pictures.

The pair disappeared inside the barn and Annette felt a tug at her heart. The man was kind to animals. It was obvious, even to her, that he had taken the old horse out of the lashing rain, giving it something extra to eat where it would be warm and dry.

She turned away, not wanting to feel anything for her unwilling host, and looked up. The room was in the eaves and high above her head the ceiling rose to a peak showing a skylight.

Her jaw dropped in astonishment. She would be able to lie in bed and count the stars tonight if it stopped raining. Flopping onto a mossy green, velvet chair, like the one where Jeff had set her bag, she hooked a footstool with one foot and pulled it in front of her. She sank into the luxurious depths, propped her feet up, and contemplated her room.

"I don't think I ever want to leave," she muttered, hugging herself with glee. If it wasn't for their unpleasant host, it would be perfect. But then she thought of Sophie and the reason they were here with Jeff. No. It wasn't ideal, she chided herself.

She looked at the phone in her hand. How unusual that she hadn't checked for messages since arriving. Except there had been too much to see and think about for that, she supposed. Besides, all of her friends knew she was on holiday. Her relationship with Philippe had ended five months ago, so there was no one special in her life that would care she was gone for the next week. She dropped the phone back in her small, quilted circle purse, letting it slide to the floor as she folded her hands over her stomach and simply gazed about her.

A light tap came at the door.

"Come in," she called, jumping to her feet, and hurrying to open the door. It must be Gabrielle, wandering over to check on her. Well, that was good. She hadn't had a chance to speak privately with her sister since landing.

But it wasn't her. Instead, a solid-looking woman, her longish blonde hair greying at the roots, and scraped into a ponytail, stood in the doorway with hands on hips. She wore a bright purple tracksuit that was, perhaps, a size too small. The lady appeared to be somewhere in her fifties, Annette gauged, with hazel eyes, an upturned nose, and a face lined from hard work in a harsh climate.

"Bun-jure," she said haltingly, and her mouth relaxed into a sheepish grin. "Sorry, my dear. I know that was a terrible attempt to greet you in your own language, but you have to give me marks for trying. I took French classes all through high school, but nothing really sank in." She tapped her forehead and rolled her eyes with a laugh. Annette liked her instantly.

"It is nice to meet you. You must be Mrs. Lewis?"

The lady nodded vigorously. "I am. I've just come up to tell you and your sister that supper will be ready in half an hour. Oh, and to check if you needed anything."

Annette shook her head. "I've never seen such a pretty bedroom," she said. "I 'aven't looked at the bath, but I'm sure it 'as everything I'd ever need. Thank you."

"You're most welcome." Mrs. Lewis backed away and turned toward Gabrielle's room, lifting a hand to knock.

"I can tell Gabrielle if you like," Annette offered, stepping into the hall. "I'd like to see 'er room anyway."

The plump little lady grinned. "Mercy," she called, and headed off downstairs.

Now that Annette had thought about food, she could smell the most tantalizing aroma and sniffed appreciatively. The last meal she'd eaten was on the plane, and it hadn't been great.

"*Oui?*" Gabrielle responded to the tap on her door. "Isn't it lovely?" she went on rapturously, as Annette opened the door and stepped inside. And it was, but not quite as beautiful as her own, she thought privately. The décor was similar, except the colour scheme was turquoise and cream. The room had the rounded doors leading outside, but no windows over the bed and no skylight.

"The rooms are wonderful," Annette agreed. "I feel quite spoiled. Is it this nice at Sophie's house?"

"No. Not really. It's a nice home, of course, and the setting is fantastic, but hers is much older. This house is something outstanding, don't you think?" Gabrielle's smiling face suddenly fell. "I am so worried about Sophie. I wonder if Jeff has heard from her yet."

"We'll know soon enough. Mrs. Lewis, the housekeeper, was just at my door to say dinner would be ready soon." She sidled close to her sister. Even though they were alone, she whispered. "I feel strange about staying with the neighbour. Especially since he isn't all that friendly. And it doesn't seem like there's anything we can do to help Sophie. Do you think we should try to get a flight back home tomorrow?"

Gabrielle raised a hand to her forehead as if she had a headache and walked to the glass doors to look outside. "I understand how you feel and I'm sorry. This was supposed to be a celebration of your achievements, a wonderful time for you and me to share. But I can't leave until I know what's happening with my mother-in-law, and offer my help." She glanced at her watch. "It's five here, so well after midnight in Paris…and too late to call Andrew. I sent him a message to say we'd arrived, but that's all he knows." She spread her hands in a helpless gesture. "There may be nothing we can do, but I can't leave either. If Andrew were here he would stand by her and do all he could…" her voice trembled. "I love Sophie like my own mother."

"Oh Gabby," Annette rushed across the room and flung her arms around her sweet sister, reverting back to the childhood name she'd called her. "I'm so selfish! Naturally, you want to stay and help if you can. We'll both do whatever possible to sort this out. Please forgive me."

They stood together for a few moments before Gabrielle stepped back and dabbed at her eyes with a crumpled tissue she pulled from her pocket.

"It's okay. I feel strange too, and I'm not entirely comfortable staying with her neighbour. But he has been kind, and you have to admit," she gave Annette a watery smile, "it's sort of like being at a resort."

Annette giggled in an effort to lighten the mood. Linking her arm through her sister's own, she tugged her gently to the door. "Let's go downstairs and see what Mrs. Lewis has made to eat. It smells divine and she's a sweetheart." She stopped and pulled her sister around to face her. "And don't give me another thought. I'm fine really. I'm with you in this, okay?" She gazed at her sister with love.

Gabrielle nodded and together they walked downstairs to find the kitchen.

The smell of roasting meat drew them like moths to a flame. Once reaching the main floor, they turned left. Altogether avoiding the living room and continuing down a short hallway till the sounds of clanging pans announced they had arrived at their destination.

The kitchen was rustic yet thoroughly modern in design. Beside them and set in front of another wall of windows, was a long dining table that could easily seat fifteen people. Curving away from it was a horseshoe-shaped bar with frosted glass lamps dangling from long metal hangers. Behind the bar, the kitchen opened up to a rock wall on one side that housed two large gas ranges and a professional-looking, indoor grill. Wooden doors with heavy black metal handles covered cupboards, drawers, and what looked like a walk-in pantry. And overtop an island workspace hung a metal rack holding antique kitchen implements, some of them resembling instruments of torture.

Mrs. Lewis had covered her purple track suit with a voluminous white apron that bore the words, '*Never trust a skinny chef,*' across the front. She bustled out from behind the bar to greet them.

"You must be Sophie's daughter-in-law, Gabrielle," she said warmly and nodded approvingly as Gabrielle spoke.

"*Oui*. I am glad to meet you Madame Lewis. The dinner smells wonderful. Thank you."

"Please, both of you call me Sandra. My husband's mother was the real Mrs. Lewis. She was a lovely woman, but a terrible cook." Sandra rolled expressive eyes and laughed. "Now, why don't you two sit here at the bar and talk with me while I finish making the meal?"

Needing no further encouragement, they hopped onto stools. Annette sniffed appreciatively. "What are you cooking?" she asked. "And could I 'ave the recipe?"

"My goodness yes," Sandra grinned at them over a pot of steaming potatoes. "But it's pretty simple. When you work on a ranch where they have all the cattle Jeff does, you get good at roasting beef." She plunked the pot down and flung open a drawer to scrabble inside. After a moment, she withdrew an electric hand mixer, fitted it with metal beaters, and plugged it into the wall.

"Excuse me a minute," she announced. "It's going to get loud in here." They stared, fascinated as she added butter, chives, and sour cream to the pot. She picked up the mixer, flipped the switch on high, and brandished it in the air as though auditioning for a part in the next Chainsaw Massacre movie, before thrusting it into the steaming heap of cut vegetable.

"My children often tell me I'm too dramatic," she proclaimed, yelling at them over her shoulder. "But if a person can't have a little fun, life would be boring. Don't you agree?"

Annette looked at Gabrielle and the sisters grinned. It was true. Sandra scooped the potatoes into a bowl and added a sprinkle of cheese to the top before popping it into an oven. She wiped her hands on her apron and faced them.

"Would you like a drink? Water, juice, tea, or maybe a glass of wine? We have most anything you could want."

They both asked for a glass of water. Sandra bustled across the kitchen to grab two glasses from an overhead cupboard and held them one at a time under the water dispenser of a massive refrigerator. Ice rattled, hitting the bottom before water splashed inside.

"There you are," she said brightly, setting them down with a clunk on the bar. "Did you have a good flight? Must have surprised you to have Jeff waiting at the airport?" She raised eyebrows at them as she hurried away to fling open another cabinet door and reach for plates. These were piled onto the counter with a handful of cutlery tumbled on top. Then she was off again flitting about to snatch a pair of heavy red oven mitts from another drawer and pull them on.

"The flight was fine," Annette answered. "But we did *not* expect to be met by...Jeff." His name was forced from her lips. She knew she should feel grateful for what he was doing, but her instant dislike of the man made it difficult.

Sandra cast her a sideways glance, but said nothing. She opened the second oven and stepped back from the heat before diving in for the dish. The meat was a sizzling, golden brown, its exterior glistening with savory juices as the mouth-watering aroma wafted through the air in waves. Annette's stomach growled.

"And you've never been to Canada before?" Sandra asked, straining the juices into a saucepan, and covering the roast with aluminum foil before setting it aside.

Mesmerized by this whirling dervish of a woman, Annette sat spellbound until she realized she could at least help out by setting the table. Whisking off the stool, she hurried around the bar.

"No, I 'ave never been outside of Europe," she answered. "It is beautiful here."

"Why thank you, Annette," Sandra said, as Annette scooped up the dishes and carried them to the table. "Just throw them down at the far end. Well," she added with a wink, "perhaps 'throw' was a poor choice of words. It might be best if you set them gently." She turned back to her work. "And I'm so glad you liked your first glimpse of the Rockies. I'm sure you two will find plenty of interesting things to see and do while you're here."

As Annette busied herself, she wondered who each place setting was for. There were six in total, but who would be occupying the chairs was none of her business. So, she set each blue plate onto the cheerful yellow mats stacked at the center of the long oval table, and kept her curiosity to herself.

Gabrielle helped by finding heavy glass tumblers and bringing them over. "I 'ave a variety of activities planned for my sister," she announced, loud enough for Sandra to hear over the busy sounds of stirring that now emanated from the kitchen, "but I'm not sure what will 'appen with Sophie's ranch. We don't want to be in the way."

Sandra turned to them with her mouth open, as though about to speak, with a metal whisk raised and dripping in the air. Any further remarks were interrupted by the sound of a door crashing shut at the front of the house. Then voices could be heard, and footsteps approached. All three women turned to the double swinging doors, much like what might be featured at the entrance of a saloon in an old western movie, to see who was coming inside.

The doors flew open, and two women marched

through. One was Sophie, but the other was a dark-haired woman dressed completely in denim and wearing a ball cap. Gabrielle rushed to throw her arms around Sophie. She was tall like her son, Andrew, with short hair that was far greyer than Annette remembered.

"My dear girl!" Sophie gushed, folding Gabrielle into a loving embrace. "It's *so* good to see you." She kissed Gabrielle's cheeks three times, before sliding an arm around her daughter-in-law's waist. The older woman led the way to where Annette was standing, wringing her hands—unsure of herself. Clearly it was a terrible time for them to visit, and part of her felt as though they ought to get back on a plane and return to France. She clasped her hands together, knowing her smile was wobbly.

But, as the two women approached, she relaxed a little. Sophie looked so genuinely happy to see them both that it warmed Annette's heart. At least for the moment she wouldn't allow herself to worry.

Sophie met her gaze with a broad grin, slipped her arm free of Gabrielle with a final squeeze, and stretched both hands out to Annette. What a striking woman. Without wearing a bit of makeup, Sophie was beautiful. Her icy blue eyes, the same as her son Andrew's, held Annette's gaze with a look of genuine welcome. Lines at their corners and near her mouth spoke of laughter and of the smile always on her lips. Today, of course, there was a tiredness in her expression, and she moved slowly across the floor. Annette's heart went out to this hard-working woman who had been struggling to keep her family ranch running smoothly after the death of her husband.

Because Annette always noticed what people wore, she took in the simple pair of jeans over cowboy boots, the long brown jacket, stained and worn from long years of use, and pulled in at a narrow waist with a drawstring. It was zipped up to Sophie's neck as though offering a thin veneer of protection from the worries that plagued this beautiful lady. Annette was swept into her arms and given the very same effusive welcome as Gabrielle.

"I am so glad you came to see me," Sophie said, still with a trace of French accent. "I am only sorry I could not be there to greet you at the airport." She shrugged and a look of sorrow crossed her lovely features.

"*Merci beaucoup*," Annette said. "Thank you for asking me to visit. I'm sorry we came at such an inopportune time."

"Nonsense," the lady said, turning to capture Gabrielle with her free hand and pull all three of them together for a hug. "No one could have predicted the future. I'm pleased you're both here." Letting them go, she ran a hand through her closely cropped hair and shook her head. "It was a difficult day, but enough of that for now."

Stepping back, Sophie closed her eyes and took a deep breath. She looked pale and tired, but her eyes sparkled as she looked across the kitchen at Sandra who had gone back to her meal preparations with renewed zeal. "I see my dear friend has been busy cooking us a wonderful meal. No doubt Jeff has told you both that you'll be staying with him until our water problem is fixed?" A cloud crossed her face.

"Yes," Gabrielle said. "It's very kind of him, but I'm worried about you. Is everything alright?"

A crack of thunder split the air, and lightning flashed outside causing the lights to flicker and her words to appear almost ominous. Simultaneously, the rain outside turned into hard pebbles of hail that clattered against the many windows of the home. The sound became almost deafening.

Sophie hurried to the window and squinted at the sky.

"It was supposed to rain heavily today, but hail is unexpected. This will make everything just a little more difficult," she added cryptically. Then, with a forced lifting of her eyebrows and a smile, she beckoned to them. "Come," she shouted over the din, "let's sit. I want to introduce you to Rosa. She started working for me a few months ago and I don't know what I'd do without her. Rosa manages the books and works alongside me at the ranch. She has been invaluable over the last few months."

At this, the tall, dark-haired woman stepped forward with her hand outstretched. She didn't look exactly happy to see them, in fact her face resembled the thunderclouds outside, but Annette put that down to the concern they were all feeling. Rosa's lips were pursed with disapproval, or so it appeared, and her grey eyes were cold as flint, but she was a pretty woman with bobbed hair and a nice figure. When she wasn't scowling, she was probably quite attractive. She wore the ubiquitous jeans and matching jacket that Gabrielle had once laughingly referred to as the Canadian tuxedo. Beneath the jean jacket was a pale blue t-shirt. At least her colour palate was consistent, although monochrome.

"Rosa, this is my daughter-in-law Gabrielle and her sister Annette. They flew in from Paris this morning."

Rosa's lips stretched across her teeth, but it couldn't really be called a smile. It was a bit foreign to shake so many hands, but Annette knew customs in Canada were different than those in France, and she murmured a polite greeting as they shook.

"I'm pleased to meet you," said Rosa. "We hope to get you back to Sophie's house as soon as possible. It's unfortunate you're forced to stay with Jeff." She moved to the opposite side of the table and sat, pushing the plate out of her way as she folded her hands on the table. Gabrielle joined her.

Annette took the chair Sophie pulled out for her, seating herself beside the older woman who dropped into a chair. "The rooms are lovely," she said, "and from what I can tell, Sandra is a wonderful cook, so we will not be suffering. But of course, I 'ope the problems are soon fixed." She looked at Sophie with lifted brows, eager for good news.

"I'm waiting for a call from our veterinarian," Sophie shrugged out of her coat and hung it on the back of her chair. "Until then, I know nothing. The animal that died was taken to the vet clinic for an autopsy. I must learn the results as soon as possible and then take whatever action is necessary."

"I'm so sorry." Gabrielle shook her head.

"Yes, my dear, I know," Sophie forced an unsteady smile. "But these things happen when you raise animals. Knowledge is power. Once we know what happened to them we can proceed." Taking a phone out of her pocket, she placed it on the table in front of her and tapped it to make sure there were no messages.

"You really think something seeped into the water?" Gabrielle's forehead was creased with worry. "Perhaps there was a noxious plant in the feed?"

"*Ne t'inquiète pas, mon lapin.*" Sophie slipped into her native French as she hastened to reassure her daughter-in-law. After all these years her accent had nearly disappeared, but her ability to speak the language remained. "Please don't worry, my dear" she translated. "To have one animal die might mean a natural cause, or something like you suggest, but when the other three are also very sick…? No. Something drastic would have happened to cause this. One must be pragmatic and look for an external reason." She shrugged. "But please, let's not talk of that now. Soon you girls will come to stay with me."

"Are you sure we couldn't stay there now?" Annette asked hopefully. "Perhaps we could help with something."

"No, no, there is no water," Sophie shook her head. "It's best you stay with Jeffrey. He'll take good care of you and can bring you to visit me during the day. Perhaps 'e will even lend you a truck, so you may come and go as you please. Everything will be back to normal soon, I promise. Then I shall 'ave you to myself." She swung around and flashed them a bright smile. "There are many things planned for us to do."

"Parties?" Annette asked without thinking. Her thoughts had immediately flashed to her pretty purple dress, but she could have kicked herself when all eyes turned to her in surprise.

"Were you hoping for a cotillion where you could wear a ball gown and satin slippers to be introduced to all the eligible males in the district?" a male voice asked dryly from the doorway.

Annette jumped. She threw a hand up to her throat to calm her racing heart and felt her cheeks flush. It was so close to the truth that she felt like a fool. Where had *he* come from? And why, of all moments, had he chosen to walk in at that one. The man was unbearable.

"Jeff," Sophie spoke his name in a reproachful tone. "She's never been to Canada before and doesn't understand how a ranch operates." Turning to Annette, she caught her hand and squeezed. "Don't pay any attention to him, my dear. I'd like both of you to tell me about your graduation and how Andrew is doing with the store."

Annette's face was hot with embarrassment. She hadn't meant to blurt that word. Clearly the foolishness of it had shocked the whole group into silence. It was all because she and Gabby had argued about the lack of social events on this trip that the word, parties, had jumped to her lips.

Jeff strode to the table and, for the first time, Annette saw him without a hat. His hair was darker than his eyes, almost black, and pushed straight back off his forehead while the back curled over his ears and collar. He pulled out the chair on Sophie's other side, sat, and was blocked from her view.

Instead, Annette's attention was caught by the sudden flurry of activity across the table. Rosa had whipped off her hat and tossed it to one side. Then she pulled the ponytail free from its elastic and was fluffing her hair with both hands, her cheeks suffused with colour.

Granted, not as flushed as Annette, but why was Rosa embarrassed? Annette narrowed her eyes. Oh, it wasn't embarrassment. She watched as the young woman darted a look at Jeff and realized Rosa was attracted to their host. Interesting. She wondered if the sentiment was shared by Jeff, then her ears picked up on what he was saying.

"Dr. Roberts was just here."

"He was? Then where is he?" Sophie craned her neck to look out the window and into the driving rain.

"He couldn't stay because he wants to go check on the three heifers in the barn. He's hoping they've improved since he treated them this morning."

"Okay…" Sophie took a deep breath. "And what did he learn from the autopsy?" Sophie's hands clenched together on her lap. Annette couldn't see her face, but she could feel the tension as the lady braced herself for the worst.

Jeff reached out and covered her hands with his large ones. "He said they were poisoned, and that it was only extreme thirst that drove them to drink the water, because it was about fifty percent pesticide."

Sophie tore her hands away and covered her face with a groan, her back heaving.

Jeff placed a hand on her shoulder. "There's more."

"More...?" Her voice was strangled.

"He thinks someone poured jugs and jugs of the stuff into your well. They deliberately poisoned those animals... and it could have just as easily been one of you that died. Of course, you would have smelled the chemicals, but the intention was there, nonetheless. This was no accident, my dear friend. I'm doubting that all the other problems you've had lately were simply bad luck. I believe someone is out to destroy you."

Grab your copy...
vinci-books.com/withlovefromparis